1

Captain Herrick
Hannah Molora Vadnais

Dear David Veatch,
Please enjoy this journey
of the high seas with
Captain Herrick and his
capable crew.

H. Vadnais

2

Dedicated to my family.
I love you all very much.

Chapter 1

I regained consciousness in a pool of my own blood, frightened and confused. A sharp smell of smoke hit my nose, the scent of charred flesh and hair. Blood filled my mouth and throat and I coughed, feeling sick to my stomach and struggling to breathe. I knew I was badly wounded, likely mortally, but I couldn't feel anything at all. For a horrifying moment my limbs would not function, I was paralysed with fear. I raised my head to see Father lying on the quarterdeck a few feet away. My vocal chords tightened in my chest, that is how I know I was speaking, all I heard was an endless high-pitched ringing in my ears. "Father!" I shrieked. I dragged myself across the deck, the sand scraping my legs as I felt too weak to stand. His chest was torn open, his gentle eyes already glazed over. "Wake up, Father," I sobbed helplessly, swallowing and choking on my own blood. Most of my face was slick with gore, my long blond braid stained scarlet. I felt sick and dizzy again, and I pressed my head to his chest as the next broadside rumbled below us and the ship trembled. "Father," I moaned. Someone took my arm and tried to pull me away, but I knew if I left I would never see my father again. "Father!" I screamed. "Father!"

"Captain Herrick. Good morning, Captain Herrick," I heard the polite, expectant voice of my servant say as he gently pressed my shoulder. I slowly opened my good eye to see his prominent forehead and straight dark hair. "Good morning, sir," he said.

I rubbed my eye then reached across to the small table by my hanging bed and slid my dentures into my mouth. "Good morning, Higgins," I replied cordially. Sleep still clung heavily to my stiff limbs and I struggled to keep my eye open. He offered his hand and helped me from the bed. I stumbled through a small hatchway to a tiny room no larger than a closet with a porcelain chamberpot and used the necessary. When I exited back into my sleeping cabin the sunlight pouring in through the starboard windows momentarily blinded me. A headache began only seconds later and I placed my hand over the shilling coin that closed the crack in my skull from an old wound. "Curtains, Higgins, curtains," I grumbled, leaning against the 18-pounder ship's gun by my bed.

"Aye, sir," he replied, obeying. The room darkened and I felt him press a cool washcloth to my head. "So sorry, sir."

"That's alright," I said dismissively.

"Your hot water is ready, sir, as you asked," he said, gesturing to a large bowl built into my vanity.

"Thank you, Higgins." He helped me undress from my nightshirt, then busied himself with powdering my wig as I quickly washed myself with a damp towel. I pulled on my undergarments then sat down and shaved, gazing at my reflection. Turning my head to the left, I could look only at the right side of my face. From this angle I thought I looked fine. I was thirty-seven, yet still had no wrinkles as I never left my cabin without wearing a hat. I contemplated my long nose, full lower lip, sparkling blue eye and rosy, prominent cheekbone, all framed by silky blond hair peppered with a few strands of grey. The long razor-blade scraped my cheek, and when it was done I wiped away the lather with a dry towel. Turning to the right I winced. A deep crease dug into my forehead from wearing an eyepatch for twenty-two years. A hideous series of scars marred my complexion. There was a short, thick one on my cheek, then a long, grotesque one over my eyelid that rendered me half-blind and the eye forever closed. Hardly any hair at all grew on that side of my head, only the white circles of burns, and the shilling glistened where my skull had cracked. I turned back the other way, quickly glancing at my better side.

I dried my cheek and slid the eyepatch on, then stepped away and turned to face the painting on the wall hanging over the 18-pounder. It was of my mother on a summer's day at home, done just after she'd married my father. She wore a light blue dress and a matching blue and white hat and carried a bouquet of roses. A gentle smile spread across her cheeks. My favourite memory is of her teaching me to play the pianoforte. I missed her dearly.

She'd passed away six months ago when she'd been taking the carriage to London. According to the letter I'd received it had been a dark, rainy night and the carriage had gone over the side of a cliff.

Higgins placed an antiquated wig on my head, so dreadfully out of fashion but necessary to cover my bald left side. I took my hat from him, a large black tricorne with gold trim.

"Your breakfast is on the table in your dining cabin, sir," he said.

"Thank you very much, Higgins, you may go about your duties," I replied, leaving for the other room. My quarters consisted of a small sleeping cabin on the starboard side, a day cabin on the left that was slightly larger than the sleeping cabin, and a large dining cabin for entertaining my officers at the aft-most part of the ship.

I sat down at the long mahogany table and uncovered my plate. A pot of hot tea still steamed in front of me and I poured myself a cup. It felt a bit ridiculous, eating alone at such a large table, as it had twelve chairs so I could entertain my officers over supper. A harpsichord sat squeezed into the corner of the room for just that purpose. Bright sunlight poured in through the aft windows behind my balcony and it reminded me of the church my family had attended when I was young. I suppose that was appropriate, as it was Sunday. I sipped my tea, my throat too dry for me to have an appetite yet. When I'd finished the tea I started on my victuals; an egg over hard and a bowl of porridge. There were a few chickens aboard the ship to provide eggs, along with a pig and two cows for fresh milk. The porridge was bland and tasteless, and I preferred to mix it with molasses for flavour. The combination of porridge and molasses was called "burgoo". There was a cabinet by the door that held my china and silverware, along with victuals and spices I had brought from home. I found my last jar of molasses on the bottom shelf then took it to the table.

The glass jar was wrapped in a purple ribbon and a note was folded between the ribbon's tie and the lid. I untied the ribbon and opened the note, knowing it was from my mother who had helped me buy furniture and personal comforts for my cabin two years ago. It read: *My darling George. Your mother loves her precious baby boy! I'm so proud of you, Georgie.*

I mixed a spoonful of the molasses with the porridge then finished my breakfast. After that I put the molasses away, then took my copy of the Bible from my room and walked out on deck. The watch, a smaller contingent of men than was usual, stood resolutely at their posts. I saw that the hammocks had been stowed in netting on the sides of the ship, though the sailors had not yet begun to do the routine chores of holystoning the decks and helping the gunners look after the guns. I checked my silver pocket-watch to find that it was only 7:52, the men were still at breakfast.

I paced the quarterdeck for a few minutes looking up at the sky. It was a glorious day, with a fresh, steady breeze and not a cloud in sight. The warm sun beat down on my face through the chilly air and I wished the heat was stronger. Above me the sails filled like saucers to the wind and the ship cruised forward with a small wake flowing from the rudder below. Looking about the clear horizon I saw that there was no land in sight, only an endless ocean. We had taken the seaward journey from the Mediterranean to Portsmouth, heading on a direct route to get there faster rather than skirting the Spanish then French coastlines. The weather on the open Atlantic Ocean was rougher than closer to shore, yet it was still early October and the usual winter storms were not to be expected. So far my risk had been justified, as the swells had been light and the wind moderate. I didn't think that my frigate could survive much longer, even in mild conditions, so the sooner we reached Portsmouth the better. We'd been in the Mediterranean Fleet for almost a year and a half without going into port for repairs. The frigate, *H.M.S. Cassandra*, had been built in 1778, almost thirty years ago. She'd not been in dry-dock for a decade and her hull was entirely reduced to rot. Only a few thin sheets of copper plating below the water-line kept us from sinking. In short, despite being old and majestic, with an unusually fancy bowsprit and gallery windows, she was as seaworthy as a wicker basket.

The ship's bell startled me from my thoughts as it tolled just in front of me and I jumped. It rang eight times in its high, sing-song-y pitch that reminded me of my grammar school teacher. The men began to file out on deck, assembling for Sunday morning's church service. I took note as my officers began to arrive, stepping up to the quarterdeck, which was raised slightly to be a foot higher than the rest of the deck. The chaplain came late as usual, followed only by the ship's surgeon, Dr. Burke. "So sorry sir," Burke said. "I had to tend to my patients. You know, the one who bruised his ankle falling from the mainmast and the landlubber who drank too much and has the jaundice."

"I know, I understand," I replied.

"We're lucky there's no scurvy, considering the state of our supplies—"

"Let's discuss that in private," I said, cutting him off before the men could hear.

The chaplain began to speak then. He read first a prayer, in this case one thanking the Lord for a safe journey thus far, then a piece from the Old Testament. Our chaplain's two favourite stories were of Noah's Arc and Jonah and the Whale, presumably because they both pertained to the sea, and were therefore relevant to his seafaring parishioners. He then read the sermon, which related to piety,

morality, and loyalty to king and country. After that he re-
cited a piece from the New Testament, and ended with a
final prayer that asked God to protect the King and bless
his people. At home, most of the prayers would be sung
rather than spoken, but as the warship did not have a choir,
we had to make do with speaking. Aboard ship the only official religion was the Church of England, though in private
some of the men practiced other faiths.

Though the church service lasted less than an hour,
I paid little attention to it, so distracted was I by the mention of our lack of supplies. That was another reason why
I'd chosen to take the shorter route; we only had enough
victuals for another three days, even though I'd already cut
rations by half two weeks ago. Any delay at all, be it the
wind dying or an error in navigation, and I would be forced
to cut rations again, down to a quarter of what my men
were accustomed to. That would create all sorts of problems which already concerned me, including scurvy, fighting, stealing, and short tempers. As the service dragged on,
I occupied myself with worrying about the supply issue.

Though I identified as a member of the Church of
England, I was not a particularly religious person. I only
held the church service when the weather was nice and otherwise seldom uttered a word in prayer. The reason I had
brought a chaplain aboard and had purchased copies of the
Bible for my men was because having a Christian presence

on the ship would help keep order. It would remind the crew of their morality, that they were subservient to God, and, most importantly, it would make the warship feel more like home to them.

I was lucky when recruiting hands, as most of my men were experienced seamen who had served under the previous captain and had stayed aboard when I transferred in. The *Cassandra* had a small contingent of landsmen aboard, however, as well as sailors pressed from a Newcastle collier ship I'd encountered entering Portsmouth harbour right before we were due to leave for the Mediterranean Fleet. There were also a dozen Austrians aboard, whom I'd found imprisoned in a French sloop that I'd encountered while attacking it in convoy with two grain transports. The Austrians were soldiers captured by the French while fighting in the Italian theatre. After being released, they'd agreed to fight for Britain. Fortunately, the well-behaved and experienced crew outweighed the insubordinate and inexperienced.

The service ended and the men went to their stations; this was the only time of the day when both watches were working. Usually, if I wished to drill the men at the guns or have them practice with small arms combat, I would do so at this time in the morning. Today, however, I had no intention of drilling them, but preferred for them to spend extra time keeping the *Cassandra* seaworthy and looking nice. The first watch was outside managing the sails while doing routine maintenance on the ship, and the second was holystoning the deck and looking after the guns under the direction of the gunner and his mates. The lieutenant who was on watch, Brooks, had the men climb the masts and fly the topsails as the wind had gone down two knots from the evening before. I decided to inspect the situation in the hull, then talk to the purser to get the exact amount of supplies we had left.

To see the purser would require me to go to the lower deck, the lowest deck of the ship before the hold where supplies were stored. I walked down the ladder to the upper deck, then down again. The lower deck was a long series of dark rooms with no windows or hatchways because it was below the waterline. I had to duck walking through, as the ceiling was only five feet high. At the most forward part of the ship in front of me was a windowless room with buckets of water outside, the most dangerous place aboard; the magazine where gunpowder was stored. Towards the middle was a place called the cockpit, where the midshipmen lived. Aft of that was the gunroom, where the officers, both commissioned and non-commissioned, had their cabins. I went to the purser's cabin and knocked on the door, but found he had already left to count supplies. I guessed he was in the slop room, which held the clothing and bedding that he would sell to the sailors.

I turned away and went down another ladder to the aft-most platform in the hold. The smell here was the worst in the entire ship, as there was no way to air it out and all the filth settled towards the bottom. It was a mixture of human odours and rotten provisions, and though I asked my men not to relieve themselves in gratings leading to the bilge, in heavy weather they did so behind my back anyway. The *Cassandra's* hold had three platforms that were used for storage, one aft, one in the middle, and one forward. I knocked politely on the door to the slop room, which was shut. "Mr. Gailden," I said.

He opened the door. "Good morning, Captain," he said.

"You can go up for breakfast, if you'd like," I told him, trying to keep the mood light.

"That's alright, I've had my breakfast. What brings you down here?"

"I need the amount of victuals we have left that are still edible; biscuits, salted meat, oranges, peas, raisins, wine, water."

"We have enough for another three days, if we keep the rations as is. The water has a bit of moss, but is still safe to drink. I had to toss three rounds of moulded cheese over the side the other day. The biscuits have the consistency of sand and are full of weevils, but other than that everything appears to be in good order."

"Thank you, Mr. Gailden. Would you mind if I inspected the stores for myself?" I asked.

"As you wish, sir," he said permissively with a wave of his hand. He picked up a shirt that had fallen to the deck and folded it, then set it on the most forward shelf. I stepped behind the first shelf, searching for provisions he might have hidden for resale, yet saw only the blankets, clothing, and bedding that he sold to the sailors, along with tobacco that he issued to them for free at the rate of two pounds per month. "You won't find anything in there, sir," Mr. Gailden said from the other room.

"Where are the provisions, then?" I asked, increasingly annoyed with his nonchalance at the supply issue. The darkness down here and the sound of the waves lapping against the hull above my head also caused me a great deal of discomfort.

"In the hold and the bread room, obviously," he said, miffed at my suspicion.

"Thank you, Mr. Gailden," I replied tactfully, hoping to inspect the victuals and return to the light.

I climbed down another ladder, then stepped onto the barrels stacked in the hold. Below them was a bed of iron ingots and shingle stones to keep the ship's centre of gravity low by balancing the weight of the masts. The first three barrels I opened were filled with salt water, as their provisions had been consumed and they were now being used to balance weight in the bottom of the ship; then I opened one of dried peas. Some had begun to germinate, spreading spindly white roots through the mixture. Digging my fingers through, I found a few were covered by a dusty turquoise mould, and others had dissolved into powder, though most were still good. The meat appeared dry and mostly gristle, but was still able to provide nutrition; we had two barrels of salt beef and one of pork. Another smaller barrel I inspected held the last of our supply of oranges. It was only half full, with many of the fruits too mouldy to eat. There were another two barrels of lemons to be used to make lemonade to ward off scurvy. Remarkably, they still looked relatively fresh.

Going back up to the aft platform, I went to a compartment just behind the slop room, the bread room. The bread, if it could be called such, were small loaves baked to be as hard as a stone and keep for the duration of a ship's voyage. They were stored above the barrels so they could remain dry away from the water in the hold. There were three bags left. To check their edibility I tapped one gently on the top of a shelf. Instantly it dissolved into dust, and weevils squirmed about in the remains. In port the food was usually better, but *H.M.S. Cassandra* was a ship of war, not Buckingham Palace. The sailors were never particularly concerned with the poor quality of the victuals unless it was absolutely horrendous; when tossed into a stew and cooked for several hours everything tasted fine, and many of them were just grateful to have enough.

As a profession, the Royal Navy had its merits. Three square meals, a hammock, and a surgeon's care were provided for, amenities that would be by no means guaranteed on land. With jobs in weaving among other professions being diminished by new technological innovations such as the spinning jenny, the navy was a means of employment. Able seamen would make 1£ 9s 6d per month, while ordinary seamen and landsmen made less. This income could also be supplemented by prize money, though the majority of this went to the officers. I had made a small fortune from the capture of two French cargo ships and their naval escort a year ago. It was my first time commanding my ship against the enemy, which led to the most money I'd ever earned in the capturing of a prize. When I was still a midshipman, I'd been sent to the Caribbean where we'd captured American vessels filled with rum and gold, which had been worth much more than my two little grain transports and the tiny sloop that had quickly surrendered. My lesser rank, however, had prevented me from getting as large a share of it as I had received from the prize money a year ago, and therefore I had earned less. Regardless of the unequal distribution of the money, the men had enjoyed the sweet taste of victory, especially with a few shillings to ice the cake.

As for officers, there was no trouble finding them for the navy. Like the men, there was the money, but also glory. For children of the lower aristocracy or even the middle class, the navy offered a chance at social mobility. It could provide increased political and financial power along with the possibility of peerages and titles, and thus ascension into the upper tiers of the aristocracy. For second-born sons of the aristocratic class, the navy offered an honourable profession with supportable pay, as only first-born sons received inheritance on the deaths of their fathers. There were extremely rare circumstances in which an officer could be promoted from the lower ranks to a lieutenancy or even a captainship. All of those individuals, however, were too old at that point to survive long enough to make admiral, which was based in a large part on seniority. There was also an officer school that I had heard of, though it must have been comparatively small because I had never personally met anyone who had attended. In short, the Royal Navy's officers represented the nation as a whole. It was a prestigious service and the King's own son, Prince William, was a naval officer. We came from all social classes, from hard-working enlisted men all the way to the royal family.

The vast majority of officers entered the Royal Navy as captain's servants, usually in their early teens as the minimum age for joining was thirteen. This age restriction did not apply to the children of men in the navy, who could nominally join at the age of eleven. Many captains chose to flout these rules, however, such as my father, who had entered me on the books at the age of nine when I was still living at home with Mother. The use of the word "servant" was an inaccurate description for most of us. Every captain had an allowance for a certain number of servants depending on the size of his ship. Some did bring actual attendants aboard, such as I had brought Higgins along with me, but most captain's servants were boys in their early teens who spent their time learning the ways of the ship. After three years of experience, they were promoted to midshipmen. Midshipmen were messengers aboard the ship during battle, and would sometimes be chosen to lead small parties of men. The rank after this was lieutenant. Lieutenants had to be at least twenty and have six years of sea experience, or at least claim to have. Again, these restrictions were often flouted. They also had to take a test in front of a board of three examiners asking questions on their service records and their knowledge of seamanship. If they passed the test, they could serve on larger ships under a captain, or even get command of tiny bomb vessels or cutters. The next rank was commander, in which they could command small vessels such as sloops.

After commander, I was made a post-captain, and thus I was given command of *H.M.S. Cassandra*, my first frigate. My orders were to assist in the blockade of the southern French coastline near Toulon with other ships from the Mediterranean Fleet and hamper enemy shipping. Frigates were a lucrative command, with the greatest chance of prize money and independence for a captain, though fewer opportunities for glory and winning the favour of admirals. My ship would be unlikely to engage in large fleet battles, as she was too small with her 36 guns to fight against a three-decked 74 or larger. With more experience, I could potentially be assigned to a ship-of-the-line in one of the big battle-fleets. From there, all I had to do was survive and wait, either to fall out of favour and onto half-pay on shore, or to make commodore and eventually admiral.

After inspecting the other bags of bread I saw that the purser was right; we had enough provisions to last us another three days at the current rate, and perhaps a few days longer if I cut rations again. My business belowdecks being done, I walked back to the ladder and climbed up to the lower then to the upper deck, where a few gratings above supplemented the light of lanterns. Heading back, I smelled a delicious stew cooking in the two galley pots. "Good morning, Carleton," I said to the cook.

"Good morning, Captain, sir," he replied, struggling to his feet to raise his knuckles. He'd lost a leg falling from a mast during a gale a decade ago, which made it difficult for him to stand. Many ships' cooks were sailors who had either grown old or had suffered injuries, or both. The quality of victuals, and thus the happiness of the men, depended on them. Carleton did an excellent job at frying meat after boiling it, and adding spices to the meals, so I tried to show my appreciation for his work as much as possible.

"That smells very nice, continue about your duties," I said with a smile, climbing back up the ladder and onto the main deck. The bright sun greeted me, blinding and beautiful. All the men were out on deck, both the watch and the tradesmen not assigned to watches, enjoying the clear blue sky and fresh air. A group of midshipmen and two of the three captains' servants who had not yet been promoted to midshipmen gathered around the master-at-arms.

I approached them. "Good morning, Mr. Kensington," I said cordially. Kensington's job was to train the men in small arms combat and look after the various pistols, tomahawks, muskets, pikes, and cutlasses kept aboard.

"Good morning, Captain," he replied, raising his knuckles to salute me.

"What are you doing with the young gentlemen today?" I asked, hoping it was the lesson in swordsmanship I'd asked him to do.

"Fencing," he said. "As you asked, sir."

"Excellent," I replied. "Very useful skill. Pay attention," I said, turning to the assembled group of boys, "it
could save your life."

The midshipmen aboard my ship were generally the
young, aspiring ones in their teenage years, rather than
older men who, for various reasons —inadequate interest,
inability to pass the lieutenant's exam, incompetence, or
sheer bad luck— were unable to earn a promotion. There
were four aboard my ship, three of the boys and one older
man named Jameson who simply lacked the skills. He'd
failed the exam twice, and in his anger and his shame had
taken to the nasty habit of drinking, which ensured that he
could never impress an officer enough to recommend him
for the test again. He was twenty-nine. Of the others, there
was an eighteen-year-old and two sixteen-year-olds. In addition, there were two young captains' servants who trained
with the midshipmen but were too young to hold the rank, a
fourteen-year-old named Haynes and a very mature thir-
teen-year-old Austrian named Matrose.

After showing the boys a few blocking and stabbing
manoeuvres, Kensington scabbarded his cutlass. "Now,
who wants to try?" He asked.

Jameson withdrew his sword. "I'll have a go," he
said, cocking an eyebrow.

"Who wants to fight Mr. Jameson?" Kensington
asked. "Mr. Larson, would you like to practi—"

"I can fight," the young Matrose replied, drawing his sword with a shaking hand. Mr. Jameson's eyes narrowed.

"Matrose," Kensington said, a bit surprised. "Alright, then."

By this time a small crowd had begun to gather around of about two dozen sailors.

"Now, gentlemen," Kensington said. "This is no mortal combat. The objective is to either *disarm* your opponent or to trap him, not to harm him. We're all British here," he said.

"Not him," Mr. Jameson scoffed.

Kensington chose to ignore his comment. "Now, when I count to three, you may begin. Do take it slowly, this is only to practice what you just learned, and executing your footwork and positions correctly is more important than winning. I expect you to try a few lunges and parrying, as that was what you've all been struggling with. Are you ready?"

Both competitors nodded. "Alright. One," Kensington began. "Two-"

Matrose took a lunge for Mr. Jameson, reaching for his opponent's sword-hand to disarm him. In a flash, Mr. Jameson pushed his arm away, driving his cutlass just a few inches to the left of Matrose's stomach.

"No rough play!" Kensington exclaimed in a flash of ill temper.

Jameson slashed for young Matrose's head, but he ducked and parried it with his cutlass. Steel crashed against steel as Matrose leaped back. Mr. Jameson stabbed ruthlessly for him; Matrose blocked him clumsily and tried in vain to counterattack. They were at it too hard, and I could see in the furious expressions that there was something personal at play.

The word to stop formed in my throat when a flash of steel glinted in the sun, and something scarlet dripped onto the deck. My blood coursed hot through my veins. "Enough!" I exclaimed, instantly drawing my own cutlass and stepping between them, blocking Jameson's next lunge with a perfect parry. Young Matrose shrieked when he saw the blood. "Mr. Jameson!" I scolded.

"I'm sorry sir," he said, the flame leaving his eyes and a look of sheer bewilderment coming over his face. "I didn't mean to, 'twas an accident."

"I understand," I replied curtly. "Back to work, all of you!" I ordered the onlookers. "Mr. Kensington," I said to the master-at-arms. "Have the young gentlemen review the use of sextants with Mr. O'Hare after dinner," I said. "I'll take Matrose to Dr. Burke."

"Aye, sir," he replied.

I turned away, holding the lad by the arm. "Follow me. I'm taking you to Dr. Burke. He's going to take good care of you," I said. We went to his cabin, which was down in the lower deck, just when I'd thought my miserable business down there was done for the day.

"Captain Herrick!" He exclaimed warmly. The walls of his room were covered in paint from his favourite hobby; currently, he sat in his chair in front of an easel painting a lady in a purple dress, his sweetheart Rosie. The only light available was from a lantern hanging from the ceiling, which he had turned up so hot that it posed a danger of setting the deck above on fire. Rosie sat on his sea-chest, posing for him.

Like a lioness gracefully getting up to stalk her prey, she stood, walking over with swaying hips and running a hand sensuously along my shoulder. Her fingers brushed my epaulettes and I shivered, the smell of her perfume an intoxicating fog. "What brings you down here, Captain?" She asked.

"G-good day to you too, madam," I stammered, then with a deep breath regained my composure. "The young gentlemen were having fencing practice and there was an accident," I explained. Matrose was visually shaking from terror. I placed my hand on his shoulder to comfort him. The little fellow could not speak English all that well, so I spoke in simple terms to him. "Don't be afraid,

Dr. Burke is a very nice man, he's going to take good care of you."

"Oh," Burke said, his voice filling with sympathy. "Hello, Matrose," he said. "Can you tell me where you're hurt?" He asked.

"His neck," I said, the neckcloth beginning to stain an inch below his ear.

"Alright," the surgeon said, opening a pouch of medical supplies on the floor. We all sat down, Rosie on the bed and Matrose and I on Burke's sea-chest, and the surgeon pulled his chair up to the boy. He undid his necktie and took a rag from a bucket of water at the foot of the chest, then cleaned the patch of blood to see the cut. "Tis just a scratch. It won't need stitches," he said reassuringly. "So, Herrick," he said to me, "is the party still happening tonight?"

"I believe so, but my personal store of provisions is all but spent, so I don't have anything the cook could prepare for dessert."

"I have a few jars of sugar plumbs left. You can have them, I won't tell. So long as your mint and rosemary sauce is there for the meat, and I can have a nip of your brandy. I seem to have misplaced my last bottle."

"I didn't bring any brandy, so you'll have to suit yourself with champagne. Otherwise, that's fine," I said. "You're very generous."

"You've always been the light drinker," he said, rolling his eyes. "But the plumbs are yours," he replied, bandaging young Matrose's neck.

"Do you feel ready to go back up for sextant practice, darling, or would you like to rest a bit? I know that may have been a bit frightening, and you lost a little blood. If you need some time to yourself I completely understand," I told him.

"I'm fine," he replied meekly.

"Well, go to the cockpit for dinner, then. Don't forget to eat your peas and drink your lemonade; 'tis important that you get your vitamins. After that you may go back to training with the others."

"Thank you, Captain," he said, quickly leaving.

"Sweet little fellow," I commented when he had gone.

"He's rather frail," Burke said. "He nearly died a few months ago. Poor thing."

"Well, what would you expect, after being forced-marched a hundred miles and imprisoned by the French for three months?"

"All I'm saying is not to get too attached," he said. Then, changing the subject, "Care to join me for dinner?"

"I'd love to," I replied, "but I'm afraid I cannot. I have work to do inspecting the hull, then the masts and rigging."

"Can't you do that another time?" He asked.

"Unfortunately not. I have to know how badly she's leaking, and what sort of pressure she can hold. If the timbers are rotten then we ought to reduce sail."

"Well, I'll see you for supper, then," he said.

I walked forward then down a ladder to the platform holding the carpenter's store. Stacks of boards lay on one end, with a worktable and woodworking tools in the centre of the room. The carpenter's mates had all gone to dinner, but the carpenter was still there. He raised his knuckles respectfully. "How's the state of the hull?" I asked.

"Not good, sir, but she'll make it to England if the weather holds. The reinforced bracing has done wonders, otherwise she would have broken to pieces months ago."

When *H.M.S. Cassandra* had last gone into port for repairs, she had been condemned as unseaworthy. Unfortunately, however, the navy had been experiencing a lack of ships. During the Peace of Amiens two years ago, the government had cut the navy's funding drastically. To make matters worse, the Secretary of the Admiralty had been Lord St. Vincent, a daring and capable admiral who had won his title in battle, but also a strongman and a skeptic. His lack of trust had caused him to launch into a series of reforms to fight corruption in the dockyards, in which many workers were fired and many more lived in fear. St. Vincent's actions to make the dockyards function more efficiently had in fact done the opposite. Fewer ships were produced due to the turmoil the reforms had caused. The peace lasted only a year, and when the fighting resumed between France and Great Britain, the navy found itself outnumbered and the ships we did have old and frail. Most would have collapsed into themselves had it not been for a new innovation; a system of reinforcing the hull using diagonal wooden beams. *H.M.S. Cassandra* had had the beams constructed about two years ago, and though it had made her seaworthy again temporarily, the underlying problem of rotten planking had not been solved.

"Do you think we should take in sail to reduce pressure?" I asked.

"It wouldn't hurt," he replied, "but I think she'll be fine. She can handle well in this, but anything more than twelve knots would stress her." The carpenter referred to twelve knots of wind speed, which was the force pushing on the sails to power the ship. However, due to the size of the ship and the drag of seawater, *H.M.S. Cassandra* would travel at a speed of six knots.

"Thank you," I said. "You've done an excellent job at keeping this ship afloat."

"Thank you, Captain," he said, his eyes softening at the thought of being appreciated.

"Now, go get your dinner. I don't believe the ship will sink out from under us if you take an hour to eat," I said, turning and leaving.

Just before I headed up the ladder to the lower, then upper deck I remembered what I had considered earlier, of having the men work the pump when the water level rose too high. "How much water is in the bilge?" I asked the carpenter. It was his duty to check the depth of the water of the bilge every hour or so, looking at a long measuring stick that went down to the very bottom of the ship.

"Two and a half feet, sir. We ought to pump soon," he replied.

Better to let the men eat before giving the order, I thought, knowing full well how taxing the duty could be on them. In order to pump the bilge, the men had to turn a lever on the upper deck up and down that activated a pump, which took the water from the bilge twenty-five feet above to the main deck where it would run over the sides of the ship and away. To power such a system the sailors were put under tremendous strain and soon became exhausted.

My eyes wandered to the wooden walls of the ship themselves. They were of long planks sealed with tar made from the sap of pine trees and buttressed with the trunks of large oaks forming a skeleton on the sides. Under the water and a few inches above, plates of copper were nailed to the bottom of the ship to help keep off marine growth. This did two things. Firstly, it reduced drag so the ship could sail faster. Secondly, it helped preserve the oak body of the ship from rot. Had we not had the copper sheath, *H.M.S. Cassandra* would have sunk a year ago. The gun ports began shortly above the waterline, with the guns as low to the water as possible for stability, which made for more accurate firing. On my ship, there was only one continuous deck of guns, but on ships of the line there could be as many as three. I'd even heard of a monster four-decker out there, the *Santissima Trinidad* of Spain, but had difficulty believing that a ship that large could actually exist.

Above the waterline, *H.M.S. Cassandra* was painted. It was the captain's preference as to colour and pattern, as there were no regulations by the navy with regards to the ship's appearance. I had decided to paint the ship mostly black, the upper deck red, and the gun ports themselves black. Truthfully, there were very few navy regulations in general. Captains could make structural changes to their ships if they wished, they could choose which guns to equip, and even had a say in how many, though this was largely determined by the size of the ship. They could set their own watch schedules as well, and assign up to twelve lashes to punish men for offences if they so chose, without having to issue a court martial. I was not fond of the lash, though I had been forced to use it a few times for drunkenness or thievery with certain problem individuals.

I ran my hand along the wood and felt the air pockets that had grown where the oak had rotted away. In one place a dampness had seeped through the boards and slimy algae had begun to grow. I checked my pocket watch, holding it under one of the oil lanterns that hung from the ceiling to read it. It was five minutes to one, when the dinner hour would be over. Deciding to head back up to the upper deck to issue the order to pump the bilge, I turned and walked back to the ladder, then stepped up the first stair and— snap! My heart caught in my throat as my foot slipped, landing on the ground. I felt a sharp pain as my knee hit the rung above. As the rush of sheer terror subsided I saw that the ladder had broken; the rotten wood had given way and the board had cracked in two. Rubbing my knee, I moaned, cursing, but the pain quickly subsided. The workers scattered about the forward platform rushed out in surprise: the carpenter, and two of the sailmaker's mates. Seeing what had happened the carpenter rushed to me. "Are you alright, sir?" He asked, voice filled with worry.

"I'm fine," I answered dismissively. "That wasn't your fault, she's rotten to the core."

"I can fix that stair this afternoon, if you'd like, sir."

"That would be good, if you please."

"Aye, sir," he replied, and I turned and climbed cautiously up to the lower deck in search of Wilson, my second to most senior lieutenant, who would have command of the first dog watch after dinner. The watch system aboard my ship, as well as most others in the Royal Navy, was structured so that after dinner, which was at noon, the watches would serve short two-hour shifts, as opposed to the normal four-hour shift. There were two watches aboard most ships, so half the crew would be in a position to respond to an emergency at any one time. One watch would have leisure time or sleep while the other was serving, except in the morning after breakfast when both watches would be employed. The dog watches were designed to switch the order in which the watches served; this was to provide the men with adequate time to sleep, as at night one watch had eight hours to rest while the other had only four. Because of the dog-watch system, each watch could get an average of six hours of sleep per night, provided they did not sleep on deck during their duty, which I allowed some of my men, especially the young gentlemen, to do so they would stay fresh. Tradesmen, called 'idlers', such as the carpenter, blacksmith, sailmaker, gunner, purser, and ships' surgeon, were exempted from the watch system and could sleep the whole night through, but could be woken when needed. As the captain, I, too was exempted from the normal watch system, but I had difficulty sleeping, and would often wake at arbitrary times, then go out on deck to check on my officers and men.

I walked up to the lower deck then aft to the gunroom, a section where the officers dined, both commissioned and noncommissioned. Their cabins adjoined the space, each squares separated by canvas bulkheads about eight feet by eight feet, though my first lieutenant, Brooks, had a slightly larger cabin. I looked around for Wilson, but did not see him. I did, however, find the master finishing a glass of lemonade. I approached him from behind. "Have you seen Lieutenant Wilson?"

"No, sir," he replied in a thick Scottish accent.

"Could you please pass the word for Lieutenant Wilson to meet me in the gunroom?" I asked.

"Aye, sir," he said, then turned to one of the other officers and repeated my message. Passing the word involved a ship's company sending a message to someone through a long string of officers and crew members. When one passed the word, he told those nearby the message, then they would go about and tell others the message, until after a few conversations the information soon reached the person intended. Sometimes the message would become jumbled, but generally in a few minutes the requested person would meet me where I'd asked. In a crowded ship only ninety feet long, one was never out of sight or sound of other people.

A few minutes later Wilson emerged from one of the cabins adjoining the gunroom, fidgeting with his neck-cloth then hastily adjusting his belt. "Sorry, sir, I was in my cabin."

"That's fine," I said, pretending not to notice Angeline, my first lieutenant Brooks' daughter, sneaking out of his cabin then away from the gunroom with great alacrity.

Wilson and Brooks, my two most senior lieutenants, had disliked each other from the start. Wilson was one of my younger lieutenants, whose maternal grandfather was a prominent Tory member of parliament. His connections had given him a lieutenancy at the age of nineteen, though of course, on his examination he'd claimed he was twenty. Now, at the age of twenty-two he was young, energetic, and incompetent.

Brooks was a family man, who'd worked his way up the ranks through hard work and capability. His upbringing was the opposite of Wilson's- the son of a prostitute and a soldier that he'd never met, he'd run away from home at an early age and had to fend for himself on the streets. At the age of sixteen the Charitable Fund had found him in a London slum, as he had travelled on a five-hundred mile journey south from his native Edinburgh looking for work. He'd had a job for a few weeks working in a textile factory but had feuded with his employer, as was his tendency, for in his youth his mercurial temper had gotten him into a number of fights. The Charitable Fund had fed him and clothed him, then provided him with a stable job and a place to live in the Royal Navy. From then on he'd thrived. Aboard a warship, his competence and assertiveness had allowed him to progress through the ranks despite his past and his lack of connections.

Having earned his rank through hard work alone, Brooks felt he was more deserving than Wilson and viewed him as a spoiled child. To Wilson, Brooks was old, taste-less, and uneducated. The main rift that had occurred between the two of them, however, was over Brooks' daughter. Wilson had feelings for her, but Brooks saw him as unworthy and thought that he was too old for her. I found it Brooks the more agreeable of the two. Neverthe-less, I approached Wilson to talk. "How are you today, Lieutenant?" I asked.

"Very well, thank you, Captain," he replied.

"I'm hosting my usual Sunday supper in my dining cabin, if you'd like to come," I said, inviting him.

"That would be lovely, sir," he replied, his expres-sion one of a pretentious lack of interest.

"Very good. I look forward to seeing you there. The ship's been leaking again. As your watch is on duty next, I'd like you to send a detachment of your men below to work the pump, if you please."

"Aye, sir, I'll do that," he said.

With Wilson looking after the pump, I decided to head back to my cabin and speak with Higgins with regards to preparation for the supper tonight. I generally invited my officers to dine with me every Sunday, and sometimes more frequently than that. I walked back to my dining cabin, which was at the aft-most end of the upper deck, where I found Higgins polishing my silverware. "Good afternoon, Higgins," I greeted him.

"Captain," he said, raising his knuckles politely. "The surgeon, Burke, brought you sugar plumbs. He said you'd asked for them."

"I've invited my officers to supper tonight, as usual," I said. "I promised Burke champagne, and he brought the plumbs for dessert, but as for the rest of my menu, I'm not yet certain. When you've finished with the silver, would you please check what's left of my personal store of victuals and see what dishes the cook could prepare?"

"Aye, sir," he replied, and I knew he had already examined my victuals, which were stored on the aft platform in the hold, and prepared a menu for tonight. Higgins was an excellent butler, and he had anticipated my needs before I had thought of them myself, as always. "We could make a soufflé with the eggs from your chicken, the one not gone broody, sir. And we do have some salt pork left, along with a few carrots."

"All of that would be fine. Thank you very much," I said, smiling. I was surprised that I had so much left.

After that, I decided to speak with the sailing master with regards to our distance from Portsmouth and how long it would take to reach our destination. I guessed we were traveling a good four knots at present, though I figured the weather could shift any day now. That being said, I couldn't see a cloud in the sky. O'Hare was standing leaning over the side of the ship, busy taking the hourly test of boat speed, having finished with the young gentlemen's sextant practice. He used a line with knots tied at known intervals. To find boat-speed, he would drop the line into the sea and measure how many knots reached the end of the ship in a minute. "How fast is she sailing?" I asked, coming up behind him. He jumped, momentarily startled.

"Good afternoon, Captain," he said, raising his knuckles. "Four knots, sir," he replied.

"That's good, very good. How far are we from Portsmouth?" I asked.

"390 miles, I believe, sir," he replied, "about three days away at this rate."

"Excellent," I said. "And is the weather expected to hold?"

"I'm no fortune teller, sir, but it should, aye," he replied.

I felt a bit of tension relieved from my shoulders. O'Hare was usually right; he had spent most of his life at sea, piloting fishing vessels in his native Dundee before joining the Royal Navy for the adventure and the pay. Fishermen were exempted from impressment, as to take them away from their profession would compromise the nation's food supply. "Good work, O'Hare, you may go about your duties."

I then decided to speak with the two helmsmen that steered the ship "Good afternoon, Captain," they said, raising their knuckles. There was a part of me that enjoyed being saluted constantly, and another bashful side that wished I could walk about the ship quietly without attracting so much attention.

"How does she feel?" I asked them.

"I 'ave to point 'er one-a-larboard, but she holds steady, sir."

"There is a bit of a current pushing her east, sir," the other translated. "Sails are trimmed as well as can be, considering the low winds, but the spars are worn, so I believe it is beneficial, if you'll allow me to say so, sir."

"I agree entirely," I said, quickly eyeing the sails. After two years, the crew all knew their duties. I had promoted the best ones to be noncommissioned officers and able seamen, and had disciplined the worst ones to be somewhat useful. I had adjusted the sails and rigging, positioned the guns, and even modified the sectioning of the hull to bring the ship to her most seaworthy. *H.M.S. Cassandra* was functioning at her maximum capability; the living, breathing organism that was the ship, which included both the vessel and its compliment, was fine-tuned to its utmost. Now there was nothing more to do but head back to my cabin and await the next development. I considered drilling the men in gunnery, but decided it would not be worthwhile at this point in the voyage and the stress to the ship would make it downright dangerous.

   "Hello, darling!" A sweet voice called. It was Margaret to her husband, the master. Her auburn hair was tied up today, and she wore a green dress. O'Hare beckoned her over. She smiled at me, curtsying politely. "Good afternoon, Captain," she said. There were seven ladies aboard the *Cassandra*, five of them wives of the officers, three commissioned and two noncommissioned and one of them named Rosie who claimed to be Burke's wife, but in reality was his sweetheart. There was a girl as well, Brooks' teenage daughter. During battle, most of them would serve as "powder monkeys", carrying gunpowder to the men at the cannons. Rosie, however, often liked to assist Burke with caring for the sailors, and expressed interest in tending the wounded if a battle occurred. I had allowed them to stay

aboard for several reasons. The first is that their presence
increased morale tenfold. Secondly, the men behaved better
when they had to answer to ladies; there were fewer disciplinary issues as a result. I had thrown out all the prostitutes
when we'd left port, so only respectable women remained.
I had grown quite fond of them, in the platonic way that
was fit to treat married ladies.

I headed back aft to the ladder leading to the upper
deck and my cabin, but before I could get there I intercep-
ted two of my men getting into an argument. Chase and
Greene, two that I had pressed from the Newcastle collier,
were almost ready to go to blows when I arrived. "Give it
back to me, you scoundrel!"

"'Tis not yours! I own you, therefore I own the
bloody shoe buckles!"

"That's my wages, not yours. You spent all yours on
the whores in Naples!"

"What seems to be the matter?" I asked, stepping in.

Both men snapped to attention. "Chase took my
shoe buckles, sir," Greene said.

"Captain, sir, the shoe buckles belong to me," Chase
said.

"May I see the shoe-buckles?" I asked. Chase
handed them to me. I examined them closely to see they
were of silver. It was one of the favourite purchases of sailors on shore liberty.

"I bought them, sir," Greene said. "With my pay, sir."

"Allow me to explain," Chase said. "We're Americans, sir. I told the men when they pressed us, but they wouldn't listen. We're from Virginia."

I cringed at the sound of the name America.

"I bought Greene here to help work on my boat," he continued. "I took her to England, but she was seized, so we ended up in the collier for employment. Then you pressed us. Greene, however, is my property, so any income he makes is mine. Because I own him, I own all his belongings, including the shoe buckles."

"But I bought them with my hard earned pay!" Greene exclaimed.

"I see," I replied, handing the shoe buckles to Greene. "But the Royal Navy owns both of you. As your captain, I would like to kindly ask that Landsman Chase and Ordinary Seaman Greene cease arguing so you can *go about your duties*. Do I make myself plain?" I asked, enunciating strongly the phrase "go about your duties."

"Aye, sir," they both said, raising their knuckles.

It was at that point that I finally walked back down to the upper deck where my quarters were located. Then, just before entering, I recognised the value of speaking a few words of encouragement to the men at the pump. I walked over to where the men were labouring away, turn-

ing the pump shirtless and sweating. "Keep at it, lads," I
said. "Make your country proud. Keeping the *Cassandra*
afloat keeps one more ship for the navy. And it keeps all of
us alive." I heard a loud huzzah, then stood with Wilson a
few minutes longer, hoping my presence would inspire
them. I went to the bilge and checked with the carpenter;
only six inches of water remained to be pumped. I waited
until the water had dropped to only two inches then relieved the men, and walked with Wilson back up to the
quarterdeck. Both of us were glad to be back in the fresh
air. Shortly after, four bells rang and the second dog watch
commenced. My most senior lieutenant, Brooks, stepped up
on deck with his watch to relieve Wilson.

For a frigate of *H.M.S. Cassandra*'s size, it was
normal to have a few lieutenants; on my ship I had four. I'd
sent two whom had started the voyage away with the prize
vessels, so while I had selected Brooks and Wilson, Reid
and Perkins had been sent from larger ships in the Mediterranean fleet. Technically these two were not lieutenants;
they had been promoted to acting lieutenants from the rank
of midshipmen but were awaiting sitting the exam in England. Thus though they had all the responsibilities of a lieutenancy, they did not yet hold the King's commission to
make the rank official. The two seniors ran the watches,
with the younger ones assisting. Brooks and Reid managed
the first watch, and Wilson and Perkins managed the

second. As Brooks was my most senior lieutenant, he also had the added duty of being my second-in-command and next in line to captain the ship should I be somehow killed or incapacitated. I also liked to go to my lieutenants for advice, a skill I'd learned from my patron.

"How's your wife?" I asked Brooks casually. I liked to make formal conversations with my officers, both to raise morale and to understand their limitations and capabilities. I never spoke of myself, or asked them anything intimate— there was a line that a ship's captain stayed behind, one that prevented him from any real friendship with any of his officers or men. It was important that this barrier of formality was never crossed; at the end of the day a captain would still have to be able to tell any one of them, "I order you to die."

"She's very well," he replied, "though feuding with Mrs. Burke."

"I see," I replied, mildly amused. So they knew about the affair.

"And Angeline is still swooning Lieutenant Wilson, even though he's five years her senior. I'm not all that worried, as she's a sensible young woman. I think she's just bored. Once we're back in port she'll have more to look at." I remembered the events of earlier that morning, the way she'd rushed from Wilson's cabin. For the sake of unit cohesion I decided not to mention it to Brooks.

"Well, it should only be another few days providing there are no mishaps," I said, changing the conversation.

"No mishaps? We've not seen the enemy since leaving the Mediterranean and the weather's been beautiful. I don't see how anything could possibly go so badly wrong as to delay us in only a few days."

"I do hope you're right," I said. Logically, of course, he was. I pushed away the ominous feeling at the back of my mind, dismissing it as unwarranted anxiety.

"I'm hosting my usual Sunday supper in my dining cabin, if you'd like to come," I said, inviting him. "You may leave Lieutenant Reid in command of the first night watch, as he got to go the past few weeks."

"That would be lovely, sir," he replied.

"Very good. I look forward to seeing you there." At that point I figured it would be a good idea to see the sails and upper rigging for myself. There was a weak section of the mizzen topsail that I was worried would tear. To fix it would be a minor inconvenience, but it would be helpful to warn the sailmaker if it was close to ripping. Normally we would carry spare sails to replace the ones that became weak or torn, but we'd had trouble procuring shipbuilding supplies in the Mediterranean, and so I'd run out of replacements for the topsails.

I climbed up the shrouds, which were sturdy lines coated in tar with smaller ratlines tied in a cross-hash pattern between them. Once I was thirty feet up the mizzen-mast I looked out over the horizon, only to see nothing but an endless blue sky and a glassy sea. The wind brushed my face and I climbed another three feet or so to the crows' nest, holding onto one of the topsail halyards with one hand and letting go with the other. A divine sense of freedom filled me, as if the entire world was mine. *This is what I live for.* I climbed out onto one of the ratlines and ran my fingers along the suspect area of the mizzen topsail, then saw that some of the canvas had frayed and was worn down, but not yet to the point of breaking. The boom that held out the bottom of the sail also creaked weakly, but I figured it would be fine in this weather.

"She'll hold, Captain," a voice startled me from behind. I jumped, almost losing my balance and falling to my death. My nerves settling, I recognised it to be the boatswain, who was responsible for looking after the masts and rigging. It was a prestigious position, and on my ship it was held by one of the oldest members of the ship's company, second only to the cook.

"Any other areas of stress I should worry about?" I asked.

"The main halyard's weak, sir," he replied. "As for booms, this is the worst, sir. The only other one of any concern in this weather is the main topgallant boom. The yards

up there are also troubled, sir, but I wouldn't recommend
reducing sail to ease the pressure yet."

"Thank you," I replied, then decided to stand
somewhere more stable. I climbed back to the crows' nest
and took hold of one of the lines that was strung from there.
It stretched between the mizzen mast and the mainmast and
looked rather odd, as it had fluffy rounds of cloth attached
to it at two foot intervals called baggy wrinkles. The purpose of this line was to keep the sails from chafing by
providing a soft barrier between them.

There were a multitude of terms for sails and rigging aboard a ship. Some common ones were halyards,
sheets, shrouds, masts, booms, jibs, staysails, topsails and
topgallants. Halyards were a type of rope, called a line
aboard a ship, that could be used to raise or lower a sail.
Sheets were another line that could pull the sail from side
to side, or in and out, to adjust to changes in the position of
the ship relative to the wind. Halyards and sheets were both
types of running rigging, or so it was called, for they were
moved and adjusted frequently. Shrouds were a type of
standing rigging, so called because they generally stayed
tied in the same position and were not adjusted frequently
during a voyage. Shrouds attached to places on the masts
and to the deck. Their job was to stabilise the masts. Masts
were the large trees that the sails attached to. Aboard my
ship there were three. In order from bow to stern they were

the foremast, mainmast, and mizzenmast. Booms were large pieces of wood that generally ran perpendicular to the masts and attached to the bottom of a sail.

Jibs were a type of sail that was special, as they were shaped like triangles, while most sails aboard large ships like my frigate were rhombus-shaped. There were three jibs attached to the bowsprit and foremast, and two that could be rigged between the masts in extremely light conditions. Staysails were triangular sails that were like jibs but had booms beneath them. They could be rigged between the masts and on the bowsprit. There were two rectangular sails aboard a square-rigged ship, which were the lowest sails on their respective masts called the foresail and the mainsail. The mizzenmast featured a uniquely shaped sail called the spanker. Topsails were the next level up, and above them were topgallants. The highest sails in the ship were the royals, which flew above the topgallants. Sails were referred to by their mast and their vertical position. For example, the main royal referred to the highest sail on the mast in the middle of the ship— the mainmast. Because the mainmast was taller than the foremast and even taller than the mizzenmast, this sail happened to be the highest up in the ship.

From the mizzenmast I could see all the happenings on deck; the officers' wives talking in a circle below, Greene taking out his fiddle and beginning to play a slow, relaxing tune, a group of four sailors playing cards, the yeoman of signals mending one of his flags, one of the sailors polishing the ship's bell, a pair of red-coated Royal Marines pacing the deck, deep in conversation. Even from here I could smell the supper old Carleton was cooking. The floating city was alive and well. We were one small speck of dust on the wide open sea, drifting calmly towards home. The breeze played in the hair of my wig and the sunlight caused the water to glint like diamonds. I stayed up there watching over my little wooden kingdom for another half-hour or so until the sky began to glow orange, then climbed back down to the quarterdeck.

After that I headed to the dining cabin, and finally made it through the door. Higgins was setting the table, though it was still two hours until supper. I made an entry in the ship's log for October 7th, 1804, then sat down at the harpsichord, opening my favourite book of Haydn's pieces and turning to his Minuet in G. The clang of the harpsichord sounded graceful, even elegant with his fast-paced, climactic pieces. I thought his music sounded better on the metallic twang of this small instrument than my grand pianoforte at home. The same could not be said for Mozart or Beethoven, and though I had taken a few sheets of their music aboard ship with me, I had left most of it at home. After playing Minuet in G, I moved on to Haydn's Sonata in B-flat Major. The music relaxed me and allowed me time for reflection. In a way this time for inner thought calmed me but at the same time it distressed me. My mind wandered back to the dream last night, the one that had interrupted my sleep for twenty-two years.

I thought of my father's body, the hole through his chest. I was thirteen. After that— only a dark void where two years disappeared. I remembered the events; the agony, the loneliness, the funeral, the many nights in hospital rooms, but they felt like a story that someone had told me, as if they had happened to somebody else.

"Are you alright, sir?" Higgins asked, placing a hand on my shoulder.

"Oh, I'm fine," I replied quickly, forcing a smile.

"Supper is in half an hour, as per your orders, sir. Would you like to be dressed now?" He asked.

"That would be excellent, if you please," I answered, standing and walking to my sleeping cabin.

Higgins followed me there. I undressed and he helped me change into more formal attire; clean white breeches, silk tights, polished black shoes with silver buckles. I wore a clean shirt with lace at the end of the sleeves, as well as a silk vest adorned with red and gold anchors. He fastened my lace neckcloth around my neck then placed a black velvet eyepatch over my left eye, then gave me a fancier wig. He brushed white powder heavily on my face, then pink on my cheeks, blended carefully so

as to conceal the scars. He placed my lace-and-gold
trimmed tricorne hat on my head, the one with the blue
feathered cockade. Finally, he slid my navy blue coat on
me, the one that matched the hat, that I'd had specially
tailored with gold trim, and gold buttons. Two gilded
epaulettes decorated the shoulders, and Higgins brushed
them so that the strands appeared straight. The hat and coat
pair had been expensive, costing almost twenty pounds, but
I liked to dress nicely. The article of clothing I was most
proud of, however, was a silver medal with a thirteen-frond
palm tree and two crocodiles that I kept beautifully polished. It was attached to a silk blue ribbon, which Higgins
slid over my head. Finally, I put on a pair of white gloves,
fine silk masterpieces that fit my hands smoothly. I took a
deep breath; parties made me a bit nervous and I always
felt exhausted afterwards.

 A knock at the door made me jump. Higgins offered
to answer it but I went instead. Dr. Burke had arrived,
dressed smartly. "You got the plumbs, didn't you?" He
asked, peering in.

 "Yes. And the champagne," I replied.

 "Good. I expect to have fun tonight. Higgins, would
you mind playing the harpsichord?" He asked my servant,
stepping into the room. "And Herrick," he said, walking to
the aft windows. "Open the windows, the weather is mar-

vellous." He swung open each of the gallery windows in turn and a cool breeze swept through the room.

"There. That looks lovely," he said. Higgins began to go through my book of Haydn. At the end of the room on the starboard side there was a table with a large clock and two decorative vases. Above it was a painting of my father, in his blue uniform coat done when he was younger than I was. Brooks arrived next, along with two of the captain's servants on his watch, Matrose and his friend Haynes. After that came two of the other lieutenants, Wilson and Perkins, then finally the Captain of Marines and his wife. Burke's lady arrived last, wearing a red dress with flowered patterns. He took her up in his arms and she kissed him passionately on the lips.

She approached me then. "Good evening, Captain," she said in a deep, husky voice.

"Good evening, madam," I said, taking off my hat and bowing politely.

"You look nice tonight," she said.

"So do you," I replied, always a little taken aback by her beauty. Burke was not the jealous or possessive type; he never took offence at her speaking to me. In fact, I think he liked to watch my reaction.

"Now, now, Rosie," he said, grinning at my unease. "Not until Georgie's had a little champagne."

"Right," I said, mildly annoyed and mildly amused. I walked to my place at the head of the table, and my guests soon followed suit, the murmurs of conversation silencing. "Ladies and gentlemen, please be seated," I said.

I pulled out Rosie's chair for her as she sat on my right and Burke took his place on my left. The cook —not Carleton, but one who served only the officers— brought in dishes on silver platters, hidden by covers, while Higgins served the champagne. I tucked my napkin into my shirt and lifted the cover over the first dish; a steaming pot of carrots. I served myself a small spoonful of them and passed the dish along to Rosie. Burke handed me the next one; a lovely soufflé, then the next, slabs of salt pork cooked in a rosemary sauce. The plates were only half-full and the victuals were scant but well prepared. This was due in part because of my diminishing personal store of provisions, but also because throwing a lavish party with copious amounts of food while the crew was near starvation on half-rations would send the wrong message. I realised I was quite hungry, having missed dinner, but knew that it would be improper to start eating without first declaring a toast. I raised my glass, and the uproar of conversation caused by the introduction of the food died down. The table looked to me. I cleared my throat, and said my usual "To king and country," then lowered my glass and sipped the champagne while the rest of the party repeated my words in assent.

"To wives and sweethearts, may they never meet!"
Burke exclaimed quickly, raising his glass to another toast.
I rolled my eyes. Wouldn't just one "cheers" suffice, and
then we could eat? Now for a whole string of them...

"To God," said the Captain of Marines, being a pi-
ous fellow and a loyal husband. His wife Abigail nodded,
glaring at Burke and Rosie. So they knew. Everybody
knew, they just didn't talk about it.

"To civility and good humour," Brooks said, want-
ing to put an end to all this, being just as hungry as I was.

"To standing up for our ideals," the Captain of Marines' wife said.

"To love," Rosie sighed in her lusty, romantic voice.

"To Britannia. Death to the French," young Matrose
piped up, his eyes wandering to the delicious carrots in
front of him. Thank you, darling, I thought to myself. Now
we can put an end to this madness and actually eat, before
we all get roaring drunk on an empty stomach. I repeated
my promise to myself that I would provide as much interest
to the little fellow as I was possibly able.

I stuck my fork into one of the carrots and raised it
to my mouth, then— A knock at the door made me jump
and I watched as Higgins answered it. It was Reid. He
entered, and I could see in his expression that something
distressed him. "Captain, sir," he said urgently. "There's
been a... disciplinary issue with one of the men."

"Alright. Let's go outside." I stood and slipped quietly away so nobody would know I had gone. Out on deck the stars twinkled in a clear navy sky. The air was fresh and the horizons endless. I turned to my subordinate officer. "Now, what seems to be the matter?" I asked.

"The purser caught a sailor smoking on the lower deck. When he asked him to stop, the sailor struck him. He was drunk, sir, when he was supposed to be on watch with me. I found an empty bottle of brandy in his coat pocket."

"Where is the sailor? I'd like to speak with him," I asked.

"I had him tied up on the upper deck, sir. Right this way, if you please." I followed him down a ladder then across the deck some ways to see the culprit; a red-faced and inebriated Chase with his feet manacled to two cannon's rings on the deck.

"Fancy seeing you again," I told him menacingly. "It seems that our little talk this afternoon didn't quite get through to you, did it?" I asked. "Do you know why you are here?"

"No, I honestly don't know why my ship was seized, I was taken from my profession by you bloody limeys and stripped of my property, then tied up for giving that rat there what he deserves!" He shouted, his eyes fixed on the purser in hostility.

I glanced up. Mr. Gailden leaned against the bulk-head, on eye badly blackened and his cheek swollen and puffy. Not that he had just stood by and taken a beating, as Chase had a bloodied nose and a cracked lip. It was clear to me, however, that the purser had received the worst of it.

"Curious, isn't it, that a common sailor comes across a bottle of brandy just as the ship's surgeon finds his is missing?" I asked.

"He ought not have the stuff anyways," Chase cursed under his breath.

"Were you really smoking on the lower deck when you were supposed to be on watch?" I asked, kneeling down and taking him by the collar. He didn't answer. "Do you know what's down there? The powder room? If that fire had reached the powder room you could have killed us all! I was at the Nile! I saw L'Orient blown to pieces and a thousand French sailors burned alive! You fool! You know now what I must do, in order to maintain discipline. What your incompetence and insubordination has forced me to do three times this voyage, and you never seem to learn. Twelve lashes for thievery! Twelve lashes for drunkenness! Twelve lashes for smoking below decks! Twelve lashes for assaulting your superior officer! That's forty-eight in total. I'll see justice carried out in the morning at eight bells," I hissed. Legally, I was only allowed to sentence a man to twelve lashes maximum for any offence without a courts-martial, but this rule was not rigorously enforced, and he had committed multiple offences.

I walked back up to the main deck, to the cool night air, feeling sick to my stomach. The power of the officers aboard a ship was not a thing to be taken for granted. Discipline was a delicate balance, with mutual duties and responsibilities. A ship with an effective system of discipline would protect crew members from each other, just as a police force and a criminal justice system would on land. By maintaining standards for safety and cleanliness, the ship could also function more efficiently and the sailors could remain healthier. The officers were the ones with the power to do this. If discipline were too lax, the sailors would fight amongst themselves and the ship would be thrown into a state of disfunction and possibly mutiny. If discipline were too harsh, the sailors would start to view their officers as enemies which could also lead to mutiny.

I took a moment on deck, and walked to the bow to clear my head. Looking down, I saw the bowsprit. It was an ornate carving of a lady with flowing black hair dressed in white robes, supposed to represent the Greek Cassandra for whom the ship was named. I remembered the myth, and her curse; she could foresee the future, but if she told anyone what she saw, they would never believe her. I thought it was an interesting choice of name for a frigate, especially one whose task was to watch the enemy and report its sightings to the rest of the Mediterranean fleet. My nerves now calmed from the ordeal with Chase, I walked back down to my dining cabin to finally have my supper.

I sat down, seeing that my guests had already finished eating and were immersed in conversation. Higgins, noticing my absence, had placed a cover over my plate to keep it warm. I looked up and smiled at him in approval, as he stood at the edge of the room. The carrots were delicious, lightly salted to make up for the fact that they were not entirely fresh. They were cut into rounds, the rotten bits having been fed to the chickens. The vegetables were my favourite part of every meal, so usually I would taste them, then finish them last after eating everything else so I could leave the table with their flavour still lingering on my tongue. The pork was salted to be almost inedible, though it had been soaked in water for hours beforehand. The sweetness of the rosemary-mint sauce, however, balanced the flavour. I ate the meat first, then the fluffy soufflé, which was filled with peas, then finished the carrots and drank what was left of my champagne. At that point, looking around at the others, I could see that they were ready for dessert.

Higgins walked over to me once I had finished eating, then I quietly asked him to bring the sugar plumbs. He left the room, and I turned to start talking to Burke, but he was too absorbed with Rosie to pay much attention to me. I swear to God, ever since he brought that woman aboard, he'd acted as though I no longer existed. Finally, after what felt like ages, Higgins brought in the large china bowl filled with Burke's plumbs. He distributed new bowls with spoons to each of the guests, and we began to pass around the plumbs. "Do take some yourself, Higgins. You've earned it," I told him.

The plumbs were strongly acidic but still a bit sweet. Some of the juices had had time to turn to vinegar, and the fruits themselves were soft and as dark-red as wine. I watched Morgan watch Rosie and had to resist my own jealousy. His eyes were glazed softly over, his face intent yet relaxed, gaze transfixed on her lips and her eyes, her eyes and her lips. He was a man in love. And she loved him back.

I decided to leave them to each other and walked over to the two captain's servants I'd invited, who stared blankly at their empty plates. "Haynes, Matrose," I said, addressing them both. "You two look bored. Would you like to hear about Lord Nelson again?" I asked.

"Yes please, sir," Haynes replied.

Matrose nodded, his sweet little face tired.

"How did you know Lord Nelson, sir?" Haynes asked.

"Well, I was stationed under him as a lieutenant. He's my patron, you see. It was he who spoke to the right people to have me promoted to commander and then captain so quickly. When I first became a lieutenant, I was sent to the North Sea Fleet, but the cold made me very sick, so I was sent home to England. That was in 1797. After that, I earned a place on Nelson's flagship in the Mediterranean Fleet after the fleet had lost men at the Battle of Cape St. Vincent the year before. He truly was an excellent commander. It was his leadership, I believe, that won battles. He trusted and believed in his officers, so we trusted and believed in him. His smile was what caught my attention, it was absolutely captivating. You felt he understood you. I've never met a man whose love of country ran so deep, it was as if his very soul was entirely devoted."

"You were at the Nile, weren't you, sir?" Matrose asked.

"Yes, I was, in 1798. That's how I got my medal. Nelson's strategy was brilliant. He had us come around behind the French by flanking them on the side they weren't prepared for, then drop two anchors, one at the bow of the ship and one at the stern, to keep us steady during the fight. I was stationed on the middle gun deck, where it was deafeningly noisy from the gunfire and the smoke made it almost impossible to see anything at all, but I remember them taking him below when he fell."

"Is that when he lost his arm?" Haynes asked.

"No, he lost his arm several years before, at a failed attempt to land and capture Spanish gold on the island of Tenerife. At this one he had a nasty head injury. I do truly think it affected him, he never was the same after that. And then, when we got to Naples, that's when the affair started."

"Affair?" Haynes asked, interested.

"Yes. He started sleeping with the British ambassador's wife, Lady Hamilton, as a married man with a stepson."

Matrose leaned with his arm on the table, half asleep and clearly disinterested with Nelson's romantic life. "Did you receive your wound at the Nile, sir?" He asked.

"No, I was very fortunate to survive unscathed," I answered.

At just that moment I saw out of the corner of my eye Brooks' daughter Angeline dancing intimately with Lieutenant Wilson. "Alright, gentlemen. If you will excuse me, I think we should join the dance," I said.

I walked over to Wilson and stood, waiting for him to finish twirling with Angeline. Just as they leaned in to kiss I interrupted. "Excuse me, Lieutenant, may I cut in?"

"Of course, Captain, sir," he said through grit teeth.

I took Angeline by the waist as Higgins began to play a waltz. She glanced away from me, over my shoulder, her lips turned in a grimace. Out of the corner of my eye I could see Brooks smiling at me with gratitude. We glided delicately across the floor until the piece was finished, and she parted from me and walked to the corner of the room to talk to Rosie. It was then that Burke was peeled away from his paramour, and he finally went to go talk to me.

"Dr. Burke," I said, pleased that he remembered that I actually existed.

"George!" he replied, embracing me. I could tell at that point that he'd had a bit too much to drink.

"That's Captain Herrick to you," I said. "Just because you're my friend doesn't mean you are exempted from the proper forms of address aboard my ship."

"Still uptight, eh?" He asked. "How about another glass of champagne?"

"No thank you, I'm to direct a flogging tomorrow morning."

"Well, then the more reason for it!"

"One of the charges is for drunkenness. I found where your brandy went, by the way," I said dryly.

"Oh? The usual suspect?"

"Yes," I replied.

"Well, don't flog him over me!" He exclaimed.

"Not over you, over the purser."

"That rat?"

"The poor fellow was beaten badly, I'd like you to examine him," I said.

"The rat or the scoundrel?" He asked. He had a penchant for using nasty nicknames for people when he'd had a bit too much. The purser was the rat and Chase, the usual suspect, was the scoundrel.

"The purser," I replied.

"He had it coming. You ought to lay off."

"Discipline must be maintained."

"But what will the crew think?"

"That justice was served. Now, I really must be getting to bed now," I said, "and so ought you."

"You're no fun," Burke said.

"I'm the captain," I said.

"Alright, ladies and gentlemen," Burke exclaimed, tapping his spoon loudly against his glass to get everyone's attention. The sound made me cringe.

I spoke when they stopped talking. "We all have an early morning of it, as per usual navy hours. So, let's all be off to bed now," I said. "The next watch with Wilson starts in six minutes." After a few last remarks between the guests, they began to file out the door, leaving my dining cabin a mess for Higgins to clean up in the morning. Rosie and Burke left arm in arm after everyone else, kissing each other passionately on the lips right before exiting the hatchway, and finally only Higgins and I remained.

"You look tired, sir. Would you like medicine to help you sleep?" He asked.

"No thank you, I'll be fine," I replied, walking back to my sleeping cabin. Burke insisted that I take laudanum to help me sleep through the night, but I chose not to, as I worried that the drug would make it too difficult for me to wake if there was an emergency.

Higgins undressed me, then washed the powder off my face with hot water. He changed me into my nightshirt, then ran a comb through my hair and slid my cap on my head. He helped me climb into the hanging bed and tucked me in, then drew the canopy around me. My mother had sewn the light blue sheets and the canopy and had embroidered blue flowers into them. Closest to my body was a wool blanket she'd knit for me to keep me warm. Higgins put out the oil lamp in my sleeping cabin and I shut my eyes, distracting myself with thoughts of Mother and of my townhouse in Portsmouth. My exhausted limbs sank into the cushion and the gentle motion of the ship rolling over the swells relaxed me. I felt safe and warm, and soon fell asleep.

I woke early in the morning to a sharp pain in my head, the old wound throbbing mercilessly. Moaning, I stumbled out of bed, then walked to the upper deck in only my nightshirt to find Dr. Burke. Before I could make it to the hatchway to the lower deck, the pain slowly began to dissipate, and I climbed up on deck to get a few breaths of fresh, cool night air. A red sun glowed in the east, spilling scarlet across the starboard side of the ship as well as the ocean and sky. "Captain, sir," O'Hare called to me, and I wondered what he was doing up at this ridiculous hour. *Celestial navigation*, I thought to myself, knowing that Venus was only visible in the early morning if he wanted to get a reading off of it. I checked my pocket watch- 5:23. "Captain sir, I have grave news, sir," he began, all in a panic. "I was just about to go find you, but thank goodness you're up."

"Yes, O'Hare?" I asked patiently, looking around me. Stars shined in a cloudless black sky that was slowly turning to blue. The long Atlantic rollers caused the ship to bob gently up and down like a leaf on a pond. No enemy ships in sight, no smell of smoke that would indicate a fire, no mutiny. The heel-angle was normal and the water an appropriate distance away; we were not sinking. Everything seemed fine, and I could not see for the life of me what was the matter.

He took me to the helm with a series of navigational instruments before it. I saw the sea-clocks, one calibrated for Greenwich and one calibrated for exact noon, a pair of sextants, and a thermometer that read forty-two degrees Fahrenheit. He pointed frantically at one instrument, a sort of dial with markings of "Fair" on the righthand side, "Change" in the centre and "Rain" on the left. The arrow rested squarely over the "a" in "Rain". He spoke before I could place in my sleepy mind what the instrument was. "The barometric pressure, sir. There's a storm coming, the likes of which could tear this ship to pieces."

Chapter 2

H.M.S. Cassandra roved softly over the long North
Atlantic swells that had grown higher overnight. A red sun
rose off the starboard bow, the light flowing like dark blood
across the sky then fading gradually to violet then to navy.
A few stars still glistened in the darker parts of the sky, as
not a cloud stood to block their light. A ghostly white halo
surrounded the moon, which glimmered coldly in the centre
of the heavens. The sea reflected the sky on the crests of the
waves but only darkness in the troughs, which seemed to
sink from day into night as the swells sunk from high to
low. A freshening breeze from the stern filled the sails,
pushing us gracefully along. The watch stood at their posts,
most of them half asleep from the rhythmic motion of the
ship and the calm, quiet night. I took a deep breath and
found the air was clear and cold. Goosebumps formed on
my skin beneath my nightshirt and I shivered from head to
toe, gritting my teeth to keep them from chattering. My
barefoot toes were so white they were almost blue, which
was partly because of my complexion and partly because of
the frigid deck. "Are you certain there was no instrument
failure?" I asked O'Hare, breaking the peaceful silence. My
voice came out harsher and more raspy than I'd intended,
but this new development complicated my already stressful
predicament.

"Aye sir, I checked several times; no broken dials, no leakage of the mercury. There's no other way to explain it, sir. Barometric pressure is barometric pressure, and it only gets low like this before two conditions: strong wind and rain."

"I doubt we could weather a storm. What would you have me do?" I asked in a low voice, stepping closer so the men wouldn't overhear.

"'Tis gotten worse as we've gone north, sir. I'd suggest you head south, then wait a few days for it to pass then turn back again for England."

"Do you think we could reach England before the storm hits?" I asked. "We're only three days away at most. If we're under the protection of Portsmouth harbour then we'll be spared the worst of it."

"If we hurry, perhaps, sir, but it would be perilous."

"Well, there are other factors at play in my decision," I said, "but I shall greatly consider your advice. You were right to inform me of the danger. Now, we should both be getting back to bed. Tis cold out here, and I need you well-rested and on the alert tomorrow morning to plot our course," I said. I was conscious of my human vulnerabilities in just a thin nightshirt, and wanted to get back inside before I caught a cold. Without the wig and eyepatch to cover the scars on my head and face, I felt as though I was standing there naked for all my men to see.

"Aye, sir," O'Hare replied.

"Goodnight," I said, walking back to my sleeping cabin.

"Goodnight, sir," he replied as I left, heading to the aft ladder to go back down to his bunk in the gunroom.

Before I reached the forward hatch to head down the stairs to the upper deck, I saw the Captain of Marines, Easton, strolling on deck with his wife Abigail. "Good morning, Captain Easton, Mrs. Easton," I said to them.

"Good morning, Captain," he replied, placing an arm around his wife's shoulders. The Royal Marines were a service separate from the Royal Navy. Though we both held the same title of "captain", aboard ship a marine captain was subordinate to a navy captain in order to maintain a clear chain of command.

"How are you both?" I asked.

"We're well, sir," Abigail replied. "And you?"

"I'm well," I replied. "There has been a development of which I wish to inform your husband."

"Go on," Captain Easton said.

"One of the men, Chase, got into a fight with the purser after smoking on the lower deck and stealing Dr. Burke's brandy to get drunk. There is to be a flogging today, forty-eight lashes for the four offences he committed. I thought I should let you know."

"Of course, sir. Serves him right," Captain Easton replied.

"Well, there's still several hours until the event," I said. "I'm going to head back to my cabin, tis cold out here."

"Goodnight, sir," Captain Easton said.

"Goodnight," I replied, finally walking down the ladder to the upper deck where it was warmer. Half the men snored soundly in their bunks, and their body heat had raised the temperature inside the ship by at least ten degrees. After entering my sleeping cabin, I crawled back into my hanging bed, pulling the blanket over myself to get warm. According to my pocket watch it was now 5:13 AM. Higgins would be up in another hour and a half to dress me; until then I decided to try to rest. I'd only slept five hours last night, but it was more than I usually managed to get. Still wide awake, I dreaded the flogging while feeling an acute anxiety about the storm. I knew there was nothing I could do at present to solve either predicament. The flogging was inevitable and I could not make an educated decision on whether to turn back or not without more information, which I could only gather once my officers were awake. The issue was not pressing enough to be worthy of rousing them from their beds and creating a panic, and doing so would inevitably alert the crew that something was up. I focused on one of the blue flowers my mother had embroidered in the curtains to my bed to distract myself from my worries, fingering the smooth stitches. Eventually my eyelids grew heavy and I sunk helplessly once again beneath the warm blankets.

Rain turned the sky a dismal grey outside and I watched it slide like teardrops down the panes of the window by my bed at Haslar Hospital. It was morning, I'd been brought in the night before and dressed in a loose-fitting blue and white striped uniform, one given to all the patients here so that they would be easy to identify should they try to sneak away and desert. An uneaten bowl of porridge and cold tea rested on the table by my bed, along with a cup with a few drops of laudanum that I had refused to take. It had been three weeks since the battle that had stripped my father from me, but the pain had not improved— the burns were aggravated at even the slightest movement and my head ached so terribly I had difficulty seeing straight. Blood occupied all my senses; I saw it as a thick red wall blinding my left eye, I heard it roaring through my ears from the damage the noise of the cannon-fire had done to my hearing, I felt it soak through the bandages on my head and dampen the side of my face, it filled my mouth constantly through the splinter-wound in my cheek so I could taste little else, its iron stench lingered in my nostrils with each breath I took. The doctor had given me some laudanum to soothe me enough to sleep, but it had made me sick to my stomach and in a frightening state of delirium I'd watched my father's corpse torn apart by crows. Too miserable to eat or sleep I'd grown weak and feverish, and by this point I could hardly lift my head. "Herrick?" A lady's voice said. It was the nurse. Still half-deaf from the battle, I pretended not to hear her. "Mr. Herrick?" She said, raising her voice. I ignored her, turning to the side and burying my face into the pillow. "Mr. *Midshipman* Herrick."

"Leave me alone. I shan't take the bloody medicine," I moaned, clinging tightly to my pillow in the hopes that she'd understand that now was not a good time.

"That's not why I'm here. You have a visitor," she said sternly.

I rolled over slowly. "Mother?" I asked, a wave of mixed emotions smashing over me.

"Georgie, darling," she said, hardly able to speak. She sat on the bed and pulled my head to her chest. "I'm right here," she said gently, kissing my forehead then my right cheek. "I love you, darling."

"Mother…" I choked as the tears came spilling from my good eye. She wiped them away with her hand.

"I love you," she repeated. "I love you. I love you." She stroked my remaining hair, holding me where I could hear her heartbeat.

"Father was…"

"I know," she interrupted, placing a finger over my lips. "I read about it in the newspaper, I know." She let me lie back down and tucked me in properly, then sat down in a chair by my bed. "Did you not like your breakfast?" She asked, glancing over the uneaten food.

"I wasn't hungry," I said, ashamed.

She picked up a covered basket from the floor then pulled off the red and white dishcloth on top. "You need to eat," she said, handing me one of her homemade blueberry scones, still warm as it was fresh from the oven. I took it from her and began to eat voraciously. The blueberries were delicious, the first fresh berries I'd had in a year. "Here's Lancelot," she said, taking out a well-loved stuffed horse that I'd slept with every night before I'd gone to sea. I wrapped my arm around him, taking in the familiar smell of home. "Now your homecoming gift," she said. My mother had a tradition of giving Father and I each a present when we came home from sea. A year ago it was a new book of music, before that a knit wool blanket. She handed me a small, ornately carved oak box. I turned the iron latch and opened it slowly. Inside was a brand new silver watch with a ship engraved in the metal on the outside and an ivory cameo of King George III on the inside.

"'Tis lovely," I replied, running my finger along the cold steel ship.

"I'm glad you like it, darling," she said, kissing my hair.

After that she sat by my bed for hours. We didn't talk. She tried to start a conversation about how nicely the flowers were growing at home and how my older brother Oswald was doing well in school, but quickly realised that I just wanted her to stay with me and hold my hand.

"Can I go home now?" I asked her when the light began to change and I knew it was getting late.

"No, sweetheart, not yet. When you're better you can," she answered in her sweet, soft voice, dashing my hopes.

"Alright, Mrs. Herrick, the visiting time is over," the nurse said, approaching us. "Mr. Herrick needs his dressings changed." I remembered the night before; I'd hated that part. The dried blood had sealed the bandages to my head. All my wounds were reopened and the flesh was torn when they'd come off— the pain had been unbearable. My heart began to race thinking of it. I couldn't go through it again, I couldn't... *I'd go mad... I'd rather die than suffer that torture again... Mother, you can't... You can't let them do this to me... Please, Mother...*

"Alright baby, I have to leave now. I promise I'll come back tomorrow morning." She kissed my cheek in calm affection. "Be brave, sweetheart, I love you."

"No," I said fearfully, taking hold of her arm. "Please don't leave me."

"Georgie, I have to. You know that. But I promise I'll come back. Tis ten hours. Eight of those you'll be asleep."

"No," I protested. "Don't leave… No."

"George, don't make this difficult. Your mother's tired, and you need your supper, then you need to go to bed," she said, stroking my hair. "Lancelot's here. He'll keep you company," she added, patting the stuffed horse. "The nurse will give you a nice hot supper, then she'll put you to bed. Supper then bed. You've done that all your life. There's no need to be afraid. Sweetheart, I have to leave now, so you're going to be brave and say goodbye until to-morrow morning."

"Don't leave me, Mother!" I cried, tears running down my cheek.

"Mrs. Herrick, 'tis time," the nurse said to her coldly.

Mother pulled away, kissing me on the head. "Be brave, George."

"Don't abandon me! I love you, Mother! Please don't abandon me!" She turned and walked away, escorted by two burly red-coated Marine guards. "No!" I screamed, climbing out of bed then stumbling helplessly to the floor. I felt strong arms pick me up and force me back into the bed.

I kicked and clawed to escape, overcome with panic. "Let go of me!" I cursed. "They're torturing me!" I screamed, my lungs aching from the effort. "Please don't leave me! Mother! Mother!"

"Captain…" I woke with a start, still struggling to get free. "Shhh, shhh… You're alright. Everything's alright," Higgins said, placing a gentle hand on my chest. "Good morning, Captain." I reached for my dentures only to realise I had already put them on, then remembered the events of earlier that morning.

"Higgins," I said, forcing a smile. "Good morning."

"Sir," he replied. "How's the head? I can send for Dr. Burke if you'd like."

"Oh, no need to. I'm fine," I replied dismissively, forcing myself not to wince from the headache I had begun to experience upon waking. Higgins could read me well—he always knew when I was worried or when my wounds were bothering me no matter how hard I tried to hide my pain. He could even predict when I was getting sick before I knew myself. I sat up in bed and he took my arm to help me as I stumbled to the loo. The pitch and roll of the ship had grown worse overnight, though I had failed to notice until now. "Thank you, Higgins. I doubt I could live without you."

"I appreciate the compliment, sir," he replied just before I shut the door for privacy. I wandered out a minute later, tripping on the end of the 18-pounder by my bed.

He undressed me from my nightshirt and folded it to stow away in my sea-chest, a heavy oak and canvas box with drawers that sat at the edge of the room. As usual, he'd already filled the large bowl on my vanity with warm water so I could wash myself with a towel and shave. Higgins then helped me into my uniform, and I sat on the sea-chest as he polished my shoes. After that I dismissed him and went to have my breakfast; an egg over hard and porridge with molasses. The jar had only a day's worth left, but that was fine; we should be home late tomorrow afternoon, or perhaps the next morning, when I could send him ashore to buy more victuals. Once in Portsmouth I would continue to stay aboard the *Cassandra* until a spring tide, then I would sail her into one of the dry-docks at the yard there, which would be drained for her to undergo extensive repair. If, however, the repairs were assessed as too expensive and the dockyard commissioner decided it would not be worth the cost to make her seaworthy again, then she would be condemned and used either as a hulk or scuttled.

Once I'd finished eating I went up to the quarterdeck for my morning observation of the weather. In just two hours the wind had picked up about half a knot more and a few puffy white clouds had appeared on the western edge of the sky. I checked my watch; it was six minutes till nine, when the men would be called up and Chase would be chained to a grating that would be propped against the foot-high edge of the quarterdeck and punished. Pacing nervously back and forth, I felt as apprehensive as if it were my own flogging to be carried out. Not that Chase was un-deserving— most captains would have him court-martialled and hung from a yardarm— but in a strange way I felt as though it were my fault. He'd committed offences before; I'd had to flog him three times during the voyage thus far, twice for stealing and once for being drunk on watch. He was the only real troublemaker aboard my ship, and I sin-cerely believed that I never should have pressed him in the first place.

When I'd stopped the collier to press a portion of her crew, I'd asked him for papers to confirm his national-ity, but he'd had none. Most likely that had been the case for his merchant ship as well, when it had been seized. Had I known about the seizure of his ship, which would never happen to a British merchant at the hands of the Royal Navy, I never would have infected the *Cassandra* with his plague of insubordination. The truth was, he was a slave-holder and a captain, used to giving orders but unaccus-tomed to obeying them. I checked my watch again and watched as the second hand ticked past twelve and the hour hand moved over the eight.

79

The ship's bell tolled and the marines beat their
drums for everyone to assemble. I stepped back down to
the quarterdeck and watched as the deck crowded. The men
were somber, which either meant that they knew little of
the punishment or thought it was unjust. Two of the boatswain's mates dragged a struggling Chase to the quarterdeck and stripped him of his shirt, then bound his wrists
and ankles to a grating that we had removed from one of
the hatches we used to lower supplies into the hold. I
watched as a grin spread across Greene's face; finally, he
could watch the slave driver face the whipping post. The
grating was propped up against the foot high raised area of
the quarterdeck and secured with lines bound to the rings
that held the guns on each side of it. I watched as one of the
boatswain's mates took the whip out of its linen bag; a rope
frayed with nine ends which had small knots tied into them
to be more painful, the cat o' nine tails. He awaited my
command.

I stepped out from under the overhang on the quarterdeck and into the light to address the men. Raising my
voice, I began to speak. "Last night, Landsman Chase was
caught in a state of drunkenness and he has therefore
earned twelve lashes." The crowd fell silent, all looking
intently to me. "In addition, he was found smoking on the
lower deck, an act which could have started a fire that
would have had this ship destroyed and its entire company

killed. For that, he is to receive another dozen lashes. When the purser caught him and tried to prevent him from this action, Chase attacked him. For fighting, he has earned another dozen. Furthermore, the bottle from which he had entered the state of drunkenness was found to be stolen from Dr. Burke. For thievery, another twelve. For the following offences, which have put in danger both the men and the discipline of this ship, he is to receive forty-eight lashes. On my command," I said, addressing the boatswain's mate with the whip, a man barely twenty years old named Goldsmith. He raised his arm and the cat o' nine tails, his face frozen in a stern apathy.

"One," I said firmly. The whip whistled through the air and slapped Chase's back. He cried out in pain, his shoulders tensing. A red welt began to mark his skin. I swallowed, glancing at the deck then back up to my waiting men.

"Two," I ordered. A piercing whiplash broke the deathly silence, the scream was more poignant now. Blood welled up this time, and I felt sick. Forty six more. I glanced briefly at the purser. Dr. Burke stood next to him, holding a damp towel over his blackened eye. Clearly they had been in the surgeons' office when they'd heard the drum tattoo.

"Three," I said, knowing that my time for reflection was up. The next stroke hit his upper back above the other

two, casting another red line over an old scar from a past
flogging.

"Four…"

"Twelve," I said, after an age had passed. Goldsmith handed the cat-o'-nine-tails to another boatswain's
mate who had stood by waiting, then stepped back. It
seemed now that every new lash hit a previous one; Chase's
entire back was swollen and bleeding. Now during the intervals between lashes he moaned. The men had begun to
mutter amongst themselves to keep from going mad from
the tension.

"Thirteen," I ordered, and little Matrose cringed as
the rope sliced through the air. Haynes held him by the arm;
the two were friends. *Better they learn the lash now*, I
thought. I tried to consider the words I would say to them
afterwards, to explain why the punishment was necessary.
Discipline is the one thing that holds this ship together.
Discipline is why our navy is the best in the world. Discip-
line means we survive.

"Fourteen." The scream caused a shiver to run up
my back. I forced myself to think of the Nile. I remembered the deck of *H.M.S. Vanguard*, the ship filled
with smoke that burned my lungs and throat and made me
feel as though I were drowning and suffocating. It was
dreadfully hot and muggy, and sweat ran down my brow
and soaked my back. My veins were supercharged with en-

ergy during the battle, so I did not feel tired despite the fact
that it was late at night and the fighting had already lasted
hours. I had seen the admiral taken below with a head
wound, a man sliced in two by a cannonball. My gloves
had been stained with blood from trying to staunch the
stomach wound of one of the midshipmen. I was completely deaf, so did not hear when the French guns ceased
firing, only saw that splinters had stopped flying through
the deck and the carnage had halted momentarily. I had
gone to the nearest gunport and peered outside to verify
that it was true; no smoke exited the enemy gun-ports.
When the night sky cleared enough for a few stars to be
visible, I'd thought they had surrendered and the bloodshed
was finished.

"Fifteen," I ordered coldly, and the Marine swung
the whip through the air to strike Chase once again. My
thoughts drifted back to the battle. It was then that the ship
had turned and I felt the deck lift a little as our cables were
cut. Then *L'Orient* came into view. She was a 118-gun
monster who had terrorised us throughout the battle.
Flames exited every gunport, climbing the masts and rigging and setting the sails completely on fire. I could see
men crowding the deck, some leaping from the ship in panic, most unable to swim. The rigging began to collapse and
the flaming sails started to fall into the crowds of sailors.
The anchor chains had begun to melt, now glowing red

with heat. I could distinctly see the quarterdeck, and the silhouette of a young boy standing on it, no older than Matrose. That was when a white light momentarily blinded me, then a cloud of flame engulfed the entire ship, at least a hundred feet in diameter. The shock wave tipped us precariously to the side to the point where I tripped and almost fell backwards, and I felt the heat wave scald my face moments later. Looking back at where the mighty ship had been, nothing remained, only ashes floating softly down from the sky and blanketing the sea. *L'Orient* had been blown to pieces no larger than flakes of snow. We turned back to pick up survivors then, those who had been lucky enough to swim away in time. All ships ceased fighting for a quarter of an hour in the wake of the catastrophe. To me it had seemed more of a natural disaster than actions taken by human hands, for the only way I could fathom such destruction was if it had been the wrath of God. Then, after all the survivors that could be found were rescued, and the shock of the explosion had swept through the fleets and dissipated, we resumed fighting again.

"Twenty-five," I ordered, the whip striking Chase once more. Blood spattered into the boatswain's mate's face, now a different man than the last, and he paused to wipe it away with a handkerchief. The duty of the lash changed from one boatswain's mate to the next at every interval of twelve lashes. A few more lashes, and the blood began to drip down to the deck.

"Twenty-eight."

"Please, mercy!" Chase cried. "I'm an American, I shouldn't even be here."

"Silence!" I ordered. "Twenty-nine."

"You bloody limey! In my country we'd tar and feather you!"

"Silence, or I'll give you another dozen for insubordination!" I hissed. "Thirty."

Chase screamed in agony.

This was nothing. In 1797 I had watched from shore as a man was flogged round the fleet and given a thousand lashes for instigating the mass mutiny at the Nore. The mutiny had been fuelled by Jacobins in support of the French, which had left the country vulnerable. Even worse, another mass mutiny had occurred at Spithead around the same time over the payment and overall treatment of sailors in the Royal Navy. I had agreed with the mutineers on that occasion; the pay of a sailor had not been raised in a century and inflation had grown to make it unsupportable. Clearly, the Admiralty had agreed too, as the mutineers at Spithead had been acquitted.

The fact that the English Channel had been virtually undefended, with the exception of two ships that had stayed loyal, had caused me a great deal of stress and anxiety. In

1797 France was still in a state of revolution and disarray under the Robespierre government and with internal strife caused by the Reign of Terror. I had been horrified by news of the guillotines murdering thousands of French citizens, and the thought of a guillotine in Portsmouth was not merely distressing but revolting. I had been convinced the situation would be better after the coup that made Napoleon Bonaparte First Consul and the Peace of Amiens had been declared. Yet my hopes had been swept away when the two countries resumed war, as they had for most of the past century, and Napoleon began massing his army to cross the English Channel. All that stood to keep his ambition of invading the British Isles in check was a stretch of water only twenty miles wide at some points, and a fleet of little more than a hundred warships already spread thin by having to defend an empire that stretched from India to the Caribbean to the southernmost cape of Africa. We could not afford to have one of those ships taken out by the incompetence of a drunk *smoking* on the lower deck near the powder room. "Thirty-one."

"Forty-eight," I counted in a hoarse voice after what had felt like hours. "Justice has been served," I said dryly. "You may go about your duties," I ordered the men, suddenly feeling overcome with exhaustion. The boatswain's mates untied an unconscious Chase and took him below to be treated by Dr. Burke. I stepped back to lean against the

hammock netting on the quarterdeck. The headache had
grown worse and I felt slightly ill.

"Sir," Higgins said, greeting me. "Are you alright?"
He asked.

"Just a bit of a headache, tis all," I replied. "I'd like
a damp towel, if you please."

I went into my day cabin and sat down in one of the
chairs at the small table there, my throat a bit sore from is-
suing the lashes and my joints feeling more tender today
than usual, particularly the knee that I had bruised yesterday when the ladder step had broken going from the lower
deck. "There you are, sir," Higgins said, taking off my hat
and wig then pressing the cold, soothing rag to my head.

"Thank you, Higgins," I said.

"You look unwell, sir," he said concernedly.

"Do you believe I'll fall seriously ill before we
reach Portsmouth?" I asked.

"Difficult to say, sir, I'm no doctor. Tis inadequate
victuals and rest, and continuous stress, sir. No one can live
getting less than five hours of sleep a night on two small
meals a day, sir."

"I'm the captain," I said. "I command this ship. My
duty takes precedent over my comfort."

"You can't perform your duty well if you're un-
healthy, sir. Would you like some tea with honey? It would
ease your sore throat."

"How did you know I had a sore throat?" I asked.

"Your voice was more raspy than usual towards the end of the punishment, sir, and you kept swallowing repeatedly."

"Well, you're very astute, Higgins. If you please, I would like some tea, just don't tell Dr. Burke I'm falling ill; he'll think I'm dying of pneumonia."

"Aye, sir," he replied, leaving the room to ask the officers' cook to prepare the tea.

After a few minutes of holding the rag, my head stopped throbbing and I put my wig and hat back on, once again able to concentrate on my duties. I decided it would be wise to examine the chart where O'Hare had plotted the course and see how far away from home we were, then check the supplies once again and observe the men to see their reaction to the flogging. With that information I could determine whether to cut rations down to a quarter or not, and also whether to follow O'Hare's advice and turn back or keep sailing straight. I cursed myself for not cutting rations sooner than two weeks ago, but we had been due for re-provisioning last month. The job of replenishing ships in the Royal Navy fell to the Victualling Board, which procured water and victuals to be sent by the Transport Board to bases in Great Britain and overseas. In the Mediterranean, our base was Gibraltar, though our commander,

Admiral Nelson, liked to procure supplies from Malta and Naples, which were allied to Great Britain.

Often admirals, or individual captains if they were independent of a fleet, would re-provision themselves by sailing into a friendly or neutral port and purchasing their own supplies. Each ship had money set aside for this, which was managed by the purser and up to the discretion of the captain to spend. Officers and crew could also use their pay to buy their own victuals and even livestock, such as I had bought my chickens. On most ships, including the *Cassandra*, officers who dined in the gunroom, or wardroom in larger vessels, had a pool of funding with which they bought foodstuffs in bulk and shared amongst each other. A captain, however, had to purchase his own victuals, as well as uniform and furniture. The costs stacked up quickly, especially as I felt it a military necessity to host my officers over supper frequently, but fortunately for me, I had no family to support at home, and only a small townhouse for which to pay taxes and maintenance. We had plenty of money aboard, but the nearest friendly port we could reach was England.

When we had been ordered to leave our station patrolling the French coastline near Toulon, a harsh wind was blowing from the west. We had to beat into the wind and it took weeks to reach Gibraltar. A few days before, however, the breeze shifted south, then suddenly died. At that point I was forced to cut rations, only miles away from a friendly port filled with victuals. After a week of this madness, I decided to cut off my attempt to resupply there, heading straight to Portsmouth across the open ocean. Now moving with the wind, I ordered my men to take the cutter out with the ship's anchor inside, towing the *Cassandra* forward. The men detested this gruelling, back-breaking labor known as kedging, but as soon as we crossed through Gibraltar to the Atlantic the southwesterly wind grew stronger, pushing us steadily towards home. It had been a gamble, certainly, but one that was better for morale than floating helplessly while waiting for starvation to set in.

Higgins returned, carrying a tray with the tea. "Here you are, sir," he said, setting it down on the table.

I took a sip and felt a bit better. "Thank you, Higgins," I said.

"Sir, if I may, what would you like for supper tonight?"

"Oh, Higgins. We're a day away from England. I'll be too busy preparing the ship and getting my papers in order." Normally a captain's clerk would prepare the papers which I was required to send to various organisations upon our arrival in Portsmouth, but mine had died of typhus early in the voyage, and so I had no one to help me with administrative tasks.

"Sir," he said. "I could have the cook fix something you can eat quickly, perhaps pork with some of the asparagus you have left."

"Oh, don't bother," I said dismissively. "It would be a waste."

"Alright sir," he said.

"You may go about your duties, if you please," I told him. He left the room and I finished the tea, then stepped out of my day cabin and climbed the ladder down to the lower deck. I passed Chase lying on his stomach next to the sailor with the jaundice in one of the hammocks in the forward part of the deck before making my way down to the aft-most platform to find the purser.

"Mr. Gailden," I said cordially. "How are you feeling? Are your injuries healing well?" I asked.

"Better now that justice has been served," he replied, forcing a smile. His cheek was still swollen and I could see a row of black stitches above his eye.

"Fancy seeing you back on duty so quickly," I said. "If you need some time to recover I understand entirely."

"I don't see the value in it; my work does nothing to upset my injuries," he replied.

"Well in that case, I came to inquire upon the state of our supplies. How much do we have left?" I asked.

"Enough for two more days of victuals; we have enough water for three," he replied.

"I'm considering cutting rations again. We're a day away from England, but if our navigational calculations are wrong then I don't want us to run out," I said.

"Has O'Hare ever been wrong?" Gailden asked.

"O'Hare knows his craft, but he's not God," I said.

"Believe me, I'm not unbiased in this matter. You asked for my opinion, sir. As it is, we're cutting it close. Most likely we'll have enough, but if anything goes wrong we shan't. If we cut rations to one quarter then we'll go from having enough victuals for two days to having enough for four days. If everything goes as planned then I'll make a profit reselling the excess goods."

"I understand that, Mr. Gailden," I said. "Thank you for your advice, and your honesty. Your opinion is not the only one upon which I shall base my decision, but it is helpful to know how much we have left."

"Thank you sir," he replied.

"Now, you may go about your duties, and I do hope your injuries heal quickly. You made the right choice in stopping Chase. Though it would have been better had you found a nonviolent means of preventing his foolhardy actions, I commend your courage and intuition."

"Thank you, sir," he said, a bit surprised.

I walked back up to the upper deck from the dark, reeking platform in the hold, careful not to bump my head on the low beams. Passing through the upper deck I could hear the men talking. The ones who saw me turned and raised their knuckles, but many did not notice my presence and remained immersed in conversation.

"made the right choice, as always. He may be ruthless but he's a damned good captain."

"not 'artless, only forty-eight lashes for offences such as those."

"…could have blown the ship to bits."

Then I heard the familiar voice of Jameson. What could he possibly be doing with the *enlisted*? The only plausible reason an officer —albeit a junior one— would be speaking to enlisted men was to give an order. Yet his tone of voice was one of complacence, not of command. "I don't know why he let those Austrians aboard. Now they're taking a share of our prize money."

"I say we kill the lot of them."

"I almost did."

"Yes, but did you really intend it?"

"Of course I intended it."

I turned and walked discreetly back to the main deck. My influence remained intact, but the rift between Jameson and Matrose had only grown deeper, to the point where it was beginning to undermine the structure of command. To cut rations now—especially the grog ration— could lead to violence or even a mutiny. Standing at his post was the master, O'Hare, writing the current speed of seven knots on the chalkboard log behind the helm. He held a map in one hand and a piece of chalk in the other.

"Mr. O'Hare," I said, glancing at the board. "Seven knots. We're making good time."

"Aye, sir," he said. "I'm surprised a line hasn't snapped or we haven't lost a spar yet."

"I could ride my horse faster than this, though I do see your point, given the condition of our rigging. I know you are busy with your duties, but, if you please, at the earliest possible convenience, meet me in my day cabin with the current chart you're using to discuss our heading and distance from Portsmouth."

"Aye, sir. I can come now, if you'd like."

"That would be excellent," I replied, leading the way to the day cabin. We stood by the table and I watched as he opened the map and flattened the corners with paper-weights. The chart featured the bottom strip of English coastline, which appeared unnaturally straight compared to the European continent. Marked in ink was our journey from Gibraltar, though the map did not go that far south, so at the bottom the line appeared from the open sea and stretched almost all the way to one of the cities inked in elegant cursive: "Portsmouth". To the left was the label in large letters of "North Atlantic" and to the right was "English Channel". The rough borderlines of each coastal European country were also visible, from south to north going

"France", "Belgium", "The Netherlands", "Denmark-Nor-way", "Lower Saxony", and "Schleswig-Holstein". The map cut off before the Baltic began to the north, and went no farther south than Ushant.

"We're 300 miles away, sir. 296 to be exact."

"So we ought to be home by tomorrow night, then," I said, doing the mathematical calculations in my head.

"Assuming our measurements of latitude and longitude are accurate and we continue to sail at our current speed, that is correct, sir."

"Very good," I said. "How is the barometric pressure?" I asked, knowing that that had been worrying the both of us.

"Still dropping, sir," he replied gravely.

"Any other signs of the storm?" I asked.

"Increased swells, clouds gathering, the temperature dropping a few degrees. That's all I've seen, sir. And red sky at morning, sailor's warning." Like most experienced seamen, he practiced the religion of superstition more than he did Christianity.

"Do you still think we ought to turn back?" I asked, the discontent of the men and our dwindling food supply still nagging at the back of my mind.

"I really couldn't say, sir," he replied. "Dropping pressure means that if the weather is fair, we ought to expect little of it. Then again, we're not far from England and we're making better time than I expected."

"Thank you, Mr. O'Hare," I replied. "Your advice is always extremely helpful. It gives me comfort to know that we'll soon be home," I said.

"Aye, sir," he replied. "Thank you, by the way, for allowing me to take my wife aboard. It has made this past year and half infinitely more agreeable for the both of us."

"I'm glad," I said. "Now, you may go about your duties."

I enjoyed speaking with O'Hare— his competence tended to reassure me. Unfortunately, I now had to address the most incompetent officer aboard my ship. I walked back down to the upper deck to find Jameson personally. Passing the word for this sort of thing would never do, as the rumours would only grow and he would be humiliated, which would only worsen his resentment further. I found him forward in the ship, gulping down his rum-ration all in one sitting. "Mr. Jameson," I said. "A word in private, if you please. Come to my day cabin as soon as is convenient."

"Aye, sir," he replied in a long sigh. "I can come now."

He followed me as I walked aft to my day cabin. I found Higgins had come in during my absence; he was now polishing my silverware. A soft breeze blew through the window. The map still rested on the table. I rolled it up and moved the paperweights to sit in the cabinet by the door and sat down in the centre of the table facing the aft windows. "You may sit down, if you please," I told the midshipman.

"Aye, sir," he replied, taking his seat in the chair on my blind left side. My chest grew hot with annoyance but with a deep breath I maintained my composure.

"We should talk," I began, trying to appear as non-confrontational as possible.

"Aye, sir," he replied reluctantly.

"I'm terribly sorry you've not yet been promoted to lieutenant," I said, turning a full ninety degrees to face him.

He perked up, his expression one of both surprise and of anger.

"I have connections who could recommend you to take the examination again. So far, I've written little of you, and what I have is only of your virtuous qualities. There is, however, a diplomatic caveat to my writing a letter and putting my reputation on the line to give you another chance."

"What would that be, sir?" He asked, his eyes filled with a fleeting hope. "I'll do anything, sir."

"I saw it in you yesterday. You were trying to hurt Matrose."

"He's your favourite," Jameson said rather bluntly.

"I don't have favourites. I don't care for any of my officers or men on a personal level. I'm the captain, their commander. I am incapable of that sort of affection. But he is strategically important to the outcome of the war."

"Strategically important? He's a child!"

"As it turns out, upon writing to the Austrian ambassador to Britain on the recapturing of the Austrian soldiers and their incorporation into the ship's company, I discovered that Matrose was the nephew of one of the generals in their army in a prominent position to direct the land war against France. If his family found out that there was an attempted *murder* of him on one of *His Britannic Majesty's ships* then the diplomatic insult could break the coalition. With Austria's army gone then Naples will fall. Without Naples, the rest of the Mediterranean, then Napoleon's Grande Armée is free to focus its efforts entirely on Prussia, Spain and Portugal. The entire European continent shall be his. With no land war what comes next? He starves us out of valuable shipbuilding supplies from the Baltic and isolates us from our colonies in India then crosses the Channel when our ships are reduced to rot and our economy bankrupt and invades the British Isles!"

I gazed directly at Jameson, neither of us willing to be the next one to speak.

"That's the sort of thing an admiral would say," Higgins said, breaking the silence.

"I-I'm sorry, sir," Jameson stammered.

"If you even touch Matrose again I'll write a letter to my friends at the admiralty that shall condemn you to half-pay as a *midshipman* for the rest of your life. If, however, you perform your duties with good conduct then I shall utilise my influence to give you another chance at a lieutenancy. You may go about your duties," I said.

He left the cabin quickly, overcome with shock.

"You can be rather frightening when you're angry, sir," Higgins said, lips curving into a smile.

A knock at the door made me jump. Higgins went to answer it and found it was Dr. Burke.

"Good afternoon, Captain," he said cheerfully.

"Good afternoon, Doctor," I replied, a bit surprised. "Please, come inside," I said when he was already three steps into the room.

"Your new chickens," he said, pulling something from the pockets of his brown coat.

"What are…" He handed me an innocent little black bundle of fluff that felt as soft as velvet. Then I saw the tiny undeveloped wings and an adorable face with big black eyes. A tiny beak extended from a long neck that was also covered in a downy fur. Burke held the other chick in his hand. "They're lovely," I said, my heart aching from their precious little baby faces. He set them down on the deck and they began to scurry about excitedly.

"Now for the serious business," he said, taking a seat in one of my chairs. I sat down next to him. He plucked something from one of his pockets and held it up for me to see. I found it was a strand of human hair. It was dark and tightly curled, and could only have belonged to one member of the ship's company. "I found this caught under the label of the brandy," he said.

"The one that was stolen?" I asked.

"Aye, sir," he replied.

"But Greene and Chase were fighting just that day."

"I saw Greene go down to the lower deck yesterday afternoon, heading forward. I didn't question him, I figured he was going to buy something from the purser."

"So you think the crime was a conspiracy?" I asked.

"Yes sir, I do," he said.

"Well, I'll speak with Greene and the purser," I said. "Something else is going on amongst my men and I need to know about it."

"May I feel your head?" He asked. "You look ill."

"Oh, don't worry, Burke. I'm fine."

"Alright, Herrick, but if you feel sick at all then tell me. I understand you didn't go to bed until late last night and I'm guessing you didn't sleep all the way through until morning either."

"I slept enough," I replied. "Now, you have more important duties attending to the sick and injured. How are they?"

"Chase just regained conscious. He wanted to go up on deck but I told him to rest. I've told the one with the injured ankle that he's cleared for duty again. Due to a strict restriction on alcohol, the sailor with the jaundice is feeling much better. The purser wanted to get back to work right away and Matrose's little scratch looked fine to me when I last checked."

"Two injuries in a day… Half-rations is starting to flare tempers and affect discipline now."

"No signs of scurvy yet, though."

"We've not run out of citrus yet," I countered. "We should by the end of the day."

"You were right to carry so much fruit," he said. "I know I was skeptical at the beginning that it wouldn't store well, and that we should pack the hold with more wine and salted meat instead."

"In the tropics more hardy provisions would be necessary," I said. "On our station the weather is temperate enough to keep the fruit from rotting too quickly."

"Very intuitive of you," Burke said. "Care to join me for dinner?" He asked.

"I would love to, but unfortunately I have work to do."

"You said that yesterday, and the day before that. Is there something in particular troubling you?"

"I need to check the hold again to see if the *Cassandra* needs to be pumped."

"I can wait a few minutes while you do that," he said.

"Then I need to speak with the purser along with Greene and Chase about the events of last night."

"Surely that can wait?" He asked.

"I'm afraid I won't have time later, as I still have to prepare the documents for the end of the voyage."

"Oh, bloody hell, George! It will take half an hour at most. Higgins!" He called to my servant. Suddenly, I felt something cold snap around my wrist. "I was afraid I'd have to use these," Burke said. I looked down to see that he had manacled my arm to the chair.

"You've gone mad," I said indignantly.

"*I've* gone mad? Look at yourself, George. You've not been eating properly and it's starting to show."

"The men are on half rations, we're out of supplies, what else would you expect?"

"You work ten times as hard as any of them. As your *physician* I demand that you join me for dinner."

"As your *captain* I order you to release me at once."

"No!" He exclaimed.

"Morgan!" I cried, rolling my eyes.

"Higgins, bring the stew."

"I could have you court-martialled for this," I hissed to Morgan.

"Yes, but you won't, will you?" He said, his expression one of complete and glorious victory.

My friend had a real talent for irritating me sometimes in a way that no one else could.

Higgins brought in three bowls on a platter and Rosie entered, smiling innocently. "The manacles were her idea," Morgan said.

I watched as Higgins set the table with great alacrity. He tucked a napkin into my coat then poured champagne into glasses. Rosie and Burke sat down on either side of me. "Champagne? This early in the day?" I scoffed.

"'Tis never too early for champagne," Burke said, grinning.

Higgins set a bowl in front of me along with a spoon. I picked up a bite of steaming stew and blew on it to cool.

Crash! Something hit the deck above, then the sound of splitting wood tore through the air. The ship shook violently, knocking the spoon out of my hand and nearly tipping my chair over. "Morgan, get me out of here!" I shouted, tugging and pulling at the manacles. He fumbled with the keys as I grew increasingly worried. *Cassandra* rocked back then forth sharply, then regained equilibrium.

Burke put the manacles back in his pocket after freeing me then we rushed on deck with Higgins and Rosie.

"One of the sails broke from the mast," she said. An icy breeze bit my cheeks; the windspeed had grown to a steady twelve knots since morning. Sitting squarely on the quarterdeck, with lines and a torn sail still attached, was a massive boom. I inspected the damage; the boom itself ended in splinters, but luckily the falling sail had just missed the helm.

My first thought was that my men might be injured. The two helmsmen and the sailing master stood off to the side, all three of them unharmed. I scanned the scene for anyone lying on the ground, my ears searching for any moans or shouts of pain. Finding nothing, I walked over to speak with O'Hare. "Are you alright?" I asked him.

"Aye, sir, I'm fine. So are the men."

"Captain, sir!" Brooks exclaimed upon seeing me.

"Lieutenant Brooks," I said, addressing him. "I heard a boom fall. Was anyone hurt?" I asked.

"No, sir. Nobody was working in the rigging at the time, and the only people on the quarterdeck were the master and the two helmsmen."

"We were lucky then," I said, the panic giving way to relief.

A herd of young gentlemen followed Brooks up the stairs to the quarterdeck. "Haynes," I said to the nearest one. "Pass the word for the boatswain, if you please." I turned to Higgins. "Higgins, if you please, put my chickens back in their coop with their mother. Burke, Rosie, you may finish dinner without me, my duties shall require me to stay on deck for some time." Burke nodded, understanding. Rosie took his arm and the two of them walked back to my cabin.

Many of the men had gathered around the scene, awaiting my orders. "Brooks, take as many men as you need and get that mast somewhere stable."

"Aye, sir," he said.

The boatswain arrived on deck then, surveying the mizzenmast and the broken sail. "Mr. Quincy," I said to him. His grey and black sideburns twitched. Navy regulations forbade beards, but many men chose to wear long sideburns in lieu of other facial hair.

"I thought that boom was weak, sir, but I didn't know it was *that* weak. It has grown breezier, hasn't it?"

"Yes, we're up to eight knots of boat-speed now," O'Hare said.

"Eight! That's certainly more than she'll handle well in this state," he exclaimed, surprised.

"Do you think we could fish the mizzen topsail?" I asked.

"I believe 'tis *possible*, sir, but the jury-rigged boom would still be weak, and it would take hours. The simple thing would be to just replace it, but we're out of supplies, so we'll have to put it back together some other way."

"How would we do it?" I asked. "If we were to mend the sail and repair the boom."

"Well, sir, we'd have to haul it up the mast first, then secure the two pieces of the boom with planking, then pitch and tar the crack, then stitch the two pieces of sail together up there."

"Why couldn't we bring the broken section of the sail down to the deck to be attached to the other piece, then hoist it back up where it is now?" I turned my head. It was Mrs. O'Hare's Scottish accent, but she was standing on my blind left side.

"That ought to work," the sailing master said, endorsing his wife.

"Aye," the boatswain replied.

"I'll have Reid take a dozen men and lower the sail. Lieutenant Reid!" I called to the junior lieutenant on watch.

He walked swiftly over and raised his knuckles. "Sir," he said.

"I'd like you to direct the lowering of the remaining part of the mizzen topsail. We're to repair it on deck and hoist it up again once we've finished."

"Aye, sir," he said.

I found the closest young gentleman. "Matrose," I said, "if you please, go find the carpenter and the sailmaker. They should be on the forward most platform in the hold."

"Aye, sir," he replied.

I watched as the men under Lieutenant Brooks raised the broken boom from the wreckage with a great heave and hauled it with straining muscles to a secure location on the leeward side of the quarterdeck. On a ship, leeward referred to the side that was lowest to the water. The side highest from the water when the ship was heeled over was windward, as that was the side where the wind first touched the ship. The reason for the heel was that when a ship was heading in any direction other than directly downwind, the sails were at an angle to the wind direction. As a result, the force on the sails not only propelled the ship forward, but also pushed it to one side. Therefore, with the round boom placed on the leeward edge, it was less likely to roll because it was already at the lowest side of the deck.

At just that moment the carpenter and the sailmaker appeared with their mates, carrying boards and boxes of tools. I walked to the edge of the deck and leaned against the hammock netting, watching as Reid's team detached the broken piece of sail from the mast. They appeared small and insignificant fifty feet up, their lives dangling on only a thin ratline. Like acrobats they worked, deftly swinging themselves amongst the lines to reconfigure the mizzen topsail halyard to safely take the boom and the rest of the sail back down to the deck. The halyard had only been intended to raise and lower the canvas section of the sail a dozen feet, rather than the sail and boom, but the whole apparatus was much lighter with half of it on deck. The men then detached the remaining sheets from the broken boom, freeing it so it could be lowered unencumbered.

"All hands to the mizzen topsail halyard!" I ordered. The crew on deck hurried dutifully to the line, passing it back so each man had a place. I looked for a sign from Reid that the men aloft had finished securing the boom. He looked me in the eye and nodded vigorously. "Belay! Steady, now!" I commanded the men. Slowly, but with more fits and starts than I'd wanted, the men let out the line and the boom lowered.

The process was agonisingly slow, but watching the men I imagined it would feel even slower participating. It was then that the next few problems began to nag at the back of my mind. I had not pumped the hold since yesterday. In a warship in decent repair that would be fine, even normal, but in rotten old *Cassandra*, especially in these swells, the water was probably dragging her down and reducing speed. Other than that, the loss of a sail would slow us and further delay our reaching Portsmouth by tomorrow afternoon. I decided to ask one of the midshipmen to find the men on watch who were not working and have them pump the hold, and immediately thought that Mr. Larson should do it, the eighteen-year-old who was almost old enough to take the lieutenant's examination.

Suddenly, the boom dropped sharply and my heart jumped in my throat. "Steady, lads!" I called, watching as the loose boom dangled from thirty feet in the air, the sail on the verge of tearing from the weight of the wood. "Hold her steady!" I ordered, walking closer to see what had happened. The halyard which the men had secured around the boom in a bowline had been pulled off and was now tangled in one of the loosely hanging sheets that the men had detached. To my shock and astonishment, one of the top-men was already sliding down the halyard, a dark figure climbing with his only foothold on a swinging boom that had already broken once today without provocation. Greene held a knife between his teeth; he took it and sawed away at the sheet until it untangled from the halyard, then tied a figure eight knot into it. With one hand, he held himself up by the knot and slid the bowline back over the boom. He swung away, his legs dangling over thirty feet of open air, then took hold of the mizzenmast, climbing back up to the relative safety of his post. "Let's give three cheers for Greene!" I shouted, celebrating his act of heroism. The men joined me;

"Huzzah!"

"Huzzah!"

"Huzzah!"

The men recommenced the labour. The sail was lowered the next thirty feet without any further complications, though by the time it rested safely on deck the men were panting and collapsing to their knees. Normally they would have been fine, considering that they had distributed the weight of the boom amongst sixty and had been working with gravity. Half-rations were making them weaker, and it was already starting to show.

"Good work, lads," I told them. "Excellent work, you're the best crew I've yet had the pleasure to serve with."

"Thank you, Captain," a few replied in muffled groans. I only imagined the task of having to haul the *whole* sail up again once repaired.

"Take a rest, lads, you've earned it," I said.

They sat on the deck to catch their breaths as the sailmaker and the carpenter set to work joining the pieces back together. The sailmaker's task was intuitive but tedious; he and his two mates had to stitch the ripped canvas back together, which was over thirty feet high and had an area the size of the entire quarterdeck when unfurled entirely. The carpenter and his mates had the more intellectually difficult but physically less strenuous problem of joining the wood back together where the boom had cracked.

First the carpenter sawed off the splintered pieces so two clean edges appeared. One of his mates then went back to the lower deck to bring large boards up. He carried them under his arm then set them next to the carpenter. I watched as the carpenter took measurements of the boom then made marks on one of the boards. It was at this point that I realised that to splice the two broken pieces of sail would take time, possibly hours.

"How high is the water in the hold?" I asked the carpenter.

"Three feet, sir, we really ought to pump now. I was going to tell you but you appeared preoccupied with the problem of the mizzen topsail, sir."

"That's fine, you've done your duty," I said, knowing I should have asked him *before* the dinner hour. Then again, I didn't know that Burke would interrupt my duties, or that one of the booms would break at just the most inconvenient time… I cursed myself bitterly for my incompetence. Trying to hide the anxiety in my voice I turned to Lieutenant Brooks. "It will be some time before the mizzen topsail is ready to be hauled back up the mast, likely when the next watch is on duty. We've been leaking badly and taking on water. If you please, take some of your men and pump the bilge."

"Aye, sir," he said. He went about the deck finding those who seemed the best rested and those who had not participated in lowering the broken sail.

I stayed on deck. With my first lieutenant occupied below, and Reid busy commanding the repair, there was no one for me to talk to. Rather than standing idly on the deck and waiting for the next emergency, I decided to take charge of the midshipmen's lesson.

"Good afternoon, young gentlemen," I said, approaching the pack of them. Jameson was nowhere to be seen; that was alright, but Haynes and Matrose stood off by themselves. "Haynes, Matrose, come over," I told them. The boys ran to the group who stood waiting attentively. "Now, lads," I said, "since most of the other officers are preoccupied right now, I will be teaching this afternoon's lesson." The boys exchanged smiles, whispering excitedly to each other. I seldom had time to educate the young gentlemen throughout the voyage, as I was usually too busy handling the ship and giving orders, but when I did the lads tended to find my lessons more interesting than those of the other officers. Larger ships often had a school teacher, but on a frigate such as *H.M.S. Cassandra* there were too few midshipmen and captain's servants to justify such an investment. In lieu of a formal teacher, the task of educating the young gentlemen fell to both the commissioned and non-commissioned officers. The lieutenants would teach them about naval command, the sailing master would teach them about navigation, the master-at-arms would teach them to use cutlasses and small-arms, the boatswain would teach them about the various lines aboard, and the cox-swains, of which there were three, would teach them small-boat sailing. Each coxswain would command one of the ships' boats when they went out, and would use the tiller. The *H.M.S. Cassandra* had three such boats; the cutter, the longboat, and the jolly boat.

"What would you like to learn about today?" I asked, as enthusiastic to teach the young fellows as they were to have a lesson from the captain. "Tell us about what happens in a battle!" Haynes said excitedly.

"Well, that would depend on the type of battle, whether it's a single ship action, a fleet battle, an inter-service operation…"

"Which ones were you in?" One of the other boys, a sixteen-year-old named Milner asked.

"I've been in all of them," I replied.

"Have we always been at war with France?" Matrose asked.

"Well, no, not always. There were a few months in 1802 and 1803 when there was peace, called the Peace of Amiens. Yet it was not a peace, only an armistice. Then the war started again."

"Were you frightened in your battles?" Haynes asked.

"Beforehand, certainly," I said openly. "During the battle, however, you're too busy to be afraid. There's too much going on. Tis the waiting that is the worst part, but the other officers and the men all appear calm, so 'tis not so bad."

"What happens if I die?"

"Tis just the same as the two men we lost to fever and an accident early in the voyage and the three Austrians that passed away under our care. Well, they put you in your hammock, like you're sleeping. Then they stitch the hammock closed and put a cannonball at your feet so your body won't float. Corpses have a tendency to do that, dear. I saw it the day after the Nile, they were washing up on the beach along with broken pieces of wood from ships and the furniture and bulkheads we'd jettisoned over the side before the battle. They put the last stitch through your nose, to check that you're actually dead, then you're thrown over the side, and as your body sinks to the deep your soul goes to heaven, and you get to be happy and play a harp while floating amongst the clouds for the rest of eternity. Yet there's no need to worry. Most likely, you won't be killed in battle. Casualty rates are only a third in the *bloodiest* ships, and that includes both killed and wounded."

"What if I'm wounded?"

"Well, you'll go down to the lower deck where you sleep and Doctor Burke will take care of you. Now, I have work to do below with Lieutenant Brooks. You all have free time now," I said, turning to walk away.

Just before I stepped down the ladder a shrill, excited voice called my name. "Captain Herrick! Captain Herrick!"

"Yes, Matrose?" I asked.

"I saw something on the horizon, I think it is a ship, sir," he said quickly, his accent almost unintelligible in his enthusiasm.

I withdrew my spyglass from my coat pocket and scanned where he was pointing, searching for the tiny white dot that would indicate a sail, but found nothing. "Did anyone else see this?" I asked the young gentlemen.

"No, sir," Haynes replied. They all shook their heads.

"Well, sometimes our eyes play tricks on us," I said. "If you're right, then she's probably a merchant vessel heading across the Atlantic, or one of our coastal traders."

"I know what I saw, sir," he said defensively.

"I don't doubt that, darling" I said, "and it would make sense that other ships would be out here, but 'tis not worth deviating from our course."

"But they might have victuals aboard!" Haynes exclaimed.

"Perhaps, but they may also be in as desperate straits as we are and have nothing to spare. I know you are hungry, but the best hope we have of getting resupplied is by reaching England on schedule. Tis only one more day. You'll survive."

I turned and resumed my journey back to the upper deck. The tired men were drenched in sweat, moving the pump slowly and stiffly. "Keep at it, lads," I said, encouraging them. "Keep at it, you're almost finished!"

The carpenter then approached me. "'Tis only a few inches deep, sir," he said in my ear. I waited a few more minutes then relieved my men. "Good work, lads," I said. At that point the watch changed, as was marked by the tolling of two bells.

Climbing up to the deck I saw that the sailmaker and carpenter were hard at work, but not yet halfway done. I decided to speak with Greene and the purser with regards to what Burke had shown me; that Chase's crime was a setup. I went first to the purser, down in his lair on the aft platform amongst the darkness and the stench. The iron ingots used as ballast had a tendency to soak up the smells of the bilge water and the rotten provisions. I found Mr. Gailden in the slop room once again. His head was turned; he stood by a shelf organising piles of bedding that the sailors had not bought. Stealthily, I crept in, shutting the door behind me without a sound. Only the noise of the waves above my head and the creaks and groans of the old ship broke the silence. "Mr. Gailden," I said. He jumped, turning his head quickly.

"Captain, sir," he said, surprised. He held a rag to his black eye with one hand and one of the thin mattresses in the other. "Come to inquire again on the state of the supplies?"

"No, I'm here to speak with you regarding a different matter."

"Oh," he said, a measure of fear entering his voice.

"What did Greene come to ask you about yesterday?" I asked.

"He-he told me that Chase had consumed all of the tobacco allotted to him, and that I should be careful as he might steal it," the purser replied tersely.

"As I recall, the tobacco was on the front centre shelf, next to the bedding," I said, running my hand along the board adjacent to me, "a rather odd place to store the substance that you'd been warned one of the sailors might steal, if you ask me. An easy place, if the purser turned his back at just the right moment, for Landsman Chase to snatch a handful to roll and smoke. Then you could emerge just in time to catch him. Yet I am a man of mercy. You knew I would only order twelve lashes for smoking below-decks, as that is all I am permitted to order without a court martial. That is why Ordinary Seaman Greene spoke with you earlier that day to coordinate a plan. Chase would be drunk from the brandy that Greene stole from the ship's surgeon and conveniently left some place easy for Chase to find right before he was due on watch. So as not to get caught drunk on watch, Chase went to one of the platforms that should have been empty because all the idlers were in their beds, and decided to enjoy a smoke in the meantime, but lo and behold, you were there, threatening to turn him in. As a result the two of you got into a fight, and the noise was loud enough to alert Lieutenant Reid to arrest Landsman Chase, and for Reid to find me so I could order four dozen lashes. Do you deny that you conspired with Greene to get Chase flogged?"

"No, sir," he said, swallowing.

"I shan't punish either of you," I said, "but I would like to know why."

"Sir, Chase has been stealing my merchandise for this entire voyage. We both know it, yet I've only caught him red-handed twice," he spat furiously. "You know I'm an honest man, Captain. I'm just a businessman trying to make a living, nothing more, nothing less, so when Greene came to me and told me how I could finally see justice served, I accepted his offer to help."

"So your motivation was justice for economic injury? 'Tis all?"

"Aye, sir," he replied.

"So there's no threat of further disciplinary issues? No threat of a mutiny?" I asked.

"No, sir," he said, a note of relief entering his voice.

"Well, that is all, then," I replied. "You may go about your duties."

"Thank you, sir," he said, his shoulders relaxing and the creases on his forehead softening.

I turned to head out, accidentally bumping my head on one of the beams holding up the ceiling before proceeding back up on deck. It did not take me long to find Greene; he was sitting with his back against the leeward hammock netting, playing a slow tune on his fiddle. There was a part of me that wanted to sit down with him and listen; his eyes were closed and his expression was one of a relaxed oblivion. "Greene," I said, addressing him. "My day cabin, if you please."

He opened his eyes. "Aye, sir," he replied, standing and following me to the day cabin.   When we were both alone I sat down. "Please, sit," I said.

"Aye, sir," he replied, taking his place across from me.

"Dr. Burke found this on the stolen bottle of brandy," I said, producing the hair from my pocket. "I've just spoken with the purser," I added. "I know that you approached him with a conspiracy that resulted in Chase's flogging. You stole the bottle and made it easy for Chase to find, the purser left the tobacco in a place where he could steal it, then knew just when to incite the fight that alerted Lieutenant Reid's watch."

"I did sir," he said bravely.

"The purser didn't try to deny anything either. You two may be conspirators, but you're the most honest conspirators I've yet seen."

"I would not lie to a man the crew claim to be akin to God," Chase replied.

"There's only one God, and he resides in heaven, not on the quarterdeck of a British man-o'-war," I said. "I understand that your grievances with Chase go back many years. Yet why did you choose to act now? Why have me flog him? Most would seek revenge with their own hand, not manipulate the Royal Navy's disciplinary system."

"Well, sir, there's something incredibly satisfying for a slave to see his master flogged. You wouldn't understand, sir."

"I understand that you knew I was at the Nile, and that Dr. Burke is my friend. You played to my sensitivities; made it *his* bottle of brandy that was stolen, made the next crime smoking belowdecks because you knew I didn't want the *Cassandra* to become *L'Orient*."

A long silence ensued in which Greene looked at his hands.

"Oh, don't worry," I finally said. "I shan't punish you. I've seen enough blood spilt today already."

"Thank you sir," he replied sullenly.

"You may go about your duties," I said, "and now that you've gotten your revenge I expect that you'll refrain from feuding with Chase for the rest of the voyage."

"Aye, sir," he replied. Greene was more intelligent and had more audacity than I'd previously thought. Here was a man who could not write his own name who had out-smarted me. The only reason I had won is because a cap-tain's power is akin to God.

It was then that I headed back out on deck. The sun had dipped to hover just above the orange horizon, the darkening sky filled with puffy white clouds with wispy cirrus higher up in the atmosphere. It had grown colder as afternoon had turned to evening. I watched as the sailmaker added the last few stitches to the canvas and the carpenter's mates hauled tools and supplies back below decks. O'Hare was at the helm, examining his instruments and messing with a thermometer. Angeline was talking to Rosie; the two were friends as they were both the youngest and most liber-al women aboard. Their conversation drifted to me from a distance.

"I think it's good that the colonies rose up in revolu-tion, but don't say that to your mother, she strongly dis-agrees," Rosie said. "They cost more than they were worth.

Those… Provincials received all the protection of our military, costing us hundreds of thousands of pounds and didn't pay a shilling in taxes until we had them under martial law."

"And the French? Were they right?" Angeline asked.

"Well, no one in these wars is ever right. If you were to ask the French, they'd say they were fighting for freedom, yet if you were to ask the British, or any of our allies, we'd say the same thing," Rosie replied.

"You sound downright Jacobin. Why is there a war at all, then, if both sides are fighting for the same thing?" Angeline asked.

"Great Britain and France are doomed to fight, tis about a longstanding struggle for power in a world that is simply not large enough to sustain both empires. Perhaps someday, after all of humanity has perished from the earth there will be peace, but until that day there shall always be conflict somewhere," Rosie said, "even if it is just a merchant fighting a thief."

"That's rather depressing," Angeline sighed.

"That's human nature," Rosie said simply.

A shiver ran up my back; the frigid breeze gave me chills. An acute headache had begun to develop, reminding me that I might be coming down with a cold. The sailmaker finally stood and stretched, his back clearly sore from mending the mizzen topsail all day.

"Alright, men," I said, raising my voice, which was surprisingly hoarse. "We're to raise the mizzen topsail. Top-men, to your stations, all other hands to the halyard," I said. Two of the men under the direction of the boatswain quickly attached the halyard to the sail and tied a bowline to secure the boom as the sailors assembled in their positions. The top-men clambered up the rigging to where the sail would go, gathering sheets that needed to be reassembled. "Ready?" I asked. The men turned, each looking me in the eye and giving a nod. "Haul away, lads!" I exclaimed. "Be careful now, slow and steady!"

The men heaved away, well-rested as they were on Lieutenant Wilson's watch and had not yet exerted themselves in the way that Brooks' watch had.

The men not on watch began to come up on deck, and though it was before supper the crew's habit of singing and dancing for exercise in the open air had already begun. One, a shorter fellow named Rockfeld with a rather dark tan on the back of his neck and two crossed cannons tattooed on his hand began to sing. "What you going to do with a drunken sailor, what you going to do with a drunken sailor, what you going to do with a drunken sai-lor, earl-y in the mor-ning!" The men joined him. "Put 'im in the bilge and make him drink it, put 'im in the bilge and make him drink it, put 'im in the bilge and make him drink it, earl-y in the mor-ning! Way, hey and up she rises, way, hey, and up she rises, way hey, and up she rises, earl-y in the mor-ning!" I listened to the sea shanty in amusement, and as the men reached my favourite verse I couldn't suppress a chuckle. "Put him into bed with the captain's daughter, put him into bed with the captain's daughter, put him into bed with the captain's daughter, earl-y in the mor-ning!"

This time, the men raised the sail without a mishap. It filled with wind, heeling the ship slightly farther over, and as I felt the burst of speed push the ship forward I wondered how much time had been lost because it had broken. Once the sail was raised, however, there was no illusion— the men were panting, falling to the deck to rest, their emaciated bodies already strained to the limit. I remembered the broken step yesterday. We had to reach England, and soon; the ship's company was growing weaker and more fatigued by the day, and the ship itself was breaking to pieces, slowly sinking beneath us. Yet only the endless, merciless dark sea was to be seen. We were utterly and helplessly alone.

I stayed on deck to watch as the sheets were re-run and the mizzen topsail readjusted, then went back down into my day cabin to begin the hours of paperwork that I had meant to start at noon today. I sat down at my table, which had four chairs around it. There were entries in the

ship's log to compile, records of sickness and injury from
Dr. Burke, records of expenditures, records of victuals and
supplies consumed, records of floggings given and disciplinary incidences, dispatches from Admiral Nelson, records
of flag-signals sent and received, records of ordinance ex-
pended, records of seamen's pay, all standard files that had
to be sent to various organisations such as the Admiralty,
Sick & Hurt Board, Victualling Board, Transport Board,
and Ordinance Board. My hand quickly grew tired from
writing so much and after a few hours I had difficulty keeping my eyes open. Higgins brought me supper, which sat on
the table until it got cold and he took it away. He sat next to
me, helping me keep the papers in order until I dismissed
him to go to bed. I worked until my candle burned so low
that I had to replace it with a new one. It flickered on into
the night, my sole companion. I heard twelve bells toll and
the watch change, but kept working. My head ached terribly and I could hardly see straight but still I continued to
work. More asleep than awake, I signed the last papers for
the Ordinance Board, which detailed my most recent usage
of gunpowder— when I had drilled the men at the guns a
week ago. Four bells rang, and the watch changed again. I
unbuckled my shoes then blew out the candle and stumbled
in the dark to my bed, clumsily climbing in and tucking
myself under the blankets without even changing my
clothes. It was four in the morning. For once, I was too

125

tired to fear my daily nightmares and looked forward to the few hours I could catch to rest. At the same time, I worried over the process of readying the ship to enter port tomorrow. I shut my eyes and quickly fell asleep.

Chapter 3

I woke to Higgins gently pressing my shoulder. "Good morning, sir," he said. The curtain at the righthand side of my bunk was open and I could see my day cabin. It showed the hellish side of captaincy; the foot-high stack of papers neatly resting on the table was a manifestation of the sleepless nights and drudgery involved with command. The 18-pounder sitting behind the table was a constant reminder that the ship could at any moment be forced into mortal combat and many of my men could be injured or killed. Yet there were sanguine objects in the room just aft of it, ones that made it difficult to believe that the ship had been built solely for the purpose of warmaking. The harpsichord resting in the corner of my dining cabin denoted an atmosphere of beauty and tranquility. The walls were painted a light yellow to make the room seem brighter and windows filled the cabin with light. All the furniture was of polished mahogany, a manifestation of my upperclass status. The curtains to my bed were embroidered with flowers by a loving mother. A frigid wind swept through the room and I saw that the gunport for the ships' gun in my day cabin had been left open.

A bitter taste filled my mouth and my eyes ached. I forced myself to stay awake. Higgins spoke softly to me. "'Tis 6:30, when you asked me to wake you, but I understand that you didn't fall asleep until late last night. If you'd like to rest a little longer then I can come back in an hour."

"No, I'm fine, thank you," I said. "I'll rest when we reach England."

Higgins offered his arm and helped me from the bed. I stumbled, and he caught my shoulders to keep me from falling. The swell had grown markedly stronger overnight and it was difficult to walk. I used the necessary, as always, and began to notice a pain in my stomach. My head began to throb and every bone in my body felt as though it were made of glass. I stepped out of the loo and walked to my vanity where Higgins was waiting.

"Sir, you look unwell," he said.

"I feel fine," I lied.

"I can send for Dr. Burke, if you'd like, sir. Perhaps there's something he could give you."

"No, thank you, though I appreciate your concern."

"Aye, sir," he replied. "I'll help you undress now, sir." He unbuttoned my coat and shirt and slid them off my shoulders. I took my pants off myself, though he helped me with my stockings then took my wig and eyepatch. "I'll powder this for you, sir," he said of the wig.

"Thank you, Higgins," I replied. I dampened a rag in the warm water on my vanity and washed myself quickly, first with water, then with soap, then with water again. I rubbed the soap into my hair then rinsed it. The wispy blond locks were trimmed to my ears. I combed them out, still wet. Goosebumps formed on my arms and legs and my teeth began to chatter. I shaved, and felt a sharp scratch at my cheek before I saw a tiny dot of blood emerge, then dabbed it dry with the end of a towel.

"Sir," Higgins said. "'Tis cold out today. I brought the warm cashmere undergarments that your mother bought you." He placed a pile of clothes on my sea chest with the ones I put on first on top.

"Thank you," I said, dressing in the red undergarments then my long white stockings. I put on my breeches next, short pants which I wore so that if *H.M.S. Cassandra* were to go into battle and I was wounded in the leg, Dr. Burke could find the injury and operate on me quickly without having to completely undress me first. Commissioned officers and midshipmen were the only personnel in the Royal Navy to have an official uniform, though the sailors tended to dress differently from landsmen. Typical sailor attire were long pants, as opposed to the more popular knee-length breeches, loose checkered shirts, and short coats called "pea-coats" or "ass-freezers" because they did not go all the way to the knee like most coats. The short style made it easier for sailors to work aloft in the rigging without having to worry about the ends of a longer coat tangling with lines. Sailors liked to wear their hair in long queues braided down their backs, which was often coated in a layer of pine tar to keep clean, as water was scarce aboard ship so it was difficult to bathe. I required my men to wear clean clothing each day so they could remain in good health, and naval regulations forbade beards, though sideburns were allowed. Many sailors also chose to wear tattoos to signify their achievements such as crossing the equator or being a boatswain. One common tattoo was a pair of crossed anchors on a sailor's hand just below the thumb; on navy ships, these were replaced by crossed cannons to indicate military service. Pigs and chickens were often tattooed on a sailor's feet; the pigs and chickens, who were stored in wooden crates aboard, would float in water, so this tattoo meant that the sailor would survive in the event of a shipwreck.

Officers didn't generally get tattoos, and many cut their hair short, a style that was growing in popularity. Our uniforms were white breeches and long navy blue jackets. The presence of epaulettes and cuff-bands was dependent on rank. As a post-captain with six years of experience, my day-to-day uniform had no cuff bands, as they were reserved for admirals, but gold epaulettes on each shoulder to distinguish me from a less experienced captain or my lieutenants. I buckled my shoes, which were black with short heels and silver buckles. After that, Higgins buttoned my shirt, which was thin with white lace cuffs, and tucked it into my breeches then secured them with my belt. The belt held my sword and a holster for my pistol. He helped me put on my vest over the shirt, which was buff and made from silk. After that he secured my silk neckcloth around my neck. Next I put on my heavy blue coat and white gloves. Higgins then slid on my eyepatch and finally my wig and hat. I felt much better having washed and dressed in clean clothing. "Your breakfast is ready, sir," he said. "Unfortunately, none of your chickens laid today, and we've finished the last of the porridge. I'm so sorry for the change of menu, sir, but I've prepared your tea and I managed to find two sausages and a sea-biscuit for you from the gunroom."

"That's alright, Higgins, we're to get fresh victuals tonight. Then we can have toast with jam, or even scones tomorrow morning."

"Aye, sir," he said. "I'm looking forward to it."

"So am I. Now, Higgins, you may go about your duties."

I could see just by looking at them that the sausages were all gristle and the biscuit was reduced to powder. As soon as Higgins left, I walked stealthily down to the gunroom and set the plate on the table there. Perhaps one of my officers was hungry enough to enjoy it. The officers were too busy talking to notice me. I went back up to the dining cabin and drank my tea, which at this point consisted of the dregs of our supply. It did little to wake me, and I sat half-

asleep at the breakfast table. I checked my pocket watch—
7:37. If I tried to go back to sleep now then I would not be
able to wake up again, though it was still too early to ne-
cessitate going outside. I walked to the cannon and pulled
on the line that hung from the ceiling and operated via a
block and tackle system to close the gunport. After that I sat
down at the harpsichord and turned through my music book
to Haydn's Sonata in F Major. I'd seen him in concert once.
I had just been promoted to commander and was coincid-
entally heading to Deptford near London to take command
of a sloop there. I was travelling through Austria on a tour
of Europe in the meantime, and had gone to hear Haydn's
Missa in Augustiis, or Mass for Troubled Times. Admiral
Nelson had reached a hero's status with the people there,
for his victory against the French at the Nile. As a result,
the Austrians had christened the mass Lord Nelson Mass. I
had gone to the concert in uniform, as I did not have any
civilian clothes with me. Several people dressed in finery
came up and shook my hand, and a lady even gave me a
bouquet of flowers. She was tall and well-built, with a
pleasant smile. I spoke only English, and knew not a word
of German, so could not say anything in reply. The best
word I could use to describe her was innocent. Strong,
wealthy, perhaps, but innocent. Sometimes that face drifted
into my mind, haunting me.

I played the first page of the sonata and the da capo, which instructed me to play it again from the top. The piece made me think of the blue-grey sea lapping at the sides of the ship on a summer's day, when a breeze comes up and the air turns suddenly cold. At the end of the first page I stopped, deciding to check my pocket watch before continuing. I pressed a button on the top above the ship and it clicked open to reveal an ivory King George III. The two moving arrows indicated 7:48.

I closed the harpsichord and walked— nay, stumbled— up on deck then headed straight to the quarter-deck. *H.M.S. Cassandra* heeled over sharply, and from my viewpoint the entire ship was tilted fifteen degrees to leeward. White caps had appeared on the waves overnight and clouds dashed through the sky on a steady wind. The swell was so deep that every time the bow went up a wave and slammed back down into the next, white dots of surf would splash onto the deck. Right now, the heel angle was fine, but if it grew any worse I would have to give the order to take in sail, else risk losing some of our guns as the force of gravity grew stronger than the lines that held them in place. A flock of seagulls flying from the east caught my attention, as a pack of thee of them beat like kites to the wind. One pressed its wings to its chest then dipped its head, gliding down then diving with a splash into the water. The sight of birds was good; it meant we were close to land, and home.

I also began to notice an awkward sideways motion with the swells that hadn't been there yesterday. The land had a way of deflecting the sea like this; I figured it was either the Cornish coast or the French side of the English Channel, and that we must not have been more than a day away from England. I searched for the master. "Good morning, Mr. O'Hare," I said upon finding him near the helm.

"Good morning, sir," he replied.

"How fast are we travelling?" I asked.

"Nine knots, sir," he answered.

"Then we should be home this evening."

"Aye, sir," he replied, "if we don't lose a sail or a spar in the meantime."

"There is certainly a risk of that. If it blows any stronger then I'll have to order the men to take in sail."

"I believe you would be wise in that decision, sir. I'm not the boatswain— 'tis not my place to judge the state of our masts and rigging, but my instinct says that the main-topgallant and the main-topsail are stressed. In fact, I'd be worried about losing the entire mainmast if I were you, sir."

"Right you are. You're the most experienced man on this ship, Mr. O'Hare. I trust your judgement."

"Thank you, sir," he replied.

"We'll be home soon," I said, "I do believe we've missed the storm."

"Aye, sir. There's still no rain, and the wind is strong but not yet a gale. It should arrive tomorrow night, perhaps."

"Yes, but by that time we should be docked safely in Portsmouth."

The toll of eight bells ended our conversation. I walked down from the quarterdeck then up again to the forecastle to speak with Captain Easton of the marines. "Good morning, Captain," I said to him.

"Good morning, sir," he replied. His wife held him by the arm. She wore a red dress today to match his red coat.

"Could you please have your men summon the crew on deck, I have an announcement to make."

"Aye, sir," he replied.

He ordered the marines to play their drums and fifes, and the crew assembled. The faces were of mixed expressions; some of the more experienced sailors likely suspected that we were close to home, though others perhaps thought that it was another cut to rations or a flogging. I stepped back up to the quarterdeck to address them.

I cleared my throat, then when they had quieted I spoke. "According to the calculations of Mr. O'Hare and I, we should be reaching England sometime tonight."

The men burst fourth in spirited applause. Rockfeld shouted through the crowd, "Huzzah!" The men joined him, "Huzzah!" I raised my fist in the air along with the others, "Huzzah!" I waited a few minutes for the cheering to die down.

When once again there was quiet I continued. "There is, however, much work to be done. The decks must be sanded and holystoned, the sides of the ship and the bowsprit repainted, the brightwork refinished, the brass polished. I expect you all to clean up as best you can before we enter port, and be the smart-looking crew I know you are. Lieutenant Brooks' watch is on deck first. Now, you all know your duties."

A second wave of cheering and applause followed this order, then the men hurried to their stations; we had established early in the voyage who was best at painting, who was best at holystoning, and so fourth, and I had assigned tasks accordingly. I figured that Brooks could handle everything happening on deck for now, but remembered a personal matter to which I had to attend.

I found the young gentlemen gathered towards the bow, talking excitedly about their plans for shore liberty. By no means was I required to grant liberty to any of my men when we arrived in port. Many captains did not due to the risk of desertion that inevitably accompanied giving the lads free reign to wander about on shore. Personally, however, I believed that allowing the crew their freedom every once in a while was a benefit to morale. Generally I didn't let all my men off at once, for that would leave nobody to watch the ship, but I allowed parties of twenty or thirty off at a time, under the supervision of one of my officers. For those who remained onboard there was plenty of fun still to be had. Merchants would take their boats up to our ship and sell the men goods, and women would climb aboard and offer their company. There would be dancing, and a large supper with plentiful spirits. I would usually host local dignitaries in my dining cabin along with my officers on those nights in port, if I was not already invited to a soirée on shore. I had important business in port, too— the purser and I had to find merchants to sell us fresh victuals and supplies. Inevitably scuffles would occur between the locals and the men, and I would have to resolve those as well.

I felt terribly for the crew; sailors were notorious for spending years of pay in only a few nights then going home broke when they were granted more permanent leave. The taverns, the merchants, and the brothels would all take advantage of my poor lads until they had not a dime left to their names. Even the little midshipmen and captains' servants would engage in these vices, if they had no adult

guidance. There was one whom I was particularly concerned about, as he had no parents awaiting him upon our
return to England.

"Matrose," I said, approaching him where he was
standing at the edge of the band of young gentlemen. "I'd
like to speak with you. You've done nothing wrong, don't
worry. If you please, join me in my day cabin."

I walked to my cabin with him following in close
pursuit, then sat down. "Sit down, if you please," I told
him. He sat in the chair to my right so I could see him
clearly. "We're going to be in England soon," I began.

He nodded in response.

"It may be some time before we can find you a ship
going back to Austria," I said.

"Yes," he replied.

"You'll need some place to stay in the meantime.
The ship is going into dry-dock, you can't stay here. Most
of the men will be going to their homes or to various inns
and taverns. You're too young to live on your own. I'd like
you to stay with me, after I'm relieved of command. I have
a nice house in Portsmouth. There's a guest bedroom where
you could live. Then we'll find you a ship going home, alright?"

"Thank you, sir," he said.

"When we're off this ship you don't have to call me
'sir'," I said.

"I don't want to go back to Austria," he said quietly. "I want to stay with you."

"Well, I have no objection to your pursuing a career in the Royal Navy. You're a good young gentleman, and I suspect you would be an excellent officer. It would be my pleasure to take you with me to my next command, and I shall support your progression through the ranks in any way I am able."

"Thank you, sir," he replied.

"Now that that's sorted," I said, "you should go back with the other young gentlemen."

"I never thought I'd see freedom again…"

"Now, don't think about that. You'll like England. We'll have fresh victuals and you can eat and sleep as much as you please. Now, go spend time with your friends."

"I should be dead… how am I alive when Franz is not?"

"Don't dwell on loss and pain in the past, think of how wonderful the future will be. Franz lives on amongst the angels. You'll see him again, a long time from now. He wouldn't want you to be unhappy in the meantime."

"Franz should be here. He was my friend and he's the only reason I survived. I miss him."

"I understand how you feel. I endured a… great tragedy when I was your age, when I lost my father. It will get easier, I promise."

"Thank you, sir," he replied. We both stood and walked out the door then up the ladder back outside.

The holystoning was gong well— the forecastle, a raised area at the bow of the ship just above the main deck, was almost finished. I went to the upper deck, my joints aching as I climbed down the ladder. Most of the men were employed washing this deck. All the gun-ports were open to allow fresh air into the ship's interior. Some of the men were below as well, cleaning the lower deck and the platforms in the hold as best they could. I would have to order a contingent of them to work the pump later, both to pump out the seawater leaking into the hold and the runoff from washing the decks.

Many men also hung from boatswain's chairs over the sides of the ship, painting her flanks black, with white around the upper deck. We would paint the gun-ports later, once we were finished airing out the ship, perhaps on Lieutenant Wilson's watch. The longboat was out, with Lieutenant Reid sitting in it supervising the painting. I walked up to the forecastle and past the working men to the bowsprit, where Rosie was painting Cassandra's dark hair. She was as much an artist as Dr. Burke, which is one of the reasons I believe the intimate attraction existed between them. "May I look?" I asked her.

"Good morning, Captain," she said. She sat on a boatswain's chair just under the bowsprit with her legs on the windward side, her dress hanging down. Shifting her weight, the dress came up a few inches. I caught a glimpse of her ankle and blushed, turning my head away. When I turned back she was giggling mischievously. I cleared my throat, then leaned over the side to see her artwork. She'd already finished the face. The coloration was lifelike in its subtle changes— the slight darkness above the eyes and the pink added to the cheeks that deviated from her main skin-tone. She wore a laurel wreath with oscillating shades of olive green and her hair was entirely black, like the irises in her eyes, and the lips were a subtle brownish pink. I looked down the rest of the figurehead, which was badly chipped as Rosie had not gotten around to finishing her repainting. In one of Cassandra's hands was a scroll, and in the other she held a shield with a crown and the initials G.R., symbolic of our king, George Regis. This same symbol could be seen inscribed on all of our ships' guns as well.

"Excellent job," I said of the painting. "She's lovely."

"Thank you, sir," she replied.

"Herrick!" Someone shouted behind me. I immediately recognised the voice to be that of Dr. Burke. I turned my head. "Hello, darling," he said softly to Rosie, then gave her a kiss on the cheek. "Not stealing my lady, are you?" He joked, elbowing me in the ribs.

"No, nothing of the sort, just checking her progress on the figurehead," I replied.

"I was trying to steal him," she laughed, "to go have dinner with us this afternoon."

"You're very kind, but I doubt I could spare the time," I replied.

"We're *not* dining in the gunroom again, I am sick to death of maggot-filled biscuits and salt pork. We've had nothing but salt pork for three bloody days, we're out of everything else!"

"I don't have much left myself," I admitted. "I ran out of porridge yesterday morning, and I have very little molasses left anyhow. Eggs are out of the question; both my chickens have decided not to lay today and I slaughtered the rooster for our Sunday supper two weeks back. I have only a few stalks of asparagus remaining and a strip of salt beef for victuals."

"I'm terribly sorry, Captain."

"That's fine, I completely understand. I've spent most of my life in the Royal Navy, I'm accustomed to poor victuals, though for landsmen they must seem awful."

"They *are* awful! The fact that you've eaten salt port and maggot-filled biscuits most of your life isn't an achievement, 'tis terribly depressing!"

"I'll have to agree with the doctor on this," Rosie said, looking up from her painting for a moment.

"Don't you have something better to do, besides pestering me?" I asked.

"Fortunately, no," Dr. Burke replied.

"How is the fellow with the jaundice?"

"I cleared him for duty again this morning," he replied.

"And the purser?" I asked.

"I told you yesterday. He's fine. I took the stitches out of his forehead as soon as breakfast was over."

"And Chase?" I asked.

"Do you actually care?"

"We flog men to discipline them, not to inflict serious injury."

"He's fine. He'll have some nasty scars but none of the lashes went very deep."

"And Matrose?" I asked.

"That scratch on his neck has almost completely healed. He was late, though. Said he was talking to you."

"Yes. We were discussing his living arrangements, once we reach England. The other lads all have families in Britain, homes to go back to. The rest of the Austrians I'm not so concerned about— they're old enough to look after themselves. Little Matrose's only thirteen. I don't want him to be alone in a country that he's never seen before. He agreed to stay with me until my next command, and I told

143

him that I would use my influence to help him through the ranks."

"So he's interested in a naval career?"

"Yes. That's what he told me."

"Lovely," Burke replied with an air of sarcasm. "I remember when we found him. As a doctor I was certain he would die."

"I suppose I won that argument," I said.

"Here I was, thinking we had won an easy victory, with no casualties, and I could go ahead and make love to Rosie while the cook prepared—"

"Dear God," I interjected, shocked by his loose tongue.

He pretended not to pay attention to my discomfort, "while the cook prepared supper, because I had no work to do, when you came down to the lower deck asking me to come to the upper deck. So, I went up, and then I saw fifteen of the most wretched beings."

"The poor things were terribly abused at the hands of the French," I said. "They were naked and emaciated, shackled to the deck at the neck, wrists, and ankles, all sick and covered in filth. I have never understood how the enemy captain could have been so cruel. I ran him through with my cutlass as soon as I saw him." Yet I did understand. I'd asked him, and with his dying words he'd said that he was avenging the deaths of his men from a previous command, who had been locked away in our prison ships. My curt reply had been that his government was at fault, for Napoleon Bonaparte had refused to engage in prisoner exchanges, and our land prisons as a result were over-crowded. I was not about to admit that in front of Rosie, however, and add fuel to her Jacobin beliefs. The bickering with Abigail Easton, who was a staunch Tory, was at present almost unbearable at my dinner table.

"Yes, they were all quite weak, emaciated and with scurvy. Most of them were ill with typhus. I was concerned that it would spread to the crew."

"I had them washed with soap and hot water, and all their clothing thrown overboard, and we didn't have any problems, *did* we?" I asked Burke. He'd been complaining vehemently that we should have left them aboard the French warship, though it had been so full of shot-holes that it sank only a day later. Fortunately, we had been able to evacuate all of the French prisoners to the two captured cargo ships before then, so not a man was lost.

"No, we were quite fortunate in that respect," he replied. "Three of them were lost under our care— thank goodness the sickness did not spread."

"The one with the injured leg, who the French shot while trying to escape, his name was Franz."

"I'd rather not know his name," Burke cut in. "'Tis difficult enough, trying to forget his face after I amputated his leg."

"He was Matrose's friend."

"Oh, *lovely*," he said sarcastically, "now I murdered the best friend of one of the little fellows. If I'd waited until he was stronger to perform the amputation then he might have lived. Even if I'd made the decision not to give him laudanum, he might have pulled through."

"If you'd waited until he was stronger then the blood poisoning would have killed him first. You allowed him to die with comfort and dignity. You never gave up on him. There was nothing more you could have done."

"Thanks *very* much for bringing it up, then," he said coldly.

"You brought it up when you commented on Matrose's poor constitution."

"Well he *is* a sickly little fellow. Not my first choice for the Royal Navy, 'tis all."

"He's just young. He'll grow out of it when he's older."

"Or a cannon-shot will take him out of his misery."

I glared at him. "I'm going to check the bilge, see if it needs to be pumped again."

"Now don't be angry, I was just telling a joke. You know, *humour*. You're supposed to *laugh* because 'tis *funny*? Laughter? Ever heard of that, Captain?" He called after me as I disappeared down the ladder to the upper deck. If I'd stayed up there a moment longer then I'm certain I would have punched him. Yet before I could make it to the next ladder, going down to the lower deck, a shout filled my ears.

"Man overboard! Man overboard!" I ran back up on deck to see one of the sailors pointing to the stern.

"Throw a line to him!" I ordered, scanning the waves. A splash of white caught my eye, and I could see the sailor struggling behind the ship, farther away than any of our lines would reach. He beat about the water desperately, unable to swim. We had only minutes. I searched with my eyes for the longboat, only to find that it was towards the bow of the *Cassandra,* hundreds of feet downwind of the struggling sailor. By the time they beat up to where the man was, he would already have lost his strength and drowned. I knew that the water was freezing, that the swell was deep and that he must have been fading fast. "Lieutenant Brooks!" I shouted up to where he was, coming down the ladder from the quarterdeck to receive his orders. "Lower the jolly boat!" I knew that my jolly boat was the smallest of the ships' boats, and could be rowed upwind faster than the longboat or cutter could sail in that direction.

"Aye, sir," he called back. This course of action, too, would take at least a quarter of an hour, to assemble the crew, lower the boat, and row to the man. By then it would be too late. Only one choice remained.

I threw off my hat and wig, then coat and shoes, then to the astonishment of my watching men I swung around the mainsail shrouds and without hesitation leaped from the ship into the dark North Atlantic water below.

For one terrifying moment I felt the air whoosh around me as I fell in free-fall, then the icy water slapped my body. On instinct alone I kicked upwards, my lungs burning. Seconds passed, seconds that felt like minutes. I wanted desperately to breathe, wondering if I had sunk down so far jumping seven or eight feet from the main-shrouds that I would drown before I ever reached the sur-face. A terrifying thought entered my mind that I might ac-tually be swimming *down*, and I opened my eye in horror. The saltwater stung but I could see that I was heading the right direction, though still far below the surface. The waves rolled and frothed over my head, and the hull of the ship sank down into darkness beside me. Beneath me was a black obscurity that made my stomach tighten. My chest was on fire from suffocation. Finally I broke surface, gasp-ing for breath.

"Captain, sir!"

"Captain, are you alright, sir?"

I felt a line fall beside me. "Don't concern yourselves with me! I can swim! All of you, shorten sail, then drop the sea-anchor. That's an order!" I shouted back to them.

I swam away from the ship, then aft as quickly as I could. The swell frightened me. One moment, on the crest of a wave, I could see all around clearly, the next, in the trough, a five-foot wall of water piled up on either side and blocked my view. It felt as though I was moving up and down more than I was gaining any forward distance. The icy water stiffened my limbs and I lost feeling in my fingers and toes. After only a minute the ship passed me by, and I found myself in *Cassandra's* wake as she cruised forward on her momentum. I knew it would be three quarters of an hour until the sails could be furled, she could be turned into the wind, then anchored. The jolly boat would catch up to her, however, long before then. I should have just ordered the men to furl the sails, as opposed to bringing her to a full stop. These thoughts occupied my mind as I pushed forward, trying to reach the sailor.

Now a hundred feet behind the ship my heart ached from the effort of swimming. I tread water, overcome with fatigue. The cold had made movement itself a trying ordeal. Furthermore, I feared that I had already lost the sailor, as I could see him nowhere nearby. I worried that I, too, would drown, perhaps for nothing. One of the white-caps sprayed over my head, and water rained down my face. I searched the waves for the drowning man in desperation. "Hello!" I cried. "Anyone out there? Any *Cassandras*?" I asked in search of the sailor. Only the sound of the roaring sea came in reply. "Hello!" I shouted, my throat tingling.

"Help!" A faint voice cried back. I swam farther forward, slightly to the left to reach him.

"Keep fighting, I'm here to save you!"

The sailor flailed about helplessly in the water, thirty feet away. With renewed strength I swam for him, then grabbed hold of him around his chest. "I've got you," I said.

"C-Captain?" he asked.

"Just relax, I've got you. The jolly-boat is coming to take us back to the ship."

I recognised the sailor as Rockfeld, though his brown hair looked black when wet. He shivered, and my stiff legs ached from the effort of treading water to keep both of us afloat.

"I-I was p-painting the upper deck," he began, teeth chattering, "wh-when the l-line to th-the boatswain's chair s-snapped. I-I c-can't s-swim," he added. "I thought I was going to die."

"My father taught me to swim before I could walk," I said. "Now, you'll be just fine," I said, turning my head. I cursed the *Cassandra's* poor condition, our lines that were rotten and torn to shreds. *She's unseaworthy*, I thought to myself. She'd been unseaworthy when we'd left Portsmouth for the Mediterranean eighteen months ago. I think she'd been in bad shape before that even. The jolly-boat was, frustratingly, just leaving the ship. I grit my teeth from the cold and the exhaustion in my legs. Dark clouds had gathered ominously about the sky throughout the day, until everything was grey and now not a patch of blue remained. After a few minutes raindrops pattered on the waves and fell in my hair. Rockfeld's breathing calmed. He trusted me to save him. A better captain would not have risked his life for one of his men. I was not a better captain. *My life is not worth more than theirs*, I thought. It was wrong thinking. *I should not care for them. I should not show affection for them.* Yet I could not help but feel a painful tenderness for my crew.

At last, the jolly-boat reached us, coming right beside us. Rockfeld clung tightly to the side of the boat, and the men hoisted him up. I swam around and climbed in by the tiller, pulling myself into the boat without help. The men had departed in such haste that they had brought nothing in the boat with them, not even blankets for the two of us. The harsh wind ran through my soaked clothing, turning it into an icy sheath. I flexed my fingers, now white with cold, assuring myself that though I could not feel my hands I could still move them. For a long, painful twenty-minutes, the oarsmen clawed their way back to the ship. The coxswain took off his coat and handed it to me, but I immedi-

ately gave it to Rockfeld. He appeared to be in shock.
"Rockfeld, when we get back to the ship," I said hoarsely,
"I'd like you to go straight to your sea-chest and put on
something warm. You have free time to stay belowdecks
and rest until your dog-watch, the second one after dinner."
I had lost track of the time, and I had left my pocket watch
on the ship when I'd thrown off my coat. To my knowledge
the watch had not yet changed, but then again, it might
already be past dinner. I tried to guess how long I had been
out there. In a crisis five minutes and five hours can feel
like the same amount of time.

"Aye, sir. Thank you, sir," he replied in gratitude.

The boat pulled up to the stern of the *Cassandra*,
and the men hoisted it back to where it hung over my balcony. I jumped out and walked immediately forward, to
order the men not to lower the anchor. The crew cheered
and applauded me as I walked across the main deck, but my
primary concern was getting the ship to move again. I realised then that the watch had changed; I had missed the dinner hour. I approached Lieutenant Wilson.

"Sir!" He exclaimed, surprised at my wet and un-
gainly appearance.

"Good afternoon, Lieutenant," I said, addressing
him calmly.

"Good afternoon, Captain," he replied.

"What progress have we made in readying the ship?"

"We finished the painting half an hour ago, sir, before the rain. All the decks are holystoned and swabbed, and all the brass has been polished. I do believe we've finished, in fact, sir."

"Splendid," I said. "If you please, order the men to fly the topsails and courses then have them pump the bilge." The 'courses' referred to the two largest sails on the mainmast and foremast, the mainsail and foresail.

"Aye, sir," he replied.

I then turned to see Higgins standing beside me. "If you please, prepare dry clothing for me," I told him.

"Aye, sir," he replied.

Higgins headed back inside to my cabin and I went to inspect my ship. The brass on the helm was polished so brightly that I could see my reflection, and so was the ship's bell. I knelt down and examined the deck to find that it was clean and sanded smoothly. I felt the raindrops pour down on my face. I went to the windward side of the ship and held onto the hammock netting; the combination of smooth planking, heavy swell, and rain made the deck quite slippery. Looking over the side I could see the coat of paint, which did not appear to be running. The ship looked new and sleek now, and the sight of her made a mixture of joy and pride swell in my heart. Rosie had finished repainting our figurehead, Cassandra. She looked young and strong, like a warrior goddess. Indeed, her features were over twice the size of those of a human. After that I headed down to the upper deck, where a hundred men, all who were not on watch, were clustered to keep warm and dry. Heating this deck was never an issue. There were two large stoves that could be lit if need be, in addition to the galley fires where pots of stew cooked endlessly, and a blacksmith's shop just aft of the galley where metal objects were made and repaired. The body-heat of the hundred or so men who would be in here at any one time was enough to provide warmth; in fact on many stations, the main issue with the upper deck was that it was uncomfortably hot.

In addition to being crowded with men, the upper deck also held tables on each side that were held up by lines and normally stowed vertically but swung down at mealtimes. The sailors' sea-chests were also stored along the walls of the ship. Ten guns sat in rows on each side, with two facing the stern at the back of my dining cabin, which made twenty-two in total. They were all eighteen-pounders, as they fired shot that weighed eighteen pounds. The upper deck, however, was not the only deck that was armed; there were fourteen guns on the deck above. In the forecastle, four of these guns were a special type of ship's gun called a carronade. Carronades had a shorter, fatter barrel than regular guns and fired large-caliber close-range shot that smashed through an enemy deck, hence they were nicknamed "Smashers". Ours were 44-pounders, which dealt a menacing blow to the enemy. Along with the 36 ships' guns we had two swivel-guns at the bow of the ship that fired 2-pound shot. Besides large ships' guns, we had muskets, pistols, pikes, tomahawks, and short swords known as cutlasses to arm the men in the event of a battle. Cutlasses were more appropriate than longer edged weapons aboard a ship of war because there was not as much space to fight aboard a warship as on a land battle-field. The tomahawks were useful for cutting lines, which might be necessary in a battle to break the lines that joined two ships during boarding. To board an enemy, one would throw harpoon-like devices with a barbed end that caught on the side of their ship and strung a line between the two vessels, which would pull them closer together.

I walked back to the hatchway. The smell on the upper deck had improved some from earlier, which is what I had wanted. With the rain, I knew I might have to have the crew pump the ship again later. Other than that, the ship was ready to enter port and my duties were done; the best thing for me to do now was to don my dress uniform and sit in my day cabin with a cup of hot tea waiting for the inevitable sighting of land to be announced. I walked to my quarters. My joints began to ache, particularly those in my fingers, though my knees and ankles were also noticeably

painful. *The old rheumatism*, I thought, the bane of all sailors. The cold, wet conditions aboard ship made it an epi-
demic, and the more time one spent at sea, the worse it got,
especially in frigid, damp climates. It had plagued me to no
end in the Baltic, to the point where I had difficulty walking. That had not been the reason I'd been sent home, however. I'd contracted a severe case of pneumonia, and had
required better care in more temperate Bath in England to
recover.

Before I went into my cabin, however, I saw Mr.
O'Hare on the quarterdeck examining his instruments.
"How far are we from home, Mr. O'Hare?" I asked.

"A hundred and ten miles, sir," he replied.

"We're making good time," I said. "You were right
about the storm," I added, "I should never have doubted
you."

"Aye, sir, and the barometric pressure is still getting
lower."

"I still hope that we reach home before the worst
weather hits."

"So do I. Tis too late to turn back now."

"Then we must press on," I said.

"Aye, sir," he replied.

I headed down the ladder to the upper deck, then
through the door to my day cabin where Higgins was wait-

ing. "I have dry clothing for you, sir, in your sleeping cabin," he said.

"Thank you, Higgins," I replied. "This weather is causing another affliction of the rheumatism. Could you please prepare a hot towel for my hands and a hot cup of tea? The joints are at present quite painful."

"Of course, sir," he replied, leaving.

I limped to my sleeping cabin. My knee had been bothering me ever since I'd hit it on the ladder the other day, now with the cold weather and the rigorous exercise involved with rescuing Rockfeld it had grown worse. I winced, sitting down on my sea-chest. With difficulty, I peeled off the freezing wet clothes and dried myself with a towel, then suddenly felt overcome with fatigue. For a moment, I was overtaken by a sudden wave of depression; I was growing old. Compared to most captains I was in my prime, and many would consider me to be rather *young*, especially commanding a large vessel such as my frigate. Yet serving with a bunch of twenty-year-olds made me feel ancient. They were so young, so foolish, many of them, unencumbered by the weight of life experiences, mere *boys*. The midshipmen, and some of the captain's servants, too, were only *children*. I thought of Matrose. He'd not even finished *growing* yet, and still had his babyface. Aboard my ship, I had started with six midshipmen and six captain's servants, not including Higgins. The captain's servants had all been promoted to either mates of Burke and O'Hare or midshipmen, with the exception of Haynes, who was still too young, and Matrose, whom I had taken aboard early in the voyage. Thinking of my age, particularly in comparison to them, and the soreness in my joints, made me feel exhausted. Almost without thinking I crawled naked into the hanging bed and pulled the sheets over me, wrapping my fingers in the soft knit blanket my mother had made, trying to get warm.

Before I could fall asleep, however, Higgins reappeared, carrying a steaming towel in his hands. He handed it to me and I held it with my fingers, the soreness dissipating. Just lying in my warm bed had caused my muscles to relax and I found myself significantly more comfortable. "Would you like a nap, sir?" Higgins asked, seeing me in bed.

"Tis best I get up," I replied, standing. "Could you please help me dress?" I asked, pulling on my undergarments by myself. I saw that he had procured one of my uniforms that was in better condition. *Good*, I thought, *I'll be prepared to impress the civilians when we come into Portsmouth.* Higgins helped me into the dry clothing, then I walked to my table in the dining cabin where a steaming cup of tea waited. I held the hot cup, waiting for it to cool enough to drink. Suddenly, I heard shouting on the deck outside.

I pulled on my oilskins, which were heavy rain-clothes to keep me warm and my uniform dry, along with my gloves, then quickly exited my cabin to go up on deck, leaving the tea on the dining table. Half the ships' company gathered on the starboard side, shouting and cheering.

"Land! Land ho!"

"We've reached England!"

"Huzzah!"

"We're home!"

"It must be Cornwall!"

Bunch of damned fools, I thought, and I saw some of the more experienced seamen walk back down to the upper deck out of the pouring rain. I walked up to the quarter-deck for a better view and withdrew my glass, then adjusted it to focus near the horizon. A small strip of brackish grey came into view. The land was small and appeared to be an island. Besides, it was to the south, and Cornwall would appear to the north. *France,* I thought.

O'Hare spoke to me softly. "Tis St. Anne, sir, the island. We're off the coast of Normandy, just as our charts say. Portsmouth is about ninety miles away, sir," he explained.

"Thank you, Mr. O'Hare. That makes sense," I replied. "Are there any rocks or shoals in this area, to your knowledge?" I asked, "I know we're still very far out."

"No, sir, only closer to shore."

"Do you think it would be necessary to take depth soundings?" I asked, getting to the point.

"No, sir, I do not," he replied, "though we should turn north onto the beam in order to head for home, sir."

On the beam referred to a direction of sailing where the ship was sailing perpendicular to the wind, about ninety degrees off the direction we sailed now. When the ship was pointed into the wind and could not sail at all, she was said to be "in irons". The number of degrees that a ship could not sail in because the wind direction was too high depended on the type of ship. For a man-o'-war, which was square-rigged, the ship could not sail any closer than 67 degrees away from the wind. The ships' boats, such as the longboat and the cutter, however, which were rigged differently, could sail closer. Even these numbers changed, as when it was windier a ship could sail closer to the wind and when the wind was lighter a ship had to stay farther off.

"You're right, we do need a slight course change," I said to Mr. O'Hare.

I then walked over and spoke to the two helmsmen, "Hard-a-larboard," I ordered, "One point large."

"Aye, sir," they both replied. They turned the helm and I felt the direction of the waves shift beneath me. The ship heeled slightly over again, and the wind hit my face at a slight angle.

"Lieutenant Brooks," I said, as his watch had just come on duty.

"I do believe, with the rain, we'll have to pump the ship for a bit again today," I said. "If you please, have Reid direct some of your men below at the pump."

"Aye, sir," he replied, going to find Reid, who was on the main-deck.

I decided it would be wise to find the boatswain to ask him about the state of the rigging. The loss of the mizzen topsail yesterday had proved the frail condition in the tops and we were about to adjust the sails to head closer to the wind by furling the courses and flying the staysail. I saw someone working up in the crows' nest of the main-mast, and decided to climb up to see if it was him.

I walked down to the main-deck, the driving rain hitting my shoulder, to find where the main shrouds came down on the lefthand side. The shrouds were a net of thick black lines that both supported the sail and were used for climbing. I grasped the lines, which were slippery beneath my gloved hands, and climbed up. My arms quickly grew tired and by the time I reached the crows' nest I was panting. The crows' nest was several degrees off centre and I leaned against the mast, which was at an angle rather than straight up and down. The most distressing thing about being this high up was that the wind was stronger here, and the brittle mast shook precariously.

The man was facing one of the sails, but I saw from the crossed cannons tattooed on his thumb and the black sideburns that it was the boatswain. "Mr. Quincy," I said, addressing him. I had to shout to be heard over the wind.

"Captain, sir," he replied, turning around to speak with me.

"Should we furl the courses?" I asked.

"Aye, sir, particularly on the mainmast, and reef the topsails, too."

"Then we wouldn't be going anywhere!" I cried.

"'Tis too rough, we ought to anchor here under bare poles rather than continue. We might lose another sail, or even be dismasted. Our rigging's too unstable and the wood is rotten."

"O'Hare said it shall only get worse. I'll have the men furl the courses, that ought to relieve some of the pressure."

"I believe, sir, that that would be wise."

"I'm going back down now," I shouted, the wind howling around us. I glanced up towards the horizon one last time, hoping to see a break in the storm, but dark clouds filled the entire sky. The mast shook violently and I held on for dear life, then the ship dipped precariously forward into a wave, jerking the crows' nest sharply down with it. I felt like a cat stuck in a tree. Suddenly, a bright shape caught my attention from the corner of my eye. It came from the west, a tiny white bubble. I raised my glass and could just distinguish the minuscule blotches that would indicate the sails of a large vessel. This wouldn't have given me cause for alarm, had it not been for the tiny flash of orange coming from her flank. I waited for another sign, then saw two more flashes, one on top of the other in quick succession. All of the possibilities ran through my mind at once. Signalling by firing guns was normal, especially in poor weather such as this. The Channel Fleet, which patrolled the waters in these parts, would also frequently partake in gunnery drills. I ruled those two possibilities out quickly— the ship was too far west for the Channel Fleet's normal blockade, and most captains would perform gunnery drills in nice weather, when the crew would otherwise have little to do. In addition, despite the fact that guns were used for signalling, typically only one gun— usually at the bow— would be fired, not two from each deck. No, only one logical explanation remained: combat.

Quickly grabbing the shroud, I hurried back down to the deck as fast as I could. "Beat to quarters, if you please," I calmly ordered the marines on watch.

"Aye, sir," Captain Easton replied, and his men began to play the rolling drum tattoo. One of the marines took up his place at the ship's bell and began to ring it incessantly. It clanged on over the wind and rain. Sailors began to arrive on deck in droves to address the emergency,

and my lieutenants joined me when I went up to the quarterdeck.

"Have the ship cleared for action. You all know
your stations," I said to the assembled officers. "After your
men have finished join me in my day cabin for a council of
war."

"Aye, sir," they each replied.

"Clear for action!" I shouted to the men. I then went
to my cabin, where Higgins quickly slid my Nile medal
around my neck. Many officers chose to wear cloth replicas
of their medals during battle so they appeared less con-
spicuous to enemy snipers in the rigging. I figured it made
little difference to my chances of survival; the smoke
would be so thick that no one would be able to see the deck
anyhow. Higgins handed me my pistol and I slid it into its
holster, then placed the cartridges in my pocket. The
weapons would be of little use to me unless we were
boarded. In fact, there was very little I could do to protect
myself once the shooting started. Snipers did not cause
most of the casualties during a battle. Shrapnel, which resulted from cannon-shot striking the wooden walls of the
ship was the most common cause of death and mutilation,
and it was indiscriminate. No, victory or defeat had been
decided months, even years ago, before a battle even started. It came from the shipyards and the cannon foundries,

the endless training and drilling at sea, the discipline we
had acquired over years of practice.

This principle of shrapnel resulting in most of the
casualties was why British ships had an advantage over the
French; our gunnery was, simply put, superior in every regard. Unlike the French, who were blockaded in port, we
had the opportunity to practice our gunnery frequently and
had learned to fire faster and steadier than the enemy. The
French also carried more soldiers, who did not know how
to fire ships' guns, as a proportion of their crews than we
did. Our guns themselves were also more effective, as they
utilised a flintlock firing mechanism rather than the more
archaic quick-match. Flintlocks were a technology in which
the gunner, who would aim and fire the gun, would pull on
a string that was attached to a flint. The flint would strike
steel and create a spark, which would ignite the gunpowder
and fire the gun. Quick-match involved the gunner standing
beside the gun and lighting a match, which would go
through to the powder and ignite it. Flintlocks had several
advantages over quick-match. When utilising a flintlock,
the gunner could sight directly behind the gun and see
where he was firing, whereas a gunner utilising quick-
match would have to stand to the side of the gun and be
unable to look through the gunport. In addition, flintlocks
were an instantaneous firing mechanism, whereas quick-
match had a several second delay in firing. On the heaving

deck of a ship, particularly if there was heavy swell, this delay could make the difference between a hit and a miss. Flintlocks, unfortunately, did not work every time, so our gunners carried a supply of quick-match to use when they didn't.

Other advantages in gunnery included the size of our guns versus those of the French. For one, the French preferred to have larger guns that fired heavier shots than we did. In addition, the French pound was heavier than the British pound, so, say, an eighteen-pounder on a British warship would fire a smaller shot than an eighteen-pounder on a French warship. With smaller shot, our crews could transport the cannonballs more easily and load the guns faster. To pack a larger punch, we had carronades, which could lob heavy shots in close actions.

We also had a superiority in tactics to the French. The French tended to attempt to dismast us, and as a result fired high, whereas we preferred to sink shots into the enemy's hull. If the French were successful in dismasting us, then they could get away and leave us floating harmlessly in the water. However, it was difficult to hit a mast, and easy to hit a hull. Considering that their gunnery was less accurate than ours, they were rarely successful. In addition, because splinters were the main cause of casualties, the casualty rate on French vessels could be as much as six times that of the British. The French also tended to station themselves downwind of our forces during a battle so they could escape easily, but our ships could come quickly to close action where our superior gunnery would take its toll, and the smoke from the battle would fall on their side and render them blind to our manoeuvres.

The real difference between us and the French lay in the fundamental purpose of our navies. The aim of the French navy was to carry out individual objectives; raid our commerce, protect their own, ferry Napoleon's army around. The Royal Navy's objective was one of complete and total domination. This difference in attitude affected everything from ship design to tactics. French ships were designed for speed, while British ships were designed for strength. French tactics involved avoiding a battle, British tactics involved total annihilation of the enemy. Tactically, of course, we always won. How could we not? Yet strategically, there was room for doubt. The grain convoy that the British had sought to destroy at The Glorious First of June had survived and made it to France. The mercury ships that we had meant to capture at the Battle of Cape St. Vincent had escaped. Napoleon's army, which we had hoped to destroy at the Nile still had reached Egypt because we had found the French fleet only after it had arrived in Aboukir Bay and offloaded the army. As far as achieving our aims went, the two navies were evenly matched.

Already the men were taking off the yellow panels that covered my walls and moving my furniture to make space for the guns. I climbed the ladder and walked outside, to see sailors spreading sand on the deck to ensure that it had enough traction so that people wouldn't slip and fall if it became covered in blood. Another group of men were installing a netting that went over the deck to keep broken pieces of masts and spars from falling on the combatants below. I walked down to the upper deck to see that preparations were well under way, and that the sailors had dressed for battle. Even in this miserable weather, they were barefoot and shirtless, with bandages around their heads to protect their hearing. It could get terribly loud with all the guns firing, and an entire ship's company would be nearly deaf for days after a battle. Without protection the deafness could be permanent.

I walked down to the lower deck where Dr. Burke was laying out his collection of knives to quickly operate on the wounded. Some of the men under the direction of Rosie were arranging the midshipmen's sea-chests to be used as operating tables. The chaplain was reading the Bible, practicing the verses he would use to comfort the dying, and I heard him murmur, "though I may lie in the valley of the shadow of death, I fear no evil…"

"Dr. Burke," I said to the surgeon, my best friend.

"Captain Herrick," he replied, his look one of sheer affection.

"I'm to have a council of war with my officers soon, and I may not see you again before the battle."

"That's quite alright. I'm certain it's just one of our first-rates attacking some tiny prize vessel and that the conflict will all be over by the time we get there."

"Just what I thought," I said. "If it isn't, if anything should happen to me, I'm making an amendment to my will that I'd like you to know about. Since my late mother's passing, I have no one to leave my money or effects to. I want you and Rosie to have my house. You may have all of my things, after I'm gone. I'd like Matrose to have the money."

"Doesn't he have enough of that already?" Burke asked.

"All that talk of him being nobility… 'tis all a lie that I invented to protect him, and my reputation." I leaned into Burke's ear and spoke in a whisper. "He's a lowly commoner. His mother passed away when he was very young, and his father was a soldier in the Austrian army, until he died of syphilis. He too joined the army, as a drummer boy at the age of ten. Matrose is illiterate in German— I taught him to read and write in English. You see, Morgan, I have everything— money, interest, a reputation, but I'm always at sea and therefore have no wife. I've no *heirs*, do you understand? I've always wanted to be a father... I loved my own father so dearly. Wilhelm is a good little fellow, he needs paternal love and care. Promise me something, Morgan. You're my best friend, my only friend. If I die, promise you'll look after the boy. I have to know that he'll have a home and a loving family."

"Of course, George," he said warmly. "I promise. Without hearing his accent, I'd assume you were father and son, you look alike. Now, you're going to be fine."

"Don't tell anyone what I've just told you, it would destroy both Matrose and I."

"Don't worry, old friend. You helped me to be with the woman I love. I'd sell my soul to the devil for you."

"Thank you," I said, then headed back up to my day cabin. I quickly took the will out of a drawer in my desk, which was next to the table, and scribbled down the amendments, then stuffed it into my coat-pocket. The men stationed in my cabin were already cleaning the guns and sharpening their cutlasses. A short time later my officers arrived for the council of war.

I addressed the four lieutenants, the sailing master, and the Captain of Marines. "Well, gentlemen," I began. "I saw a warship from the crows' nest in the mainmast, firing its guns. The nature of this fire was not that of signalling and a captain would be barking mad to do drills in this weather. Therefore, we can deduce that the shots were fired in anger. As to the details of the situation, that is all I know."

The officers nodded in assent.

"Most likely, she's one of ours, capturing some lowly French vessel as a prize who was foolish enough to put up resistance. If that is the case, as it probably is, then the fighting will all be over by the time we get there. Now, there is an unlikely possibility that the man-o'-war is French. If that is the case, we shall engage with her in battle. Luckily for us, we are aboard *H.M.S. Cassandra*, the finest frigate that has ever set sail, and our British tars are the best in the world. I am certain of our superiority in training and discipline, and that if we can come to close action with her quickly then we shall be victorious. I would like to say, gentlemen, that it has been an honour and a pleasure to serve with you all. I trust that you shall conduct yourselves with courage and zeal for duty if there is to be an action. O'Hare, if you please, have the helmsmen hold the course thus," I said. "Fly the staysail and furl the mainsail. After that don't adjust the canvas in any way— any more would be dangerous, any less and we'll never catch her. The rest of you may go about your duties."

"Aye, you're the courageous one," Mr. O'Hare said.

"Yes, you're the one who's held this ship together for two years," Brooks added.

"It has been an honour and a pleasure to serve with you, too, sir," Wilson said.

"Your perseverance and capabilities are difficult to match, sir," Perkins said.

"I hope someday to be a captain like you— serving under you when you're an admiral, of course, sir," Reid said, kissing my hand.

"God bless you, sir," Captain Easton said. "Your love of this ship and of your country are an inspiration to us all."

My heart glowed with affection for my officers. At that point I was inclined to turn back to avoid bloodshed; I could not bear thinking of any of my men lying dead or writhing about in agony. Then I stopped myself; I was a captain. They were not men, they were means to a victory. If I ordered them to fight, and some perished, then that was the price of that victory. It had to be worth it. Victory was always worth it. The only alternative was defeat, and defeat equalled annihilation.

I climbed back out to the quarterdeck. The rain had softened to a light drizzle. In the distance, the dot had grown larger, though it was still too far away to see details such as a ship's flag. I ordered the yeoman of signals to raise our colours. It was customary to raise the flag of your nationality before firing your guns at an enemy; to neglect to do so was a severe breach of etiquette. Down below I could hear the men, and I climbed down the ladder to the upper deck.

The mood was jovial. Greene was playing his fiddle and the men were dancing and singing "Rule Britannia". Some were eating large meals. The cook had already put out the galley fires, as was customary before a battle to avoid a fire hazard, so it would take time to prepare victuals after the battle, which could last for hours. Some men sharpened cutlasses, some of the more religious ones prayed. Rockfeld took a swig of grog and sang the first verse to "Rule Britannia" in an operatic voice. "When Britain fir-ir-ir-ir-irst at heav-en's command… arose from out the a-a-azure main! Arose arose from out the a-azure main! This was the char-ter! The charter of the land! And guardi-an a-a-angels sing this strain!" The rest of the men joined in, stomping their feet wildly. "Rule Bri-tannia! Britannia rule the waves! N'er shall Britons ever ever ever will be slaves!" Greene played the next few notes on his fiddle, his expression one of contentment. Even Chase was dancing.

Heading back out to the upper deck, I could feel the rain bead on my oilskins. We were still miles away. I was glad that the men were enjoying themselves. No one was afraid. They felt that as British tars they were invincible. The newspapers, the stories, their own experience had taught them little else. In fact, I was the only man aboard, to my knowledge, who had actually *been* in a full-blown sea-fight. This was not uncommon. Fleet battles seldom occurred and they were often years apart (except in 1797-1798 where three fleet actions had occurred within about a year of each other). Even so, most of the fighting was concentrated on only a few ships. The Royal Navy had around a hundred ships and no more than twenty participated in any one battle. Similarly, it was the same ships that were in many of the battles. Some household names were *H.M.S. Royal Sovereign, H.M.S. Victory, H.M.S. Captain, H.M.S. Vanguard,* and *H.M.S. Agamemnon*, to name a few. Single-ship actions were much more commonplace, but were usually just a man-o'-war firing two shots at a helpless cargo ship and taking it as a prize. They did not often occur between two fighting ships because the French fleet was to a large extent blockaded in port. That being said, individual French vessels did escape occasionally, and sometimes even whole fleets.

I headed towards the bow, placing my hand on Cassandra's black hair. *My beautiful ship*, I thought, *my crew*. I pushed those worries away. Most likely, there wouldn't be a battle. The man-o'-war was probably ours. We would meet them, then see they'd taken a prize. We'd ask them for victuals and water, then head home and be in Portsmouth later tonight.

I saw then that it already was night. The sun had been hidden behind the clouds and I hadn't seen how low it had gotten. In the meantime, the sky had darkened. I knew that it would never get truly dark, as the clouds would reflect any light there was, but the last fading rays of an orange sunset glowed behind us. I went back to my cabin. From the stern I watched as the ships' boats floated away in the distance, along with a few sea-chests and some furniture. The corpses of the two cows, the pig, and the chickens all floated on the sea— we'd killed them before setting them adrift to be more merciful. Having live animals running wild on the upper deck would be dangerous during a battle, and jettisoning the boats and furniture made more room for the men at the guns. It would be a while before the details of the other ship would even be visible. She was heading north, evidently chasing some sort of prey, and had likely not seen us. There was little difference in our speeds, which meant catching up would take hours. I could tell by now that she was French-built as she was moving quickly, most likely a converted prize vessel that had gone into the service of the crown. Smaller ships, however, tended to be faster than larger vessels. We would catch up eventually. With the ship readied for battle there was nothing more to do than continue our approach. I did not dare fly more canvas, as that would heel us over and we'd risk losing our guns.

To pass the time I went to my harpsichord and played Haydn's Sonata in D-Major then "Heart of Oak."

The men cheered at that from the rest of the upper deck; I knew they could hear me. Afterwards I wandered through the ship, carefully examining the guns to see that they were in good repair, and that the decks were cleared of all obstructions. Not a man in the ship showed an inkling of fear or doubt. I went down to the lower deck to see that Burke was ready and that the ladies along with some of the younger seamen were standing by at the powder room to distribute the gunpowder if the fighting started.

I then walked up to the quarterdeck to watch the sky. No stars were visible, but the clouds glowed in pretty shades of blue and grey. There was a chance, albeit minuscule, that I might never see the sky again. I took it all in, the smell of a fresh sea breeze, the taste of the wind and the clear, crisp air flowing through my nostrils. Most of all I savoured the quiet, with nothing but the waves and the rain, and the familiar creaks and moans of the ship's planking to fill my ears. The party below drifted to me in a faded melody through the gun-ports, but the merriment of my brave crew was a comfort rather than a distraction. I sent a prayer to God that He would forgive me for risking the lives of my men. In a way I felt responsible for them, as a good king feels responsible for his countrymen, that his decisions can determine their fate, and that if they suffer he and he alone must answer to God for it. I had no envy of the lower ranks, for it was a difficult life, yet there was something to be said for the fact that they could confide in each other. I could speak to no one of the sickening feeling in the pit of my stomach, the apprehension that set me on the edge of the precipice of insanity. Logic dictated that the ship was ours, that everything was fine, that she was in the Channel Fleet and had drifted off-station capturing French prizes. Yet the small voice at the back of my head begged to differ. Deep down I knew that this night was likely to be my last. Never had I felt more alone than captaining my ship on the eve of battle.

It was 5:40 in the morning, and the sky had just begun to fill with light when Matrose approached me. I turned, seeing that his jaw was set in firm determination.

"Sir, please, come with me," he said urgently, "'tis important."

We walked to the bow. I realised that he must have been watching the other vessel as we had approached it. *Revenge*, I thought. He did not yet have the experience to see the structural differences between a French and a British warship. British ships carried anchors that were shaped like a sharp "V" at the bottom, whereas vessels originating from any other nation had "U" shaped anchors. British ships tended to be wide and short, whereas French ships tended to have a long, thin build. Many French ships had adopted the new technology of the lightning rod, which they attached to the top of one of their masts, whereas British ships had not. For ships that had been taken as prizes from the French and had been recommissioned for reuse, it was more difficult to tell friend from foe, as was the case with the vessel ahead. As soon as an ensign was visible, however, we would know. If the ship was firing its guns in anger, as I suspected it was, then as an etiquette of war it was required to fly its true colours.

"You can see the ship better," Matrose said, raising his glass to his eye contemplatively. His expression was one of an icy sang-froid, and his lips curved into a smile as he looked at the ship. My stomach churned and I feared the worst.

I withdrew my own spyglass and held it up to my good eye. Adjusting the lens, a few details came into view; the rudder, the shape of the hull, the three sails, the two decks of guns, all French in appearance, and one more thing. The tricolour fluttered off the line attached to her spanker, the aft-most sail. Watching the ship, a new development emerged. I could see the smouldering wreck of a British East Indiaman in the water only a hundred feet away. So the French man-o'-war had fought and won. Now I could clearly understand our situation. I counted forty-four guns, which meant that if she was fully manned then she would outnumber us by over a hundred men and eight guns. We'd been so keen to rush into battle, so certain of our superiority. Now the roles had reversed, and the predator had become the prey.

Chapter 4

I lowered my glass in shock, then put it back up to my eye to confirm what I had seen. The tricolour billowed out onto the wind, threatening us. Matrose stood staring at it, transfixed, as if he were seeing a mirage. His expression was one of hunger, nay, starvation for vengeance. Without a word I headed to the quarterdeck. I ordered the helmsmen to head fifteen points to larboard towards the wreckage of the East Indiaman. We had already jettisoned all of our boats. Had we not, I would have sent them in. Instead, we would have to search for survivors from the deck of the *Cassandra*. As we neared the few charred remains of the trading vessel I ordered the men to furl all sails to slow the ship. Burned corpses floated through the water and bounced off of our flanks. "Hello!" I called. "Anyone out there?" I paced the larboard side of the ship, searching for any sign of life in the bodies below.

"Help…" a faint voice moaned from forward.

I ran to where a group of men stood clustered on the larboard side. "There's a man, sir," one of the men said. "He's alive."

"Throw him a line," I ordered. Two of the men took the slack from the main-halyard and tossed it below. I saw the fellow then. His face was blackened with smoke and his body was limp. He seemed more dead than alive.

The man looked desperately at the line but refused to move from the piece of wreckage he clung to. I realised then that he must not be able to swim. "Pass it to him again. A bit closer now," I told the men. They pulled the line back up and threw it so that it fell next to his shoulder. He took hold of it and swung to the side of the ship, hanging on for dear life. "Lower a boatswain's chair," I ordered them. The sailors did so, but he lacked the strength to climb into it. Greene slid down the side of the ship then sat in the chair, pulling him up by his waist.

"Pull them up," I ordered.

When the chair reached the deck the man collapsed, unconscious. I could see now that he was badly burned and both his legs ended in ragged tatters at the knee. Greene stood up, his white trousers covered in gore.

"Greene, if you please, carry him down to Dr. Burke," I said. "If you men on deck see any more survivors, then alert Lieutenant Brooks."

"Aye, sir,"

"Aye, sir," they all agreed.

I followed Greene down to the lower deck.

"Who is-" Burke began, confused.

"I don't know," Greene replied.

"Well, set him on the table, if you please," Burke said, gesturing to the midshipmen's chests that had been readied to receive the wounded.

"Is he breathing?" I asked.

Burke placed two fingers on his neck to check for a pulse. "I'm afraid he's dead- wait…" he paused. "I feel a heartbeat, 'tis very faint."

"Greene, you may go about your duties," I said, dismissing him.

"He's very weak, sir, he's been hurt badly. Mortally, I would say."

"Try to get him as comfortable as possible, and pre- serve his life as best you can."

"Aye, sir," he replied.

"I'm going back up on deck to see if the men found anyone else," I said. *More importantly, I'm going back up on deck because I hate the lower deck and I hate watching people suffer,* I thought to myself, though I would never admit it for fear of being called a coward.

We searched the wreckage for another twenty- minutes or so, then finding not another living soul, I real- ised the necessity of going back down to the lower deck to question the man we'd rescued. The idea of causing yet more distress to a man who'd already been through mutila- tion and shipwreck did not sit well with me, but I needed to know precisely what we were up against, and if there were any other British ships who he'd seen in the area that might need to be defended. I saw no one on the midshipmen's chests, only Dr. Burke cleaning up blood with a rag.

"Rosie and I set him down in a hammock," he said when I arrived. "We dressed his wounds as best we could. He's been unconscious this whole time. I don't believe he'll wake up again, for he has not long."

"Can you wake him for me, so I may speak with him?"

"He'll be in terrible pain. It would be a cruel thing to do. He'll die at peace as it is, surely you wouldn't deprive him of that, Captain?"

"If his ship was in convoy with others, we ought to know about it. He might have seen how many guns the French vessel has, her condition, her men, her strengths and weaknesses. Now, 'tis not easy to give the order to wake him, but as I am your captain you must obey."

Burke did not respond, but his expression was one of blatant refusal.

"Morgan, the Captain is right," Rosie said. "He could have knowledge of the enemy that could save lives. If you won't wake him then I shall."

"No, I'll do it," Morgan said, approaching the man. In a gentle voice he spoke to him. "Wake up, dear sir. Wake up, you must wake." Burke took his hand.

I knelt beside him, then heard a low moan escape the man's lips. A tear slipped down his face and he shifted about restlessly.

"Water…" he moaned.

"Rosie, get the man some water," I ordered her.

She nodded, going to find some. For an age it seemed she was away, and he refused to speak, only to moan in anguish with increasing misery. "Water… water…"

Finally she returned, and Burke held the cup to his lips. He drank thirstily. When he'd finished, Rosie refilled the cup, and when he'd finished that he calmed some.

"Can you tell me your name?" I asked him.

He muttered "John" something, though the last name was unintelligible.

"I am Captain George Herrick, of *His Majesty's Ship Cassandra*. Tell me, are you a merchant seaman?"

"East… India Company," came his weak reply. His chest heaved with the effort to breathe, and I knew he was fading fast.

"Who did this to you? Who attacked you?" I asked.

"French… Ah!" He cried out in pain, a tear sliding down his other cheek. "Forty-four… Tried to fight… Ah!" His expression was one of agitation, as though remembering the battle only aggravated his wounds further. Morgan glanced at me to see my response. I knew he could read my discomfort.

"Did you travel alone or in convoy?" I asked him fervently.

"Convoy... Nine others," he moaned through grit teeth, eyes clamped shut to fight back the pain.

"Do you know where they are?"

"West... North-west. Bound for England..."

"Did you have a military escort?" I asked.

"Yes... Frigate... Sunk... Cape... Good Hope," I saw he was choking, then a stream of blood dribbled out his mouth. I wiped it away with a handkerchief.

"Herrick, please," Burke said. "We ought to give him some laudanum."

"Yes!" He cried. "Yes, laudanum! Please, laudanum! Please!" He sobbed.

"No! It would weaken him and he would die! Remember Franz?" I exclaimed in frustration. Now that that idiot Morgan had brought up anaesthesia the John fellow would think of little else. The interview was effectively over, and I still had no idea of the French vessel's armament or condition.

Morgan glanced at me as though I had taken my cutlass and driven it right through his heart. His face reddened in anger. "How dare you?" He scoffed. "You'd withhold laudanum from a dying man? You sick, murdering, barbarian! All you do is run people through with your damned cutlass and whip men half to death. I hate you!" He shrieked. "You monster! I hate you!" Then in a low voice he muttered, "You don't even look human."

My stomach twisted itself into a knot. I felt sick, and my face flushed. I turned back to the man, practically shouting at him. "Tell me about the French vessel. What was her name? Her armament? Her condition? Did you inflict any damage fighting her?" I asked. East Indiamen were armed to keep away pirates, albeit more lightly than most warships.

"Laudanum," he begged.

"I'll give you a spoonful as soon as you've answered my questions," I replied firmly.

"Laudanum," he moaned.

"Answer me, damn you!" I barked, shaking him vigorously.

"Fire shots…Attacked… so quickly…" he muttered something unintelligible. "No damage…"

"Alright, enough of this!" Morgan exclaimed, pushing me aside. He held a spoonful of the laudanum and the man swallowed it quickly. I turned and glared at the doctor.

"*Forêt Argonne,*" the John fellow moaned. He shut his eyes, a peaceful expression coming over his face.

Dr. Burke checked his pulse. "He's dead," he said matter-of-factly.

"Apologise at once, both of you," Rosie demanded.

I ignored her, storming back up on deck, biting my lip from rage. I walked up to the quarterdeck deck and rested my eyes on the white ensign flying from the spanker halyard as I collected myself. As soon as the urge to head back down to the lower deck and tear Burke's throat out with my teeth had dissipated I walked down to the quarter-deck.

"Good evening, sir," Higgins said calmly. He could tell that I was agitated.

"Good evening, Higgins," I replied.

"Your commission, sir," he said, handing me a leaf of paper.

"Thank you," I said, placing the paper in my coat pocket with my will and testament. I always carried my commission with me into battle, so that if I were to be captured I could prove to the enemy authorities that I was an officer and therefore deserved to be granted more hospitable living conditions than my men. Officers, both commissioned and noncommissioned were generally given parole so long as we agreed not to return to our home country. The men, however, would be locked away in prisons. The British policy in this regard was the same as that of the French. Just by looking at my uniform, an enemy officer could tell that I was a captain, but I liked to keep the papers with me as extra proof of my identification. I glanced over my will again, noting the additions I had made for Matrose to receive my entire fortune and Morgan to receive my effects. I considered writing Burke out, but thought against it. Matrose would have no idea what to do with my house in

Portsmouth or my cabin furniture. Morgan's words flashed through my mind again and my face flushed.

I knew I needed to stop thinking about the argument, that I needed to focus on what to do about the *Forêt Argonne*. If the man, John, had been speaking the truth, which I assumed he was, then the enemy ship would be after that convoy. Without a naval escort they would be slaughtered, being attacked by a ship as big as her. The thought occurred to me then that the enemy might not know about the convoy, but I pushed it out of my mind. East Indiamen never travelled alone if they could help it. No merchant vessel travelling any distance away from the English coastline did. Ships not in convoy with a naval escort were much more frequently captured than those that were. The enemy knew this. Likely, the French captain thought that *we* were the escort. If that was the case, then he would turn to attack *us*. If he knew about the convoy to the northeast he would run from us and attack *them*. We would not be able to catch him before he had either taken or sunk the lot of them. I had to act quickly, to convince him that the convoy was not to the north, but to the south. I walked over where the yeoman of signals stood at his station on the quarterdeck.

"Utilising the Howe signal codes, fly the signal: "Ships in convoy, close in with *H.M.S. Cassandra.*"

"But sir, we're not in convoy."

"Don't question my orders, just do it," I said.

"Aye, sir," he replied. He searched for the three-number codes in the alpha-numeric signal book. There were fourteen signal flags we used; the numbers, 0-9, along with a flag for affirmative, one of negative, one for preparation and one for substitute. In the book, each word had a three-number code. The words were approximate meanings, so one code could mean any number of related words. For example, the three-number code for "defend" could mean "defend", "defended", "defending", "defensive", or "defenders". It was up to the receiving yeoman to piece together a coherent sentence from the words. Also in the signal book were signals for each of the 26 letters of the alphabet, so words not listed could be spelled out. This took more time, however, so an alternative wording was usually found. Ships in convoy would all use the same signal book, as the Royal Navy used both the Howe code and the system developed by another admiral, Sir Home Popham.

"Now signal: *H.M.S. Cassandra* sailing for close action, ships in convoy avoid action."

"Aye, sir," the yeoman replied. The flags went up the mast in an array of blue, white, red, and yellow shapes. The French would have no idea what we were communicating to our phantom convoy, only that we were signalling someone. The captain would likely deduce that the convoy was behind us to the south, just over the horizon that he could see, as he was in front to the north and could see no one. The signal books were highly classified, and in the event of a warship being taken, a captain would throw the signal book along with his orders from the Admiralty over the side of the ship in a weighted bag so they would sink into oblivion and remain a secret. The French captain, however, would have reason to assume that we were the convoy's escort, and that we were signalling the ships under our protection.

I raised my glass to my eye and watched as the French man-o'-war turned, her menacing bows coming to face us. I shifted uncomfortably. It was unnatural for the French to be aggressive in this manner and go after a British warship unless they were absolutely certain of their superiority. Even then, they would avoid a fight if at all possible, unless their orders specifically told them to attack. I saw another layer of canvas unfurl, and the colossal beast grew larger as it approached. I stepped back down to the quarterdeck and ordered the helmsmen to steer ten degrees to larboard. After that I ordered my men to trim the sails. We were heading as far into the wind as it was possible to go and still be moving. The heel angle increased to a dangerous degree, where the windward hammock netting was a full six feet higher than the leeward hammock netting. The enemy seemed to be on the verge of capsizing but remained sailing smoothly. I judged her to be in good repair, or the

French captain was a reckless fool. I hoped the latter but feared the former.

The waves crashed over the bow and seawater slid across the deck. We could not put on any more sail in these conditions without straining the mainmast to the breaking point. The knot in my stomach tightened further and I felt nauseous and dizzy with terror. I grasped one of the hitches on the mizzenmast that was currently unused, clinging to my sanity. The French ship was now only two miles distant, and though the jib blocked half of her from view, I could now see the tricolour flying without my glass. A piece of me wanted to run down to the lower deck and apologise to Morgan, knowing that one of us might die and we'd never have the chance to resolve the fight. Most likely, it would be me. The lower deck where he worked was the safest part of the ship, whereas the quarterdeck where I stood was the most dangerous.

The most frustrating part about my position was that there was now little I could do but wait. We would be in range of her bow chasers before we would be able to fire back. Higgins stood on my blind left side, an invisible guardian, and Lieutenant Brooks, my second in command, stood on my right. If I was wounded, then Higgins would take me below to be cared for.

Brooks spoke in apparent calm. "'Tis very windy, Captain, and cold. I should like a hot supper and a cup of tea when this is all over."

"Yes, I do say, perhaps we shall find plentiful provisions when we take the Frenchy. I think it would be wonderful, to invite my officers to a party celebrating our victory."

"I think I'll buy my wife, Mary, a new necklace with the prize money, and perhaps Angeline a shawl. When we were last in Portsmouth, Mary couldn't take her eyes off of this one diamond beauty in the jeweller's store."

"Surely you'll treat yourself to something nice?" I asked the lieutenant.

"Oh, no, certainly not. I'm going to add any of the money left to my investments at Lloyd's of London."

"Spoken like a true Scotsman," I said, laughing at his miserly nature.

"And yourself, Captain?" He asked.

"Oh, I'll spend it all on my next command. Perhaps I'll be able to buy some sort of uniform for my crew, make the ship look even more well-managed. I was thinking of black shoes, white trousers, checkered shirts, and black pea-coats, and perhaps some sort of hat they all could wear with the name of the ship painted on them."

"Yes, I do agree that the Royal Navy could do with a uniform for the enlisted and the noncommissioned officers."

"Oh, I've been petitioning the Admiralty for ages, but they never seem to listen."

"'Tis important, you know, to distinguish the sailing master from the landsmen."

"Aye, I'm sure that Mr. O'Hare would agree with you there."

"Did someone mention me?" O'Hare asked from his position near the helm.

"Yes. We were discussing the necessity of uniforms for non-commissioned officers," I said.

"Oh, right. Certainly we do," he replied.

"I've been petitioning the Admiralty for it," I said.

"My wife's been petitioning the admiralty. Margaret thinks that we should pay the women aboard ship, and include them in the official rank and rating system," the master said.

"That sounds very radical," Brooks replied. "Angeline and Rosie want to take it even farther and give women the vote."

"I would be fine with—" I began, but a sudden roll of thunder and the splash of a cannon-shot just thirty feet off the starboard bow interrupted me. My heart writhed in my chest.

I turned to Lieutenant Brooks and we both began to walk casually down to the main deck. "You were complaining about the weather," I began, then flinched as the roar and splash of another cannon shot fell ten feet closer than the last. "I don't believe we'll have a problem with the cold much longer. In fact, I dare say that 'tis about to get quite hot in this climate!"

The four of us, Higgins, O'Hare, Brooks, and I all laughed. I could hear the men still singing "God Save the King" below, now with an air of ferocity.

"Mr. Larson," I said to the eighteen-year-old midshipman trailing behind us with Haynes and Matrose. The other young gentlemen were stationed on the upper deck. "Tell Mr. Wilson to have the men hold their fire until my command," I ordered.

"Aye, sir," he replied, scampering below.

I walked back up to the quarterdeck with the rest of my entourage. The courses and topsails still filled with wind. Once the enemy was in range I would order the men to furl the courses, but until then we needed every ounce of speed we could get. I checked my pocket watch. It was 6:45 in the morning, and I had slept hardly a wink in two days. I did not feel tired— the energy of a thousand suns coursed through my veins and cleared my mind. A feeling of utter peace and clarity filled my thoughts. I realised then that I was no longer afraid, that I had crossed the barrier of fear to that rapturous euphoria called courage.

The next cannon-shot whistled through the air, and I heard the sound of canvas tearing before it splashed harmlessly with a *ca-thunk* over the bow. Walking to the edge of the quarterdeck looking forward, I could see a singed hole about the size of a person's fist in the staysail. "What did I tell you, Lieutenant?" I asked him with chagrin.

"Quite hot indeed, sir," he said, assessing the damage to the sail.

"The sailmaker will have his work cut out for him when this is done," I said.

"Aye, and the blacksmith and the carpenter in not too short a time," he agreed.

We continued pacing the quarterdeck, mocking the enemy with our cool, almost idiotic courage and disregard for danger. Three more shots whizzed through the air above us. One passed too far to larboard, the next too far to starboard by about twenty feet, and the final one was aimed much too high and though it was in the right position to hit the mainsail and shred more canvas, it went clean over the top of it without doing any damage. I stepped up to the quarterdeck and raised my glass, scanning the enemy quarterdeck to see if I could identify her captain. The two ships were still a mile and a half away, and though I could distinguish tiny ants that appeared to be the French crew, the deck was too shaky from the swells for me to pick out any details from the blur. We were heading straight for each other, though the *Cassandra* was coming at a slight angle to windward of the enemy vessel, so we would have the weather gage. The French captain did not even appear to care, though by her zig-zag course I guessed that her helmsmen were mediocre at best.

"Send up another signal," I ordered the yeoman. "Say: Convoy stay back, *H.M.S. Cassandra* engaging in close action."

"Aye, sir," he replied, looking up the words in the signal book. *We should keep the ruse going, clear the enemy captain of any doubts,* I thought to myself. I trained my eye on the *Forêt Argonne.* She pitched and rolled in the swells, and though looking down I could clearly see a good six inches of copper plating on the *Cassandra* at the highest parts of the waves, on her I could see none, and her lower gun-ports were extremely close to the water. That told me that she was heavily laden, and therefore our speed and manoeuvring capabilities would outmatch hers, despite her more slender, streamlined French build. Being to windward and being the smaller ship would increase the *Cassandra's* sailing qualities as well.

The shipwrecked man, John, had spoken of a special shot type aboard her, called fire-shot, or red-hot shot. These shots were heated so they were red-hot going *into* the ship's gun. When fired at an enemy they were an incendiary. The weather, however, was on our side. I glanced up at the sky and a raindrop fell on my cheek. In the distance I could see the enemy getting drenched by a wash of grey. Fire was the bane of wood-and-canvas ships, especially ones filled with gunpowder such as ours. My experience at the Nile had only confirmed this belief. British tars had a particular hatred of red-hot shot, because although splinter wounds were bad enough, serious burns were even more painful. The best that Dr. Burke could do to treat burns was to apply olive oil to the sailor's wound. I had learned that, too, the hard way, when a piece of *regular* grape-shot had struck me in the head at close-range as a midshipman and I was severely burned. The use of black powder heated up shots to smouldering temperatures anyhow, and fire was always a risk during a battle.

I walked down to the quarterdeck, then asked the helmsmen to turn two degrees to starboard, in order to gain speed as we were high enough upwind of the enemy to clearly have the weather gage. Sailing ships travelled faster the farther away from the wind they were pointed, with the best point of sail being at about a 45-degree angle from having the wind directly behind. Any farther from the wind and the sails would overlap and lose power. The top-men readjusted the control lines accordingly, loosening the sails slightly. I wanted to get out of the precarious position of being within range of the enemy's guns but not yet close enough to fire back. At a mile distant we would be able to return fire and effectively hit our target. Ideally, I wanted to be as close as possible, in a situation called "close action", where my crew's faster rate of fire would take its toll against the less-disciplined French crew. Movement on the starboard side caught my eye and I walked down to the main deck on the leeward side to see around the staysail and get a better view. A puff of smoke emerged from one of the *Forêt Argonne*'s upper gun-ports, and a flash of orange appeared shortly after, then a low rumble. The shot was followed by five more. I could tell just by the angle of the flames that one of those shots might be a hit. "Incoming!" I shouted. "Get down!" My words were drowned out by the sound of splintered planking and a loud *crash* belowdecks. I felt my legs give way from the impact of a large object, but Lieutenant Brooks caught me instinctively before I could fall.

"Are you alright, Captain?" He asked, searching me quickly for wounds. My ears were ringing and I figured that I might be in some sort of shock. I surveyed the damage and saw that one of the hammocks, which was filled with bedding, had been torn through. Burned cloth and goose down floated to the deck. A body lay at my feet, that of Higgins. The frightening thing was, he had no head. His neck ended in a bloody pulp, and I felt a hot dampness as the blood that had been sprayed from his decapitation soaked through the sleeve of my coat. I saw pale pink strips of gore reveal themselves against the blue fabric and wiped them away desperately with my hand.

"Higgins!" I exclaimed. The head had rolled down to the very leeward hammock netting, leaving a scarlet trail in its wake.

"Captain, are you wounded?" Brooks asked in a harsh voice, pulling me back to my senses.

"No, I'm fine," I replied. I then saw two people limping from the forecastle to go below, one wearing a red dress. Her head was rather bloodied up, and it took me a moment to recognise that it was Abigail Easton. Brooks' expression was one of deathly terror, his face almost green from angst.

"Abigail Easton," I told him. "'Tis not Mary or Angeline, I stationed them carrying powder to the upper deck.

The crease in his brows softened and he resumed his apathetic expression.

I put my glass to my eye and examined the *Forêt Argonne* again. Now I could distinguish individual men aboard, though they were very small. "Matrose," I said to the youngster by my side. "Go to the upper deck and inform Lieutenant Wilson that the men may fire at will, if they please."

"Aye, sir," he replied, hurrying below.

"Haynes," I ordered his friend. "Inform Lieutenant Reid that the men on the quarterdeck may fire at will, if they please." I knew that Reid was only about fifteen feet behind me, but I didn't want to leave the helm for too long.

"Aye, sir," he replied, heading aft. I retained Mr. Larson at my side in case I needed to send an emergency message after the boys. I would not order the men on the forecastle to fire quite yet because their guns were carronades, which fired a heavier shot that was closer range than the long Blomefield-type 18-pounders on the rest of the ship.

I could hear the rumble of the men loading the guns below, and took note of the time on my pocket-watch. I'd heard of well-trained crews that could fire a shot every minute but the best my men had been able to do during gunnery drills was two minutes fifteen seconds. During a battle, however, their blood would be up, and perhaps they'd do better. Captain Easton was down by the forecastle, facing forward. Occasionally he looked up at the rigging, at some of his marines stationed there as snipers. We were still much too far away for them to do any good, or the four guns' crews in the forecastle who were stationed at the carronades. The sooner we closed in with the enemy the better.

I watched the second hand tick in infuriating slowness, glancing up occasionally and watching with my glass as the enemy guns went in to be loaded again. My ears would not stop ringing, and by the end of the battle I knew it would only be worse. Higgins' body lay lifelessly on the quarterdeck and a stream of blood soaked the sand. Brooks remained at my side, and I tried to forget the terror that had been in his face minutes ago. Raising my glass again I saw one of guns run out in the enemy forecastle, now ready to fire.

Suddenly a rumble filled my ears and the ship rocked precariously. A deafening roar erupted from below and I stumbled, holding the nearest hammock netting for support. Smoke and fire billowed out the side of the *Cassandra* from three of the forward gun-ports. I could hear the cannon shots whistling through the air and ran to the main-deck in excitement, training my glass on the *Forêt Argonne*. To my disappointment the first one fell twenty-feet short, and the second was too far to starboard. Then the third… I saw a black hole and a puff of smoke in the side of the enemy ship. "We've hit them!" I exclaimed, shouting through the grating that led to the upper deck. I checked my watch. "Two minutes eight seconds! Excellent time!"

I heard shouts of "Huzzah!" below, and the men stationed on the main deck and in the rigging soon joined the cheering. They were sharply interrupted by a rapport from the enemy gun that had first finished readying. The shot passed forward, and I heard splintering oak as it grazed the bowsprit, then splashed harmlessly into the water. If it had been just two inches higher then the bowsprit would have broken in half and our forward rigging and jibs would be torn to pieces. One of our guns went off next, and the planking beneath my feet shook violently before the flame spit from the barrel and the shot fell short a few seconds later.

I examined the *Forêt Argonne* again with my glass. She had furled all of her sails but for her topsails, and was now slowing down. We were close enough at only a mile distant for me to distinguish individual men aboard her. Surveying her quarterdeck I saw one fellow wearing a red, white, and blue feathered cockade in the style of the revolutionaries. His shoulders were decorated with gold epaulettes, and I identified him as the captain. He raised his glass, watching us. That was when the frightening detail emerged. I watched as the helmsmen aboard her spun the helm hard over to larboard. Slowly, but assuredly, she rotated onto a broad reach, turning all of her menacing broadside on our vulnerable bows. I ran to the quarterdeck, shouting to the helmsmen. "Hard-a-larboard, if you please!" I ordered them. The ship began to slowly turn, but we were not fast enough. I watched in horror as both decks of the *Forêt Argonne's* guns were run out.

An inferno of smoke and fire spewed fourth from her. "Get down!" I ordered the men, my lungs aching from the effort of shouting with all my voice. A hail of lead struck the *Cassandra* and I dropped down to lay flat on my stomach, scraping my knuckles against the sanded deck as I went. Splinters flew every which way around me and the smoke made it impossible to see. When the hellish storm of death and peril had ceased I raised my head, surveying the carnage. I'd gone completely deaf and heard nothing but a sharp ringing in my ears, and I felt weak and disoriented, as though I was about to faint. Matrose lay on the ground a few feet away, screaming and clutching a wound in his shoulder. I could not move, I felt detached from my body. A wave of blood rolled across the deck as we pitched up and down along the swells. Smoke billowed from one of the sails and the staysail had shredded and now lay over the bow in the water.

Someone shook me and I regained my senses. "Captain, sir, are you wounded?" Brooks asked fervently.

"No, I-I'm fine. Matrose!" I called to the young gentleman. I knelt by his side. His face was grey in a smoky pallor and he screamed, sobbing. "Matrose!" I cried desperately. He was covered in blood and shaking from terror. I tried to take hold of his hand but found that two of his fingers were missing. "Brooks," I ordered my lieutenant. "Take him to the lower deck." I turned back to the boy and kissed him on the head. "Be brave, sweetheart, Dr. Burke is going to take good care of you."

On shaking legs I stood, limping up to the quarter-deck. I did not feel any pain that would indicate that I had been wounded, and as far as I could tell all my limbs were intact, but I had difficulty keeping my left leg steady. "Dead down wind," I ordered the helmsmen. "One hundred degrees to starboard, if you please." By turning onto a broad reach the enemy had sped up to be on a course downwind and to starboard of us, heading east southeast. If we headed directly downwind, we would intercept her quickly before her men had time to reload their guns. Then our full broadside, with the forecastle carronades, would tear them to shreds. The animosity I had felt towards the enemy earlier in the morning had now evolved to full-blown hatred. I would not stop until the *Forêt Argonne* was a smouldering wreck. In the meantime, I had orders to give.

"You lads on deck," I ordered the men whose station was to manage the lines hauling sails up and down during the battle. Many were readjusting the sails under the direction of O'Hare from our course change, but there were still some who were not busy. "Put out the fire in the mainsail then cut loose what's left of the staysail. 'Tis slowing us down."

"Aye, sir, Aye, sir," they replied.

"You at the carronades," I ordered the two forecastle guns' crews. "Prepare to fire. The enemy will be in range soon enough. Captain Easton!" I called to the Captain of Marines. "Have your men load and prime their muskets, we're closing for action."

"Aye, sir," he said, carrying out my orders with a smile.

I saw then that Brooks had arrived back on deck, his face pale. "We've many wounded, sir," he began.

"Not here," I said, cutting him off before the men could hear. We all knew that casualties had been heavy, but discussing the matter openly or worse, naming names, would only lower morale. I needed the men to focus all their energy on the task at hand. There was no point in worrying about injured comrades until the battle was over. If the men, or the officers, began to dwell on death and mutilation prematurely then we would most assuredly lose.

"Aye, sir," he said, biting his lip, as if there was something he wanted desperately to ask but dared not say a word.

I heard the fizzle of smoke as one of the men poured a bucket of water on the mainsail to douse the last bit of the fire, then checked my watch again. Only two minutes had passed, but now we had closed to be within 200 feet of the enemy. We were closing quickly with the French vessel, though she seemed determined to stay on her present course. Logically, if she wanted to keep fighting at long range she would head downwind with us, or even turn and go back the way she came. I knew then that she must think us beaten. Glancing down at the blood running through the scupper holes from our dilapidated deck I could see why. I studied the French captain with my glass. He was standing on the quarterdeck with five other men, perhaps two lieutenants, a servant, and two *aspirants*, the French equivalent of midshipmen. The tricolour momentarily obstructed them from view, then I could see them again. The French captain was of average height, and paced the deck with an air of pride, his shoulders held back in regal dignity. Watching him fight his ship I could see that we were likeminded men. We both shared the same ambition, the same physical courage, the same sense of duty. Perhaps in another life we could have been friends. There was a certain coldness in him, however, a degree of ruthlessness that I both despised and feared. It was a demon within me that I had struggled my whole life to hold back. The fact that he displayed it openly and unabashedly only made me hate him more.

Looking over the hammock netting, I watched as the guns were run out. I checked my watch, finding that it had only taken the men one minute and fifty-two seconds. "Fifteen degrees to starboard, if you please!" I ordered the helmsmen.

The *Cassandra* turned, and I held the mizzenmast, bracing myself for the impact. "Fire all she's got!" I shouted. The men at the quarterdeck, main-deck, and forecastle guns heard me immediately, and Mr. Larson rushed down to the upper deck to give my orders to Lieutenant Wilson. We turned so that our full broadside came to bear on the enemy. A few moments later, a massive earthquake struck the deck followed by a deafening thunder. The ship rocked precariously to the side and my throat leaped in my chest for fear we would capsize. Smoke billowed up blindingly, clouding my throat and stinging my eyes. For a full mesmerising minute the eruption of all the fire and fury of hell spewed from the barrels of the guns aboard ship, one after the other. I watched the carronades in the forecastle surge forward and back, straining the lines that held them in place. When the roaring of the guns had ceased the ship slowly regained equilibrium. It took a few seconds for me to recover from a deaf and dumbstruck shock at the sheer power of the noise and the recoil. Sweat beaded on my temples and under my arms from the oppressive wave of heat now emerging from the upper deck. Conditions down there would be hellishly hot, hence the sailors stripping to a state of half-nakedness beforehand. "Reload!" I shouted to the men on deck. "Mr. Larson, Haynes. Inform the guns crews to reload, this time inserting double shot, if they please."

"Aye, sir."

"Aye, sir," the boys replied.

I could pick out specific features of individual men now on the *Forêt Argonne*, and the sixty foot gap between the two ships was continuing to close quickly. Double shot, as I had ordered, was a method of loading the ship's guns with two shots in the barrel simultaneously. It did not have nearly the range of a single shot, but by firing the guns in this manner we could throw iron at the enemy ship with a greater efficiency.

Other than different ways of loading the guns, there were different shot types, which I quickly considered using but chose not to at the present time. The shot type we were currently using was called round shot, which was a simple round ball that fit smoothly into the gun's barrel. Another shot type that could be helpful in the present situation was grape or canister shot, in which many small balls were cased in either a bag or a canister. The balls would go different directions after being shot, and would act as an array of death and destruction striking the enemy. Using grapeshot to decimate the enemy crew could even our numerical odds, but I decided against it. In these seas damaging the *Forêt Argonne*'s weak French hull with the sturdier round shot, which penetrated the planking more effectively, would force her captain to draw men away from the guns to work the pump. There was a third type of shot as well, which I didn't even consider using, called bar or chain shot. Bar shot consisted of two cannonballs connected by an iron bar, and chain shot consisted of two cannonballs connected by a chain. Despite their differences in appearance, bar and chain shot were both designed to accomplish the same purpose, that of disabling an opponent by wreaking havoc in her sails and rigging, or if the gunner was particularly lucky, dismasting her. It would make no difference to our chances of victory if the enemy was dismasted or not. To take her even crippled, we would still have to board her. She outnumbered us by a hundred, and many of her men were trained as soldiers. That would be a challenge in which success would be improbable unless we seriously reduced her numbers through gunnery first.

Close enough now to observe the enemy without my glass, I regarded the destruction aboard the *Forêt Argonne* with grim satisfaction. Blood ran down the sides of her decks and flowed in a steady stream from her scupperholes, staining the water around her in clouds of red ink. Smoke wafted in the air between us, and I watched as flames fluttered up her foremast and the crew struggled to put them out. The top half of her mizzenmast had collapsed and plunged into the sea, with the mizzen topgallant boom catching on her leeward hammock netting to avoid the piece of mast completely falling in. Shot holes riddled her flanks, and I saw a bent piece of copper plating and a hole exactly on the waterline. There could be more underneath which were obscured by the waves. I wanted her as a prize, but if sinking her meant fewer casualties by avoiding boarding her, then I was all for it. The captain remained alive, but his movements suggested an anxious distress.

Less than thirty feet away, our next broadside would be even more potent. Looking down, I saw that two of the guns had been run out. The first went off, veiling the larboard side with smoke. I watched as the orange flashes that lit the smoke aglow recommenced. The thunder of the guns rumbled once again beneath me, all that power surging and trembling under my feet. I shivered in awe, the hairs raising on my back from amazement at the sheer force of destruction H.M.S. *Cassandra* could deliver. Grasping the mizzenmast, it was all I could do to stay standing as the ship quaked precariously every which way.

When the last of the show of smoke and flame had cleared, I raised my glass, still deaf from the roar of the guns, watching the enemy. She'd now lost her mizzenmast entirely, and her hull had been shot up so badly that I could see the men wandering about through the shot holes on the two decks of guns. Brooks placed a hand on my shoulder and I turned sharply, momentarily startled. His lips moved but I had completely lost my hearing. I nodded respectfully. The heat from the guns was so strong now that sweat soaked through my clothing. Between the deck planks, the tar that held the deck together had expanded and entered a viscous state, where it stuck to my shoes when I walked.

Watching the enemy, I could see something peculiar happening on deck; the men were gathering in a cluster. I knew what this meant. Another telling sign was that the *Forêt Argonne* had turned higher into the wind to close the gap between us entirely. She meant to board us.

"Hard-a-starboard, if you please," I instructed the helmsmen, practically shouting at them. We headed upwind. I knew that we could outmanoeuvre the enemy, especially since she had been dismasted. "Haynes, Mr. Larson. Instruct the guns' crews to reload, if you please. When they've finished firing their next broadside then have the master-at-arms prepare the men for boarding."

"Aye, sir."

"Aye, sir," they replied, running in different directions. Just then, glancing to my right I saw the French guns finally being run out.

"Incoming!" I cried, watching as smoke and flames flashed from her gun ports.

I remained standing with Lieutenant Brooks, watching resolutely as the lead and splinters flew about every which way. It felt like a harsh wind. I heard the sound of splitting wood, then a loud *crash* as the mainmast shattered and fell from the side of the ship, bringing the netting over us down with it. Something buffeted me, and Brooks and I stumbled, falling. Debris rained down on my head, and I was buried by canvas. "Captain, sir! Lieutenant!" a Scottish voice shouted in desperation. It was O'Hare pulling a col-lapsed sail off of us. Brooks and I helped each other up. To my infinite relief the master and my first lieutenant were both relatively unscathed, though both were a bit bruised. I caught my breath, winded, surveying the scene around me. One of the helmsmen moaned, cursing in his cockney jar-gon, knocked off his station at the helm by a splinter to his side. The helm had been torn in two but remained function-al. Dead and wounded men covered the main deck below and our rigging was in shambles. The deck was so badly shot up that it resembled the surface of the moon. A tear came to my eye at the destruction wrought on my beautiful ship.

Mr. Larson returned, unharmed, though his face was entirely black with powder smoke but for his ghostly eye sockets which remained unnaturally bright. "If you please, Mr. Larson, inquire of the condition of our guns to Lieuten-ant Wilson," I ordered him.

"Aye, sir," he replied, walking quickly, his body sagging from exhaustion. Now *H.M.S. Cassandra* was a sitting duck, but perhaps we could get in one more broad-side before the enemy boarded us.

"Sir," the yeoman said, coming down from his post on the back of the quarterdeck. "There's been a shot to the rudder, sir," he said.

"Can we still steer her?" I asked him.

"Aye, sir, though not as effectively."

"Thank you, yeoman," I told him.

We had lost our advantage in both speed and man-oeuvring. I would not sacrifice our advantage in gunnery lightly. The enemy drew ever closer, testing my nerve.

"Haynes," I said to the young fellow. "Instruct the men at the guns to load with grapeshot but to keep firing at the enemy."

"Captain Easton!" I called to the Captain of Marines.

"Aye, sir," he replied, walking quickly to me.

"We're to be boarded soon. I'd like you at my side when we are. You're the most experienced man on this ship in the more… military fighting style."

"Aye, sir," he replied.

"Sir," Mr. Larson replied, returning.

"How many guns can still fire?" I asked.

"All on the starboard side. On the larboard side, eight of them below, along with both the carronades in the forecastle, and three of four on the quarterdeck, sir."

"Good, very good," I said, relieved that we were still at such a strong fighting capacity.

Yet would there be time enough to use them? We were now only twenty feet from the enemy. I watched as a French sailor threw a line with a barb attached to it onto the main deck. It scraped across the deck and stuck in the hammock netting. The line was followed by two dozen more. An army of boarders crowded on their side, shouting an cheering. They were matched by a thin line of Royal Marines and a motley collection of sailors. I walked to the front of our crowd, preparing to lead my men into battle. "God save the King!" I shouted, rallying the men. The words filled my veins with energy.

The men cheered heartily, then bullets began to fly from the enemy side, presenting a new kind of danger, a more targeted sort. I knew that the two gilded epaulettes on my shoulders and the Nile medal around my neck painted me as a prized target. As soon as the thought entered my mind a shot whistled through the air and sliced through a lock of hair in my wig, just missing my cheek. I drew my cutlass, preparing to defend myself. A roll of thunder shook the *Cassandra*, and I heard the shouts and screams of wounded from the enemy's lower gun deck.

The French captain stood ready on his side. I cringed as a crash and a moan struck the two ships, and they surged suddenly back and then forward as hull struck hull. "Vive la France!" The enemy captain shouted. The French line surged forward, and smoke and chaos erupted all around.

Captain Easton's red coat was a comfort to me in the confusion, as well as Lieutenant Brooks' bright red hair. He fell back to stand on my left, defending my blind side. I jumped, startled, hearing steel strike steel on my left, then turned my head to see Brooks block a stab at my side. I lunged at the Frenchman, who was a dark haired fellow, and ran him through, blood gurgling from his mouth instantly. Easton drew his pistol and loaded it patiently, then shot at something through the smoke. I jumped to the side, startled by a tomahawk slashed in my direction. The Frenchman who carried it looked like Greene. Stripped to the waist, I could see his muscles tensing for the kill. He held the tomahawk in his right hand and a knife in his left. I lunged for him with my cutlass, but he jumped back agilely. A flash of steel and he slashed for my chest with his knife, tearing through my jacket as I was not quick enough to block him. Raising my sword to avoid his next blow, I managed to cut him lightly on the arm before he struck my wrist and disarmed me. I tripped over something soft on the deck, falling on my back. He was on me in an instant, and I caught his wrist before he could stab me through the chest. Glancing desperately to my right I saw that Captain Easton was preoccupied with fighting one of the French lieutenants.

The Frenchman's leg pinned my knees and I could not hope to escape. My strength was giving under that of his powerful arm, he would soon be free to drive the knife through my heart and end me. Suddenly, I felt my legs freed as he was pulled up. I scrambled to my feet, snatching

my cutlass from the ground. Lieutenant Brooks tried to slit
the Frenchman's throat, but he was too quick and the fight
was soon veiled once again by gun smoke. I was entirely
alone. I wandered warily about until I found a familiar object; the shrouds. I climbed to the crow's nest of the
mizzenmast to get a better view. From here I could see the
battle below, which had now spread across both ships'
decks, but could not tell which side was winning. Too much
smoke, and too many men fighting in it. I sheathed my cutlass and loaded my pistol, pouring powder into the pan,
ramming the rest of the cartridge and ball home, then cocking it. I aimed for the enemy captain, who was now fighting
some of my men from his quarterdeck. A whiff of smoke
blocked him before I could tell if I had hit him or not, but I
climbed down the ratlines attached to the mizzen-sheets,
then drew my cutlass and rushed into the fray, taking one of
the lines that had been shot in half and swinging to the enemy quarterdeck. I blocked a lunge for my neck from one
of the French lieutenants, then went straight for the captain.
Seeing him in person I could tell more details about his
physical appearance.

    He had a long, regal nose and fierce green eyes,
with high cheekbones and tufts of dark brown hair. There
was something captivating about those sparkling, intelligent eyes, perhaps beautiful even, if he hadn't been looking
to kill me. I lunged straight for his heart but he dodged me,

albeit rather clumsily. I could see then the blood staining his breeches; he'd already been wounded in the leg. He bared his teeth, hissing at me. He tried to lunge, but I pushed his blade away with my cutlass. It scraped across my stomach, tearing my jacket but I saw no blood. I stabbed for his chest but he blocked me, knocking my attack harmlessly to the side. I was about to go at him again, when suddenly I felt a punch to my arm. I stumbled back, falling, then looked down to see blood dripping to the ground from a gunshot wound a few inches above my elbow. The cutlass slipped from my hand, falling then clattering on the deck. Already I felt weak from the blood loss. I watched through blurring vision as a figure in a red coat shot the French captain in the side at point-blank range. From my position on the quarterdeck I could see the French sniper who had shot me reload, aiming for my chest. I tried to move but my limbs refused to work. I knew it was the end. Then, suddenly, Captain Easton stepped in front of me to take the bullet. His body collapsed, and blood spattered into my face as he fell on top of me, dead. Someone dragged me out from under him, then across the deck and behind an 18-pounder. Mrs. O'Hare shook me back to my senses.

"Let's get a tourniquet around your arm, dear," she said in her thick Scottish accent, taking my cutlass and cutting away a strip of cloth from her dress, then setting it on the ground. She tied it quickly around my upper arm, pulling it uncomfortably tight to staunch the bleeding. I tried lifting my sword but could not move my fingers, and I realised that the bone must be badly broken. I tucked the useless arm into my coat between two of the buttons.

"There you are, Captain," she said. My chest tightened as a Frenchman discovered us, coming around from the side of the gun. She picked a pistol up from the floor, one that she had been carrying, and shot him squarely between the eyes.

I stood on shaking legs, just in time to see the French captain shout something and her yeoman ran back, striking her colours from where they flew from halfway up the mizzenmast. I realised that Brooks held a cutlass to a French *aspirant*'s throat, who bore a striking resemblance to the captain. The tricolour came flying down, and though I had expected a feeling of elation to accompany the sight, all I felt was sheer exhaustion crashing down upon me.

My first thought was to issue orders to my lieutenants. "Lieutenant Brooks!" I shouted to him hoarsely.

"Aye, sir," came his reply, which I struggled to hear over the endless ringing in my ears.

Lieutenant Wilson approached me then, along with Reid and Perkins and the remaining young gentlemen. Haynes' eyes were glazed over in some sort of shock, and he looked as though he were about to faint.

"Brooks, you're to direct the men in repairing the damages to the *Cassandra*. Wilson, you're to take command of our prize. Perkins, you're to secure the prisoners belowdecks on the *Forêt Argonne*. Reid, if you please, take your men from the quarterdeck guns crews and load supplies from the prize vessel to the *Cassandra*."

"Aye, sir," they each replied in turn.

"Mr. Jameson, you're to be an acting lieutenant under Lieutenant Wilson. The two of you shall escort the *Forêt Argonne* to Portsmouth."

"Aye, sir," he replied. "Thank you, sir."

"As for me, I must now speak with the enemy captain. Gentlemen, you may go about your duties." They all went off in their separate directions, and I was left alone on the enemy quarterdeck.

Both ships had been smashed to a pulp, each down a mast with the rest of the rigging and sails in tatters. It looked as though it were once again about to rain, and enormous thunderheads gathered in the distance. The motley collection of men on both sides, and women, as Mrs. O'Hare stood off to the side, were blackened with powder smoke and covered in blood and gore. The dead lay in fantastic positions on both decks, some without arms, some without legs, some like my poor Higgins missing their heads. The planking lay in shambles all about, with sharp bits of wood coming up through the deck. Now that the gunfire had stopped the cold wind once again closed in on the two ships, and I shivered, my clothing soaked through with blood and sweat. The young *aspirant* lay weeping with his head on the French captain's chest. I placed a hand gently on his shoulder and spoke to the captain. "Do you speak English?" I asked him.

He shook his head weakly.

"My father does not," replied the boy in a heavy French accent, "but I can translate."

The two exchanged a few words in French, looking at me worriedly. Now that the necessity to kill to survive had passed, I felt no more animosity towards the French captain. In a strange way, in fact, I felt an inclination to like him, or at the very least pity him. The captain then withdrew his sword, offering it to me. I shook my head. "No." I spoke to the boy. "Tell your father that he is a brave man and a good captain. I respect his courage and his abilities. He may keep his sword as a sign of that respect."

The two spoke in French and the captain opened and closed his eyes, nodding his head in gratitude.

"We should get your father to your surgeon to treat his wounds. When he's comfortable, then we may discuss the terms of your surrender."

The boy translated, then the French captain spoke to him urgently, his voice filled with angst. The lad remained insistent, glancing to me to read my expression. I waited patiently, as their conversation lasted a long time. Finally, the boy turned to me and spoke.

"The captain does not wish to go to the surgeon. Our casualties were very heavy. He says it will take hours until his turn will come to be treated. He does not wish to wait to discuss terms. He fears... The wound is bad, he has lost much blood." The boy's eyes filled with tears and he struggled to speak.

"He's dying," I said.

The lad nodded, weeping.

"We should get him comfortable, then, perhaps take him to his cabin?"

The boy translated, the tears still streaming down his cheeks. The captain replied, then struggled to stand, but fell to the deck with an anguished scream. I offered my good arm and helped him up, taking his arm across my shoulder to help him walk. We limped down to his upper gun deck then inside his cabin, both of us wounded, both of us fatigued, both of our ships torn to pieces and both of our crews decimated. I knew that if he survived, he would likely lose his leg, and I knew... it distressed me to think of it, but I knew that I must lose my arm.

It did not hurt much at present, truth be told, for I was still in a state of shock from the battle. The loss of blood, which the tourniquet had helped prevent but did not stop entirely, was so great that I struggled to see straight. I

pulled out a chair and helped the French captain into it,
then fetched another to prop up his leg. The boy took a pillow from his bunk and slid it under his foot, and the tension
in the captain's brows dissipated slightly. I searched the
captain's cabin to find a cabinet like the one I kept in my
dining cabin, and found a bottle of madeira inside. I set the
bottle on the table, then managed to procure the last three
unbroken glasses. Opening the bottle, I tried to fill each of
the glasses, but my hand was shaking so badly that I spilled
wine all over the table, ruining the white table cloth that
covered it. I then realised that it was already stained per-
manently with blood.

"Mrs. O'Hare," I said to the lady who had followed
us in. "If you please, inquire if Dr. Burke is busy. As soon
as our wounded are looked after, have him come here to
examine the French captain. If he is occupied, then send
Rosie over with water, bandages, and a bit of laudanum, if
you please."

"Of course, sir," she replied.

"Thank you," I said.

She hurried out the door.

The French captain took a gulp of the madeira, then
a shiver ran through his body. The boy took his hand. "Tell
your father," I began, "my name is Captain George Herrick
of *His Majesty's Ship Cassandra.*"

The boy spoke, translating my words into French. The captain replied, looking me in the eye, though knowing I could not understand a word.

"He is Jean-Etienne Valeurais, *captaine de vaisseau* commanding the *Forêt Argonne*. I am his son, Jaques-Louis Valeurais, *aspirant*."

"Tell him that he may remain in his own cabin, and his men will be allowed to keep their possessions and remain in their quarters for the duration of the voyage."

Jaques-Louis translated for Captain Valeurais. The captain spoke to me, watching my expression.

"Thank you, Captain Herrick," the son translated. "He says that he thinks you a man of honour. He says that he is grateful for your kind treatment towards him and his crew. He has one request of you."

"What would he like?" I asked warmly.

At that moment Mrs. O'Hare returned, followed closely by Rosie. The captain jumped, startled by the sound of the door opening. Rosie carried a bucket of water, along with a rag and a leather pouch of medical supplies.

"Captain Valeurais, this is Rosie Burke. She is an assistant to our ship's surgeon, Dr. Burke. The doctor is still busy with our own wounded, but she can look after you." The boy translated and the captain's eyes widened with fear as she set the pouch on the table, revealing an array of knives and metal instruments.

"Rosie, this is Captain Valeurais. He doesn't speak a word of English so his son, Jaques-Louis will be translating for us. Now, the captain was just giving me a request. Once he's told me what he'd like, then you may operate on him."

"Aye, sir," Rosie said tersely.

"Alright, Captain," I said. "What would you like?" The boy translated for me, then the captain spoke in French, and the boy spoke to me.

"He hears that you use both ships for prisons and land prisons. He hears that prisoners are treated better on land, that many die in the ships. He asks that you speak to the authorities to ensure the fair treatment of his men, and try as best you can to have them sent to a land prison."

"I will try," I agreed. "The decision is not mine to make, it is that of the authorities on shore, but I will beseech them to treat your men well."

"Thank you, sir," he replied after translating to his father.

"Now," I said. "Your father has been badly wounded. This nice lady will take excellent care of him."

"Thank you, sir," the boy replied.

"I'm sure Miss Rosie would like to know where he is wounded."

To my surprise, before the boy could ask she spoke in fluent French to the captain. His expression relaxed some, then she pulled up his breeches to reveal the wound, a deep, gurgling mass of blood that was two inches above the knee. She dampened a towel and cleaned it to see better. I stood, limping to the cabinet where I had procured the wine, unnerved by Captain Valeurais' anguished howls behind me. There were two drawers in the cabinet, and I opened them to find his papers, though all I found were his commission and a map. Opening the map I saw that his ship had indeed escaped the blockade about three weeks back, and had headed north towards Ireland, then cut into the North Atlantic. Something had turned him back a few days ago, however, eastwards back towards Europe.

I walked to his day cabin in front of the dining cabin where I'd set him down, then opened his desk and was surprised at what I found. The entire thing was filled with sketchbooks and paintings. The stack of canvases and papers, charcoal, brushes and pigments, was a full foot high. I looked through them, finding them to be quite good. There were many of ships, the tricolour, even a few of Napoleon Bonaparte. There was one subject, however, he kept coming back to. She was an almost unnaturally beautiful French lady, with auburn hair and fierce blue eyes. The feature that most stood out to me were her luscious, full lips. Here she was in one painting, at total peace sleeping nude in a field of flowers, the next, her teeth bared in ferocity as she waved the tricolour in one hand while brandishing a cutlass in the other. I found a handful of letters stuffed into one of the drawers written in a long, sweeping cursive, addressed to an Aurélie-Océan Valeurais. It was then that I found the letter of value, along with a notebook. They were orders direct from Napoleon and the ship's log.

I did not understand a word of French, but knew that they were important, and that the men at the Admiralty would be interested in reading them. I stuffed them both into my coat pocket, then headed outside to check with each of my lieutenants. Stepping out the door to the upper gun deck, the scene of carnage astounded me. It was so full of dead men that it was difficult to walk across without stepping on the corpses. The planking on the sides was riddled with shot-holes, and light poured in from outside. Wilson's men worked tirelessly at the pump, and in the forward half of the deck the uninjured French prisoners were changing into warmer clothing, guarded by Lieutenant Perkins and some of his men. On the lower deck, I shivered. Shouts and screams penetrated the darkness, voices filled with so much agony it made my blood curdle. There were hundreds of wounded, and I could see the surgeon and his mates were covered from head to foot in blood. I climbed quickly down to the aft platform in the hold, where I found Lieutenants Wilson and Reid allocating the supplies to be brought to the *Cassandra*.

"I say we should bring over as much as possible," Wilson said. "She's overloaded as it is, and the men need victuals."

"I concur, though the *Cassandra* is so full of holes that adding any weight would only make the situation more precarious. Besides that, repair will be slow as the blacksmith's been badly wounded so it will be his incompetent mates replacing the damaged copper plating."

"Gentlemen," I said. "How is the transfer of supplies going? Can I order the cook to return to fixing the men their full rations? Perhaps some extra to celebrate our victory?"

"Sir," Wilson said, looking me over. His expression was one of shock. After an awkward silence he replied. "Yes, sir, of course Captain. The supplies were meant for us anyhow."

He gestured to one of the smaller barrels. It was labelled in paint. "Salt Pork. Gibraltar." Underneath it I read "Victualling Board."

"Bloody Frenchies," I cursed. "Have you secured the prisoners?" I asked Lieutenant Wilson.

"Aye, sir. Perkins is watching them with a guard detail now," Wilson replied, seemingly distracted. Reid refused to meet my eyes.

"Have I said something?" I asked.

"No, sir," Wilson replied.

"What is it, Lieutenant?" I asked.

"You're covered in blood, sir," Reid replied tersely. "There's a splinter in your leg, and your arm…"

Suddenly I felt very weak, as if I would faint before them. Looking down at my battered clothing I could see now that I was an absolute mess. A large splinter ran through my calf and bullet-holes along with cutlass slashes had torn through my coat. Blood ran from the wound in my arm and dripped onto the catwalk we stood on. I felt it trickle down the side of my head, staining my wig, which was filthy and blackened by powder smoke. Wilson reached to take my good arm but I stepped away. "Don't touch me," I ordered him. "I'll see the surgeon as soon as I'm able. You both may go about your duties."

"Aye, sir," Wilson replied.

"Aye, sir," Reid replied after a moment's hesitation.

I walked back up the many ladders to the quarter-deck of the *Forêt Argonne*. I was lightheaded, and the world with its spinning horizon appeared an unusual shade of yellow. My ears rang, and voices slurred around me until they were unintelligible. I could hear very little, except for my own heart pounding in my chest. Passing through the quarterdeck I saw the lifeless body of Captain Easton, then heading across to the *Cassandra* I passed Higgins' head on the deck. I knelt down and shut the eyes, a final tribute to my servant. Going down to the upper deck, I saw several men grieving one of the bodies—Rockfeld, who'd been delighting the ship with his voice singing "Rule Britannia" only hours ago. Corpses abounded; my ship, *H.M.S. Cassandra*, had become a floating coffin. Seeing my men, my brave, handsome young lads strewn about the deck, their bodies desecrated by shot and splinter, tore my heart to pieces. I didn't realise the tears streaming down my cheeks until I reached the lower deck and the screams of the wounded broke me entirely. I saw a frantic Lieutenant Brooks push through the crowd to his wife Mary, then took the hand of his daughter Angeline as she lay half-dead in a hammock. The cockney helmsman lay moaning, clutching his side. Abigail Easton screamed with anguish, learning of the death of her husband from a shocked Mrs. O'Hare, after already suffering a terrible head wound. The blacksmith was nearest me, coughing up gore, blood already seeping through a layer of bandages around his stomach. Matrose had passed out, his face as white as a sheet. I remembered his shoulder. It had looked more like raw meat from a butcher's shop than human flesh. His hand was tightly bandaged, but I could see where two of his little fingers ended in stumps halfway.

"Herrick," a familiar voice said through the horrors around me.

"Dr. Burke," I said, turning my head.

"Herrick!" He exclaimed in surprise, looking me over. "You're covered in blood, are you hurt?"

"I'm fine," I lied. "Have you finished tending the wounded?" I asked.

"Aye, sir," he replied.

"You're to join me in my cabin as soon as is convenient. Tell Lieutenant Brooks to come with you, I need your help in writing my official dispatch."

"Aye, sir," he replied, turning to get the lieutenant.

I headed back up to my cabin. I'm not sure what I'd hoped for; all my papers in order in my day cabin with my furniture unscathed, a return back to normal, but the destruction penetrated here as well. Looking through the hatchway to my dining cabin I saw that my chairs had all been knocked over, and shards of glass covered the floor from my broken windows. Several shots had singed my bed and curtains in my sleeping cabin to my left, and my harpsichord music was scattered about the deck, covered in blood. The light yellow bulkheads were all gone, jettisoned earlier to reveal the bare wooden walls of the ship. The bodies of six of my men lay on my floor, one against the harpsichord, and a shot had crashed through the music stand on the instrument. My china had all been smashed to bits, both by the shots and the splinters, and by falling from the shelf as the ship had been tossed about so badly from the broadsides. It all seemed so unreal, as though the aftermath of the battle were some terrible nightmare, and I could open my eyes and it would all go away.

A knock on my door made me jump, and I opened it to allow Dr. Burke and Lieutenant Brooks to enter. "Lieutenant, how badly are we damaged?" I asked.

"There's several shots below the waterline, sir, but the carpenter's fixing them as we speak. Most of the men still fit for duty are at the pump, and the others are repairing the rigging as best they can."

"That's excellent. Thank you," I said. "Doctor, how many wounded have we?" I asked, dreading the answer.

"Forty-five, sir," he replied gravely.

"'Tis awful," I said.

"I counted twenty-three killed," Brooks said.

I winced, the high casualties tearing me in two. That was a third of the ship's company unfit for duty. "Lieutenant," I said. "I myself have been wounded." I turned to the doctor. "I didn't want to say so in front of the men. I will return to command as soon as I am able. As my first lieutenant, you have command of the ship until then."

"Aye, sir," he replied.

"Conduct repairs at sea, then continue on our course to Portsmouth. Prepare the dead. I shall conduct the funeral service for them as soon as we're seaworthy again. 'Tis imperative that we reach Portsmouth as soon as possible.

There's a storm coming, and we're in no shape to ride it out at sea."

"Aye, sir," he replied. "I'll do the best I can."

"Thank you, Lieutenant," I said. "You may go about your duties."

"I hope for your quick recovery, sir," he added before leaving. "Your officers and men care for you deeply."

The door shut, and my strength suddenly failed. "I've been shot, Morgan," I cried, collapsing into his arms.

"I know, I saw the tourniquet," he said, leading me into the dining cabin and helping me up to lie on my dining table. He opened his bag of knives and took one of the pails of water used for cooling the guns, bringing it to the table. I watched him warily, my heart about to burst through my chest. I was so overcome with dread anticipating the operation that I felt sick to my stomach. "Alright, we have to get this off now," he said of the tourniquet. I nodded, watching as he untied the strip of cloth from Mrs. O'Hare's dress. Blood immediately began to spill from the wound and flow across the table. "I'm going to undress you now, dear. I promise I'll be gentle," he said, untying my neckcloth. After that he pulled my gloves from my fingers, the white silk soaked through with blood. He untucked my arm from my shirt, and I clamped my eyes shut to avoid the pain. First the coat came off, then my vest, then shirt, and I lay half-naked and shivering on the table. I felt helpless and vulnerable without my uniform, which only added to my unease. "Alright, Georgie darling," Morgan said. "I have to feel the wound, see if the bone's broken. It will hurt terribly but I promise it will be over in only a few seconds. Try to hold still, it will make it easier for the both of us." I nodded in response.

Morgan stuck his fingers into the open wound. I shrieked in pain, and survival instinct made me try to push him away but I quickly forced myself to lie flat on the table. In only a moment it was over and I lay gasping for breath.

"Alright, 'tis badly broken," he said, only confirming what I already suspected. "I'm afraid we'll have to amputate your arm, dear." A shiver ran through my body and I grit my teeth stubbornly to withhold a scream. A knock at the door startled the both of us. "Just a minute!" Dr. Burke shouted. "I'm with a patient!" The knock came again, more fervently this time.

"Answer it," I ordered the doctor.

"Alright, try not to move, dear."

I lay on the table, studying the ceiling, and heard Rosie's voice. "I heard a scream. Are you alright?"

"Herrick needs his arm amputated. Can you hold him down for me?" Burke asked. I could hear the anxiety in his voice and it only deepened my own agitation.

233

"Certainly. Hello, sweetheart!" She called softly to me.

"Rosie's here, darling. She's going to help us." Burke withdrew a long leather object from his surgeon's kit. "Alright, dear, I'm going to put this above the wound to stop the bleeding." I watched as he fastened what looked like a belt around my upper arm, pulling it tightly through its buckle. "There we go," he said. "Now, look at that portrait of your father on the wall," he said, pointing to the painting hanging on the wall near the entrance to my sleeping cabin. A bullet hole had torn the canvas right through his chest and the paint was singed around it. The glass frame had been shattered by the shot, and part of the frame had been shot away. "You've been very brave. Your father would be proud of how brave you are. Look at your father. Isn't he handsome? You look just like him. He'd be very proud of you." I could feel Burke washing away some of the blood with a damp towel to see the wound more clearly. Rosie took hold of my good hand and placed her other hand on my chest. "Alright, now 'tis time for the worst part." Burke placed a hand on my cheek. "Try to hold as still as you can. This will be terribly painful, but I promise it will all be over in only a few minutes. Rosie's right here. She's going to hold your hand. Now, are you ready?" He asked.

"Aye," I replied, fighting back my terror.

"Alright, then. Rosie, are you holding him?" He asked his sweetheart.

"Yes," she replied. "I've got him."

"Let's get this over with, alright, Georgie?" He asked.

I nodded, then felt a stab of pain as he plunged the knife into my skin. I screamed, thrashing about without control. Rosie pinned my chest to the table with her hand, holding my good arm so I could not move my upper body at all, despite my struggles. The screams came to my throat uncontrollably, and tears coursed down my cheeks. Burke cut the flesh and muscle around the bone in a circle. Sheer, excruciating pain ran up my arm and I shrieked, trying with all my might to get free as he folded the flesh upwards away from the bone. I had no control over myself anymore, I'd gone mad from the agony. I gripped Rosie's hand tightly, then a wave of sheer terror came over me as I felt the bone saw grinding away at me. I grit my teeth so hard that with a crack I felt one of the ceramic pieces break and powder filled my mouth. My vision had blurred until I could only see red, and my muscles weakened. Finally, I felt a release as the skin was pulled back down over the severed bone, then a few moments later strings touched the stump when Burke had finished tying off the arteries.

I turned my head at just the wrong moment and saw my severed arm in a pool of blood. My arm, that I had known all my life down to every last freckle, lay out of my control a full foot from my body. Burke quickly wrapped it in a blanket and set it on the floor. I let out a cry, finally realising that I had lost my right arm forever. A sickening feeling filled my stomach at the sight of all my blood flowing over the table and forming a puddle on the floor, and I coughed, suddenly vomiting all over the deck. "Shh, shh," Morgan said, gently rubbing my upper back. "We need to bandage that now, dear. This part shouldn't hurt.

I lay on the table, moaning, shivering, gasping as I caught my breath. I felt soothing bandages wrapped around the stump.

"That feels good, doesn't it?" He asked in a soft voice. I nodded weakly.

"There's still that splinter in his leg," Rosie said. My heart sank.

"Yes. We're going to have a look at your leg now," Morgan said.

"I'm cold, Morgan," I moaned.

"I know, darling, but that's because you've lost a lot of blood. There's nothing we can do for that. Your leg is still bleeding, we have to fix it now."

"I'm tired. I'd like to rest a minute first. I'd like some water," I moaned.

"Rosie, why don't you find him some clean water to drink? Even better, a hot cup of tea? Perhaps the officers' cook has heated the fires."

She nodded, leaving to head downstairs.

"A hot cup of tea, that sounds nice, doesn't it?"

"I want my blanket," I sobbed, the tears rolling down my face.

"It won't help you get any warmer," he said, "but if it helps you relax then I'll get it for you."

"Thank you," I said, and watched as he walked to my sleeping cabin.

He cleaned the blood off of the table before sliding a pillow under my head then spreading the knit blanket over my body. I clutched the folds with my good hand, thankful for something at last to cover my bare chest and restore some shred of my dignity. "Try not to fall asleep, you've been badly injured and you won't wake again if you've not had water and victuals first. 'Tis a miracle you've remained conscious for as long as you have, considering how much blood you've lost."

Rosie then returned with the tea along with a plate of hot victuals. "Oh, excellent," Burke said. "You're brilliant, darling. We'll give him his dinner as soon as we've finished tending his wounds. Here's you tea, dear," he said to me. I held out my hand to take the cup, but Rosie grasped my fingers in hers. "I'll do it," Morgan said, raising the cup to my lips. The tea burned my tongue but I was so cold and thirsty that I gulped it down anyhow.

"Would you like more?" He asked.

I nodded, then he let me finish the cup.

"Are you ready for me to look at your leg now?" He asked.

"He was walking on it earlier, I think that is a good sign," Rosie added to Morgan.

Morgan cut away my stockings with a knife, isolating the splinter. I saw that it had punctured the edge of my lower leg, away from the bone.

Rosie held my hand and I tried to focus on the blue wool my mother had knitted to make the blanket. I thought of my mother, tried to think of happy memories with her, but all I could remember were the two marine guards escorting her away from me at Haslar Hospital, and it only distressed me more. I screamed in pain as Morgan tore the splinter from my leg. "He'll need stitches," Rosie said simply. I watched her thread a needle then felt it jab into my skin.

"So, what are you looking forward to most when we get back to England?" Morgan asked, taking my hand.

It was a simple question, but I was too weak to answer.

He continued talking anyhow. "I'm looking forward to fresh meat. You, know a nice fresh steak with eggs in the morning. And sugar, for tea. Personally, what I miss most are plants. You know, flowers and such? Then again, I have the most precious rose in the world right here on this ship." An image flashed through my mind of the Austrian lady who had given me flowers, then I thought of Matrose. I cried out in pain at Rosie's next stitch, not so much from the needle but from the thought of the little fellow's bloodied shoulder and mutilated hand.

"How is Matrose?" I asked Burke, seemingly out of the blue. The effort from speaking made me dizzy.

"He's going to be just fine, just like you," he said, though his eyes said differently. "Don't you worry. We cleaned him all up and gave him some laudanum. Last I saw he was resting comfortably in his hammock, just as you will be in only a few minutes."

I felt Rosie wash my face with a damp towel, finding that the blood staining my head was not my own. Morgan found my nightshirt and cap in my sea-chest, and the two of them dressed me as I was too weak to lift my head. Morgan half-walked, half-carried me to the hanging bed and I slid beneath the sheets, exhausted.

I moaned, then felt Morgan massage open my jaw and slide a spoon into my mouth. With difficulty, I swallowed a liquid that tasted so bitter that it made me want to retch, then instantly felt the tension in my brows relax. The pain dissipated with it, but so did my strength.

Something warm brushed my lip and I opened my mouth for Morgan to offer me a sip of tea. I drank it down, the warm liquid easing my throat that stung from the powder smoke I'd inhaled earlier that day. Rosie held my hand, rubbing my palm. The feeling comforted me. Someone dressed me in gloves and socks, then my night-cap, and I felt a bit warmer. Morgan held something else to my mouth, and I smelled steak, but I had no appetite. In fact, the thought of eating repulsed me, and I felt as though I would be sick if I tried to chew the steak. Morgan pressed it to my lips and massaged my jaw to open but I refused. "You need to eat, darling," he said, stubbornly holding the steak. "Alright, then," he said in resignation. "If you won't eat meat, then perhaps some vegetables? The carrots are fresh, they're very good," he said, setting down the meat and picking up a softer foodstuff with the fork. I opened my mouth and took the carrot. The sweet, fresh taste was a shock to my tongue. "Good, very good. Can you eat anoth-er?" He asked. I managed to swallow one more carrot be-fore collapsing into my pillow. He carefully pried my jaw open and slid my dentures out to clean them. I did not fall asleep immediately, however.

It took a few minutes for the laudanum to set in completely, and it was then that a memory returned to me, just one scene. The sailors had dragged me screaming to the lower deck and set me in a long line. I counted the men

left to be looked after; fourteen in front of me. I waited for
a long time, I don't know how long exactly, until my turn
came to be seen by the ship's surgeon. I walked to the midshipmen's chests, but then I was immediately thrown off
and sent to the other side of the deck. I screamed, grabbing
his coat, begging him to take the splinters out of my eye
and cheek, but he refused. "You're coughing up blood,
you'll be dead within the hour!" He shouted, pushing me to
the ground. I'd been given up for dead. An hour later, once
everyone else was tucked safely in their hammocks and the
mortally wounded I had been placed with had all breathed
their last, I remained alive. I'd been coughing up blood
from a cut in my cheek, not an internal injury. I'd survived.
But I also knew that I was living on borrowed time. The
movement of the swells that rocked my bed also reminded
me that the storm was destined to arrive tonight. Both our
ships were shot to pieces and we were still over seventy
miles from Portsmouth. Sheer fatigue fell over me and I
soon fell fast asleep.

Chapter 5

A wave of pain overtook me and I woke with a start from a dream I couldn't remember. An electrifying agony ran up my arm and I moaned, trying to grasp the focal point just above my elbow but unable to feel anything but my side. I screamed, my thoughts muddled in a confused terror as it hurt so badly. A blinding red clouded my vision, and I tossed and turned about in my bed, still trying to find the arm that was afflicting me. In my writhing about the blanket slipped away from my chest and I saw the empty sleeve in my nightshirt, which only frightened me further. Screams racked my chest until my throat ached, until finally someone tore through the curtains around my bed.

Burke raised a spoonful of medicine to my lips, which I took without hesitation. He wrapped his arms around me and with one hand stroked the back of my hair. "Shh, shh. 'Tis alright. You're alright. I'm right here. Morgan's here."

My chest ached and I started to cry. His presence relaxed me and slowly the pain dissipated. When I could breathe normally again he slid my dentures into my mouth, the extra pair I kept in the event that my normal ones were lost or broken. "I-I could feel my hand, and my elbow. It-it hurt terribly. H-How is that possible? I-I've lost my arm."

"That happens to many of my patients who lose limbs. We call it ghost pains. I'm afraid there's nothing I can do for you, as there's nothing physically wrong with you. The best thing you can do is relax. It gets better, I promise."

I jumped, hearing a knock at the door, then it opened. Reid entered, walking to my bed. "I heard screams and immediately woke the doctor. Are you alright, Captain?" He asked.

My face flushed, ashamed of having given in to my pain and of forgetting my position as captain.

"His wounds were troubling him. He's fine now," Burke replied.

"Yes, tell the men on watch that I'm alright," I added. "I appreciate your concern, and thank you for sending for Dr. Burke."

"Aye, sir," Reid replied, then headed for the door. He had taken over Lieutenant Wilson's watch, as Wilson and Perkins were both now stationed aboard the *Forêt Argonne*. The events of yesterday came back to me, and then I remembered the destruction aboard my ship and the death and injury that had been brought upon my crew and I wished they hadn't.

Gazing through a window to my right, I saw that one pane had been broken through completely and the other was badly shattered and covered in dried blood. Storm clouds gathered menacingly over a grey sea, and fear tugged at my heart. The wind whistled through the broken glass, only adding to my apprehension. We could not have travelled very far during the time I had been asleep, as we'd had to make repairs on the two ships. That process would only have been extended as we were vastly undermanned after having a third of the crew killed or wounded. I remembered then that we had not yet held a funeral service for the dead, as I'd asked Lieutenant Brooks to wait so I could do it. The thought of the bodies waiting on the deck to be released to the sea filled me with anguish, and I swung out of the bed quickly to go outside.

I screamed, then fell gracelessly to the deck, my wounded leg unable to support me. My knee struck the planking, then what was left of my right arm. A wave of pain rushed through my body from the injuries of yesterday and I lay curled up on the deck, moaning.

"Careful!" Burke said, kneeling beside me. He held my good arm, then gently raised me to a sitting position. "Take it slowly, or you're going to hurt yourself."

"I think I already have," I groaned.

"I can help you out of your bed, and it will aggravate your wounds much less. Now, I know you had a nice long rest and you must be feeling better, but you still shouldn't be walking yet. I'll have the cook prepare you some breakfast. We have loads of fresh victuals aboard from the Frenchy you captured."

"Not until I've performed the funeral service for the dead and have written my dispatch," I countered.

"You don't need to do either of those things. You're incapacitated. Brooks is therefore in command, and it is his duty to hold the service and write the dispatch. You need to focus on your recovery and rest as much as you can. After breakfast we'll change your dressings, then clean you up, then I want you to try to fall back to sleep, alright?"

"The only way I shall relinquish command of this ship is if I'm dead!" I shouted. "I'm holding the funeral service this instant!"

"No need to get angry. Let's come to a compromise. You can use a cane to help you walk outside to give the funeral service, that will keep weight off of your leg. Then we'll come back here and I'll change your dressings, then you can have breakfast in bed and you can dictate your dispatch to me while I write it."

"Surely in a ship with forty-six wounded men you have better things to do than mothering me?"

"You're right. Rosie can help you with your dispatch."

I rolled my eyes. "Very well, then. Where is my coat? My hat and my wig? I have to get dressed now."

"Let's get you into a chair," he said, walking to the other room and picking up one of the chairs from my dining table then setting it down in my sleeping cabin. With one hand on my waist and the other cupping my elbow he helped me up then set me down in the chair. I realised then that I had to use the necessary. I once again tried to get up, but fell on my good arm, a stab of pain shooting up my leg. Burke caught me around my chest.

"I must use my chamber pot," I groaned.

"I've got you," he said, propping me up on his shoulder. "You're absolutely the worst patient I've ever had the duty to attend to. Please don't try to get up again without help."

"I'm the captain," I said. "I'll get up if my duties require it."

"Yes, I know you're the captain, you remind me every five minutes. You're also severely wounded. 'Tis alright to ask for help, that's what I'm here for." Infuriatingly, he set me back down in the chair. "I'll bring you your chamber pot, you can use it here."

"I'd rather not," I said, but despite my objections he went to my water closet and fetched it anyhow. I tried to unbutton the pants that went with my nightshirt, but with only one hand I found the task impossible. To my increasing frustration he unbuttoned them for me. Why must Higgins be dead just when I need him the most? I relieved myself, then Burke emptied the chamber pot out the window, the broken glass on the deck crunching beneath his shoes as he walked. He returned, then went to my sea chest and dug through it for a fresh pair of clothes, taking out my books and my toiletries and setting them in an inglorious heap on the ground.

"I-I'd like to wash my face and shave, if you please," I said hesitantly. Higgins knew my needs without my having to ask for assistance. It felt strange asking Morgan for help.

"Excellent idea. I'll find you some warm water, then maybe we can clean you up a bit?" Burke said.

He walked below and was gone for a long time. Higgins had everything ready before I woke up; a bowl of warm water, clean clothing, my breakfast… The waiting annoyed me. Finally, my door opened, through it was not Burke who entered but Rosie.

"Good morning," I said politely, a bit surprised.

"Morgan sent me," she said. Her shoulders sagged and her eyes were bloodshot from exhaustion. Her hair and her dress were both bloodied up, and I realised that they were the same clothes she'd been wearing yesterday. Thinking back I realised that Morgan had not bothered to change either, and that the two of them had probably been up all night looking after the wounded.

"You look tired," I said.

"So do you," she replied with a sigh. "You went through a terrible ordeal yesterday. I'm glad you're alive."

"I'm glad you are, too. Thank you for helping me."

"'Tis my duty," she said.

"No, 'tis not. The regulations say that you shouldn't even be here. 'Tis Morgan's duty. You did more than your duty required. What you did was heroic."

"I'm so sorry you lost your arm," she said, "yet I'm eternally grateful that you didn't lose your life. When I saw you on your table, covered in blood, I realised that you could have been killed. Knowing that... I realised that I might never see you again. I like Morgan, he's my friend. But the thought of losing you nearly killed me," she said, a hint of desperation entering her voice. "I love you, George. I've loved you since the moment I saw you. I love you now and I always will."

I was in too much shock to reply. Then, finally, words exited my lips. "You're exhausted. We both are. Morgan is my best friend. I would never confess to having feelings for you, or encourage yours for me. I would not betray him as such, after all we've been through." a knock at the door interrupted me. Burke entered, carrying a pail of water. "Let's get you cleaned up," he said, as if Rosie wasn't even there. I turned my head, only to find she was gone.

"Have you seen Rosie?" I asked.

"Yes, she's sleeping in my cabin," he replied concernedly. "Why do you ask?"

"I thought she was just here."

"I saw her only a moment ago in my cabin," he replied. "I went down to the lower deck to get clean bandages for you and I checked on her while I was gone. Poor thing was exhausted. We stayed up quite late last night. She was particularly distressed after Angeline was wounded, the two are friends you know?"

"She was just here," I said, confused.

"That's the laudanum talking," he replied. "I gave you a heavy dosage. Now, let's get you undressed." He raised my nightshirt over my head, gently prying it around the stump of my arm, then slid my trousers off my legs. Looking down at my body I could see that I was badly beaten and covered in dried blood and black powder. Morgan took off my eyepatch, which was the same one I had worn yesterday… and the day before that. "I think this might be a little easier if you were lying down," Morgan said. "That way I could wash your back as well."

He helped me up then led me to my hanging bed, then held it for me as I climbed back in.

"Let's start with your face," he said. "Would you like a shave?" He added, dampening my cheeks with water then soap.

"Yes, if you please," I replied. I shut my eyes and felt the razor gently scratch at my face. Morgan ran the warm towel along my whole body, wiping away the blood. He started talking about the weather, though there was a touch of anxiety in his voice and I knew that he must just now be coming out of shock from yesterday. The ringing in my ears had also not yet stopped, but I only payed attention to it now that it was relatively quiet. The gentle motion of the warm towel on my skin relaxed me so much that I almost fell asleep again. Finally, he placed the water under my head and washed my hair. After drying it with a towel he combed it out. He put me in my lower undergarments and breeches, then to my surprise began undoing the bandages around my leg.

"What are you doing?" I asked, wincing as I felt the bloodied part tear stubbornly away from my skin.

"I think it would be best if we changed your dressings now, dear, before you go out on deck. It has been a full eight hours. If we get it over with now, we can wait until after supper to do it again," he said simply.

My stomach ached from anxiety. I didn't want my dressings changed, I was in enough pain as it was. I didn't want Burke to even touch my leg, for fear that he would bring out the knife. I'd already lost my arm. I didn't want him to find some infection and take my leg, too. I'd rather die than lose another limb. Shivers racked my body and I felt dizzy from sheer terror as he unwrapped the last of the bandages to see the leg clearly. I glanced down briefly to see a bloodied mass of flesh that was red and swollen around the outside, then quickly looked up again, choking in an effort to hold back a scream. I wished that I was dead.

Seeing my misery Burke stepped toward me and took my hand. "What's wrong, Georgie?" He asked. "Surely that didn't hurt too badly? The wound looks much better than I thought it would. There's no infection, and I'm already seeing the edges start to heal. You should be able to keep your leg. Even better, at this rate you'll be off your cane in only a few weeks."

"But the red? 'Tis swollen. It looks awful. How bad will the scar be?"

"There's no infection. A bit of redness and swelling is normal after an injury. It would be much worse if it was infected. I was a little concerned as you're a bit feverish, but that's likely due to the cold and fatigue more than any-thing. You should be just fine."

"I-I don't w-want to lose my leg," I sobbed.

"You most likely don't have to," he said reassur-ingly. "Now, be brave. I'd like to wash the wound with a bit of warm water. It looks much worse than it is, because the dried blood covers much more than the cut."

I grit my teeth as he dabbed the cut with a damp towel, every little motion agitating the wound. After my leg he moved on to my arm, which only caused me further pain. I distracted myself by looking out the window, trying to focus on the storm clouds moving swiftly in. The dark

underbelly of the storm swooped menacingly down, drawing ever closer. The rumble of a full broadside being run
out startled me, and I could see an enemy ship to stern of
us, a 74-gun ship-of-the-line. "Incoming! Get down!" I
cried, turning sharply in my bed as I tried instinctively to
hit the deck. A flash of light erupted from her gun-ports,
then I felt Morgan's hand on my shoulder.

"Shh, shh. You're alright, Georgie," he said com-
fortingly.

I turned back over, looking back out the window.
Only clouds closed for action with us.

"'Tis just a thunderstorm. You're alright. You're
safe now."

"No, we're not safe now. The storm's destructive
power is worse than that of the *Forêt Argonne*. The weather
knows no mercy. It shall sink us without hesitation if we
don't ready the ship. You must finish changing my dressings quickly, so I can issue orders to the men."

"Alright, I'm almost done," he said, finishing by
wrapping clean bandages around the stump. I kneaded my
blankets impatiently, my anxiety building by the minute.

He then dressed me in a clean uniform, then handed
me a decorative black cane. I hobbled out to the upper
deck, then up the ladder and outside, searching for Captain
Easton to have him order his men to call the crew on deck.
A long row of brown hammock bags lined the deck from

bow to stern, filled with our dead. I remembered then that Easton was in the one with the Union Jack draped over it, and it was his lieutenant who was now in command of the marines. "Lieutenant," I ordered him. "If you please, have your men call the sailors on deck."

"Aye, sir," he said. The remaining drummers and fifers played their instruments, and the men still fit for duty came wearily from the ladders to the main-deck. They looked beaten and exhausted, and their numbers were sparse. When normally the entire main-deck would be filled, two-thirds of it lay empty. A third of the original Cassandras were now stationed aboard the prize vessel, though the other third lay either broken on the lower deck or stitched in the hammocks that rested by the starboard side. Lieutenant Brooks soon found me where I stood on the quarterdeck and discreetly held the list of casualties for me to read. A crash of thunder echoed overhead, and I turned to see a streak of lightning strike the sea. Rain began to patter down on my hat, and the chaplain arrived from below, late as usual. He began to read a verse from the Bible, though between the rain and the ringing in my ears I could not hear a word he said. The men stood with their heads bowed solemnly, and an achy feeling filled my heart.

The cold and the rain reflected my mood, and I gazed down at the bodies. *I killed them*, I thought. *The*

*French fired the shots, but if I'd not given the order to at-
tack then they would still be among the living.*

I felt Brooks place a hand on my shoulder, and I
realised then that the chaplain had stopped speaking. "I-I
will now read the names of those who have sacrificed their
lives in the line of duty defending our country," I said, my
throat tightening.

"Captain…" I stopped, choking back tears. "Captain
William Easton, of the Royal Marines." I walked to the
stitched hammock on the quarterdeck and brushed my fingers along the flag.

As Easton had been the only commissioned officer
killed, the rest of the list was organised by rank and alpha-
betically, and the men did not get flags. I began to read off
more names, my thoughts scattering in different directions.
I avoided the eyes of the crew, fearing that they blamed me
and hated me for the deaths of their comrades and friends,
just as I blamed and hated myself. At one name I stopped,
unable to go on. "J-John…" I felt a tear slip down my
cheek. "John Higgins." I continued, my throat in a knot,
hardly able to speak.

I hoped that the rain obscured the tears that
streamed down my face. *So many killed… So many of my
brave crew… Good lads, all of them. Good young lads
struck down in their prime, innocent fellows who did their
duty selflessly and without hesitation, who followed me,*

who trusted me… Only for my orders to close for action to slaughter them. Brooks placed an arm across my shoulders, and I leaned heavily on my cane to keep weight off my aching leg.

I finished reading the list, a full page and a half in length. "We-We shall now…" I struggled with the words, feeling lightheaded as though I would faint, so overcome was I with grief. "We shall now…" I choked on my sobs, my throat burning as it contracted, cutting off my air so I struggled to speak. "We shall now commit their souls to the deep," I said, then watched as the hammocks were thrown over the side. The bodies sank quickly from the cannon-balls laid at their feet. Lieutenant Brooks embraced me, crying into my arms. The men below moaned and sobbed in sorrow, the whole ship awash with anguish. I allowed them to grieve for a few minutes, then spoke to Lieutenant Reid, who was currently on watch. His eyes were red and swollen from crying and from a lack of sleep.

"Lieutenant Reid," I said, my voice raw and hoarse. "Have your men batten down the hatches and prepare the ship to weather a storm."

"Aye, sir," he replied. Each watch had been reduced from a hundred men to only thirty.

"Lieutenant Brooks," I said to my second in command. "You're to have your men pump the bilge."

"Sir, we've been doing that continuously since last night. Twelve men from Reid's watch are at the pump now."

"Very well, then," I said. "Have your men check that the guns are secure, and try to patch the hull as best you can."

"Aye, sir," he replied.

"We're to have all hands on duty right now, until we're out of the storm or safely in Portsmouth," I told my two lieutenants. I turned then to address the crew. They now looked to me for orders, as I had not yet dismissed them.

"There's a storm coming, lads," I said. "You shall have time to properly mourn your dead comrades, though we're not through the danger yet. The *H.M.S. Cassandra* has been shot to bits, and the rigging is in tatters. The battle delayed our reaching England, and I'm afraid the storm shall reach us while at sea." A rumble of thunder interrupted me, then a flash of lightning ignited the sky only a few seconds later. "We must ready the ship to ride out the weather, else risk her sinking. The storm will show no mercy, for it knows none. We won't last without serious repair, and men at the pump in the meantime. Aside from that we're severely undermanned. I need all hands still fit for duty at work. The normal watch schedule is officially superseded, you are all on duty now. I know you are exhausted, cold, hungry. We've all lost close friends in the recent action, or have others who are fighting for their lives below. I know the task at hand may seem impossible, but we are Cassandras! We are men of the Royal Navy, and we shan't relinquish our ship, not to the French, not even to the wrath of the sea!"

The men on deck gave a weak three cheers of "Huzzah!" They were clearly fatigued, yet still spirit remained in their voices.

I stepped down from the quarterdeck, and Brooks followed me to issue orders to his men. "Lieutenant, I still must write my dispatch," I said. "If there's any new developments, you may find me in my cabin."

"Aye, sir," he said.

"I suppose I haven't had the chance to properly thank you," I continued. "I know your family is in a time of crisis, that you must be terribly worried about your daughter. I thrust the burden of command on you at what must have been the worst time, and you rose to the occasion with clear-headedness and zeal. You're an excellent officer, and knowing that the ship was in good hands made my surgery much easier. I'm in your debt."

"Thank you for trusting me, sir. You've been through a lot as well. It would be my honour to continue to relieve you of some of your duties, as I know you've been badly wounded."

"Oh, there's no need. I appreciate your offer but I do believe I have the strength to resume command."

"As you wish, sir," he said.

I turned and hobbled back to my day cabin, leaning heavily on my cane. When I reached my table I took out one of the chairs and sat down, then pulled up another one on which to prop up my leg. I reached back into my desk and found my quill pen and paper, along with the ink. Before dipping the pen in ink I considered my words carefully. *The Hon. William Marsden, Secretary of the Admiralty. We have achieved a Victory...* No, not strong enough. *We have achieved a Most Glorious Victory in a Single Ship Action the 10th of October 1804.*

I clumsily dipped the pen in the ink. My remaining left hand was unaccustomed to writing, as I was right handed. I thought that perhaps if I was careful, and worked slowly enough, then I might be able to write a coherent sentence. I took the pen out of the ink then lowered it to the paper, accidentally dripping black splotches all over the paper before I even began to write. I balled up the paper and took out a fresh sheet, then attempted again to write. *Th-* the letters were large and scratchy, the lines thick and smudged and completely illegible. I crumpled this piece, too, dropping it by my feet, then tried again, *Th-* I cried out in frustration, chucking the paper at the window above the 18 pounded in the room, then throwing the feather as far as

I could. It went up about two feet then fluttered off to the starboard side, spinning slowly to the deck. My throat tightened. *I'm bloody useless,* I thought. *The men must either consider me a murderer, a fool, or a hopeless wreck, and my officers think me unfit for command.* I realised then that my career was likely over after leading my ship into a slaughter, then being severely wounded. I thought with dread of the years dragging by on half-pay, imprisoned on shore, wasting away in Greenwich Hospital if I was lucky, else in some London slum as I waited for my savings to dry up. I thought of the civilians walking on the streets who would refuse to meet my eye, the other men who would laugh at me behind my back, jeering, *the failed captain.* So great was my distress that I didn't notice when my door opened.

"George." To my surprise it was my brother Oswald, whom I'd not seen in years.

"How did you…" I began.

"You're in Portsmouth now. The rain made it difficult to see. Lieutenant Brooks landed while you were trying to write your dispatch."

"Where's Mother?" I asked. She was always the first person to see me when my ship came into port.

"I think you know where," he said, his voice turning suddenly to anger.

"No, I honestly don't," I said.

"You killed her," he said, his voice deepening to a dark growl. "She died trying to get to London, to petition the Admiralty for *you*. And Father. He died protecting *you*. You killed our entire family. You killed Higgins, you killed Rockfeld, you killed Easton. You even killed the little one, what was his name? *Matrose*."

"Please, stop!" I moaned, unable to take any more.

"You killed me, too," he said, then suddenly a bloody, gaping hole filled his chest. "If you'd resolved the duel as my second, then I wouldn't be dead," he growled. Then an eery, sucking voice filled my thoughts, a hollow gasping from years back. "Where's mother?" It moaned. "I want... Mother. I-I can't breathe. George... George..." the voice stopped, then my brother dissolved into blood, which formed a puddle on the deck then rose up as ashes, blinding me and choking me. I coughed, suddenly falling out of my chair to vomit on the ground.

"Captain Herrick!" A lady's voice said. Rosie ran to my side as I wretched, coughing up my stomach. "Are you alright, Herrick?" She asked, feeling my head. "You're awfully feverish."

"Go..." I said miserably, a bitter bile lingering in my mouth, "get Dr. Burke, if you please."

My head hit the deck and I fainted.

I found myself in my hanging bed, then felt as Burke pressed a damp towel to my head. "How are you feeling?" He asked.

"Quite ill... I'm afraid."

"You're feverish. Rosie said you were sick to your stomach."

"I think you gave me too much laudanum."

"Perhaps a bit. 'Tis difficult to tell. For a man of your size you should have been fine, but you've lost a lot of blood, so maybe it was too much," he replied. I knew he didn't measure out doses, and Burke tended to err on the side of too much rather than too little.

"How is Matrose?" I asked worriedly, suddenly remembering my brother's haunting words.

"'Tis good of you to ask. He lost two fingers, and his shoulder's been torn to shreds, but the bone was not broken so I think he'll be able to keep his arm. He was in a lot of pain when we woke him to give him breakfast, but he's resting comfortably now."

"That's relieving to hear. I've been quite worried about him. Can you help me write my dispatch?" I asked.

"Of course," he replied, "but let's start with some breakfast. I've already eaten," he added, handing me a bowl of porridge with fresh molasses.

"They had loads of fresh victuals on the *Forêt Argonne*," he added.

"Can we start with the dispatch now?" I asked.

"Of course," he said. "Why don't you dictate what you want to say, then I'll write it in your letter."

I nodded. "Thank you," I said.

"Alright, who shall I address it to?" He asked.

"Say: 'The Honourable William Marsden, Secretary of the Admiralty'," I began.

I watched his hand move quickly and effortlessly as the pen scratched the paper. He dipped it in ink mid-phrase, then continued. With the bowl burgoo resting in my lap I took a spoonful and swallowed, the sweet molasses filling my mouth. The warmth travelled through me to rest in my stomach, and I already felt better.

"Now, to begin," he said.

"Say: 'We have achieved a Most Glorious Victory in a Single Ship Action the 10th of October 1804.'"

"I would hardly call the events of yesterday glorious," he said.

"From the lower deck I doubt they were. I agree. Yesterday was no triumph, it was a tragedy, yet 'glorious' is what the Admiralty wants to hear."

"They don't care about us, do they?" He asked.

"Of course they do," I countered, "but the taking of a French '44 by a 36-gun frigate is more important to them than the heavy casualties we suffered to do it. Just write what I tell you to, I've had a lifetime of experience with these sorts of people."

"Very well, sir," he replied. I sensed Rosie's influence here. The Jacobin she'd spawned in him still wished to slight our superiors.

The dispatch writing continued, in which I explained how we had attacked and taken the *Forêt Argonne* of forty guns, but that we'd suffered twenty-three killed and forty-six wounded, myself included in the latter. In addition, I described the masts and rigging of both ships to be much wounded, and the hulls of both of them to be in poor shape. I complimented each of my officers individually on their good conduct, recommending a captaincy for Lieutenant Brooks, and wrote condolences for the death of Captain Easton. In the end, to safeguard myself in the event of a court of inquiry, I explained that a storm was coming, and I described my doubts that the *Cassandra* would survive it. By the time Burke and I had finished, I had eaten my breakfast.

"You really don't think we'll survive?" Burke asked in surprise, "And you're willing to include that in your dispatch?"

"'Tis to protect myself in the event of a court of inquiry, that if the *Cassandra* were to sink it would be as a result of damage from the battle and poor weather, not for incompetence on the part of myself or my men."

"A bit defeatist, isn't it?" He asked.

"A bit realist," I replied. I listened as rain began to patter on the roof of my cabin. A roll of thunder roared overhead, then a few seconds later I watched as a flash of lightning streaked down from the clouds and lit up the sky. The waves had now begun to grow choppier, causing the ship to bob up and down sharply. Little white dots of spray flew off their tops. The wind whistled softly through the bullet holes in my broken windows. Someone had cleaned up the blood and the broken glass on the deck while I had been unconscious. I checked my watch to find that it was just past one in the afternoon. From the darkness outside, it was impossible to tell if it was midday or midnight.

"Can you help me out of bed?" I asked Burke.

"Of course, sir," he replied, finding my cane then offering his arm. I took his hand, and slid more gracefully from the hanging bed than I had this morning, then took the cane.

"I'd like to visit Matrose," I added. "You may go about your duties."

I stumbled to the larboard bulkhead. The sharp pitch and roll of the deck made it difficult to stay standing, especially with a bad leg. With my shoulder pressed against the planking, I could maintain some semblance of stability. I walked out of my cabin to the upper deck. My ears still ringing, I could not hear the conversations of the men around me, and so could not listen in like I usually did. The turned and raised their knuckles as usual, and I could see a new emotion in their eyes. Pity? Admiration? A bit of both?

I climbed down to the lower deck, struggling to keep my footing on the rungs as they shifted about. The worst part was in the middle of the ladder, where a shot had torn away a rung, and I had to fall down a full two feet to the next rung. I continued walking. If Higgins were here, he would hold my arm to keep me steady, yet he was now at the bottom of the sea in a hammock bag. The sight of the lower deck crowded with wounded brought tears to my eyes. Even my impaired hearing could not drown out the moans and screams of my poor lads. I found Matrose on the starboard side, his head buried in a pillow. Sensing my presence he turned, taking me in with surprise and horror. "Your arm," I heard him cry.

"I'll be fine," I replied quickly. "How are you, darling?" I asked.

He didn't answer, so overcome was he with shock. I leaned down and kissed him softly on the head. "I'm alright, sweetheart," I said gently. He remained silent, frozen with fear. "How are you feeling?" I asked again.

He shook his head. "I'm frightened. I don't want to die."

"Don't be ridiculous, you're not going to die."

"My first time in England is ruined," he added.

"We'll make the best of it," I said.

"Sir," someone said behind me. I turned my head to see Lieutenant Brooks.

"The weather is worsening, sir, I do believe the storm is about to arrive. Should we reef the topsails and furl the courses, sir?" He asked.

"I'll come back on deck with you," I said, realising that the best way for me to make a decision would be to go up and see the situation for myself. Brooks helped me up the ladders so we got outside faster. I walked to the quarterdeck to find Mr. O'Hare.

"Wind's blowing twenty-five knots, sir," he said.

"Twenty-five knots! Dear God!" I replied. I felt it whip through my wig and my coat-tails.

I looked up at our two remaining masts to see them shaking violently.

"Top men!" I ordered the men on deck. "Furl the courses and reef the topsails!"

Twenty-five knot winds would be fine for most ships but the *Cassandra* was in such bad shape that I knew it must be stressing her. I watched the men climb the shrouds hundreds of feet up, then perform stunning feats of acrobatics as they climbed the ratlines to the sails. A wave crashed over the bow, and seawater rolled across the deck. It reminded me of the blood that had completely soaked the deck the day before. Then, directly off the larboard side I saw a blackness gathering.

The cloud was completely black on the bottom as it was so dark. It stretched endlessly back and endlessly up. Lightning flashed with a torrent of rain and thunder beneath it, and the waves were so high that they seemed to almost touch the base. Worse than that, it was moving in quickly on a harsh wind. The storm appeared to be only two miles off, closing fast. The cloud front stretched across the horizon in both directions; there was no way we could get around it, and we could not outrun it. An icy wind blew in my face, and I had to hold my hat so it wouldn't fly off. The planking beneath my feet creaked and groaned in an anguished cacophony. Our trials had only just begun.

I hurried back down to the main deck, dragging my injured leg behind me. "Lieutenant Brooks!" I shouted. "What is the condition of the ship? How have repairs progressed? Are the hatches battened down and the guns secure."

"Aye sir, hatches are secured. We've reinforced the lines holding the guns in place as best we could. As for patching up the hull— we're low on supplies, sir, but everything should hold. The masts and rigging are still terribly stressed; we've jury-rigged the forward part of the bowsprit, as it had taken severe damage during the battle. As for the mainmast, well, there was nothing we could do.

The mizzenmast is in as good of a condition as can be had, and the foremast is battered but should hold if we keep the canvas down to a minimum."

"Aye, sir. The masts should survive," the boatswain said, joining our conversation. "I've finished splicing the lines for the topsails, courses and jibs only so I doubt you could use the topgallants, or royals, but everything else appears to be holding up fine. I'd say you were right to reef the topsails, sir, as the rigging up there is still rotten."

"Thank you Mr. Quincy," I replied. "Thank you Lieutenant," I added to Brooks.

Knowing that we were as prepared as possible for the storm, I went to my sleeping cabin and found the bloodied jacket I had worn yesterday. The bullet hole was stiff with dried blood where it had torn through my sleeve to strike my arm, and the fancy silk stockings I had worn with it were ruined. I found my Nile medal on the ground under the clothes, and slid it around my neck.

"Sir," Brooks said when I walked back outside to the quarterdeck. His eyes rested on the medal.

"I won it in battle with the French, and if I drown this afternoon I should like to die with it. Don't be afraid. I trust the seamanship of the men to pull us through, and though the *Cassandra* may be old and broken, she's not yet beaten."

"Aye, sir," he replied, though behind his mask of courage I could tell that he, too, was afraid.

Glancing to stern of us I saw that the *Forêt Argonne* was in similar straights as us, if not worse. She, too, had been dismasted, though the boatswain's less experienced mates were aboard her, so her rigging had not been spliced as well as ours. While we were running on a third of our usual manpower, she was being managed by even less, as her compliment was normally a hundred more than ours, and I had sent a third of the Cassandras aboard her. In addition, most of the damage to the *Cassandra* was to our masts and rigging, but in the *Forêt Argonne* it was to her hull. And while we had transferred some of the supplies to the *Cassandra*, the *Forêt Argonne* was still heavily laden with her gold and treasure, and her heavy French guns. I didn't intend to give up the prize, but I decided that we should evacuate the French prisoners to the *Cassandra* and leave a skeleton crew aboard the *Forêt Argonne.* I walked to the aft part of the quarterdeck where the yeoman of signals was mending one of his flags.

"If you please, utilising the Howe signal code, signal the *Forêt Argonne:* Approach the *Cassandra*, arrange prisoners for transfer."

"Aye, sir," he replied, taking out his book to find the signals. I knew that one of the first things Brooks would have done upon taking command was to make one of the men a yeoman and send him aboard the *Forêt Argonne* with a copy of the signal book so we could communicate to her.

I watched as the flags flew up the mizzenmast, then waited for a response. The rain smudged the writing in the signal book, and the yeoman closed it quickly. I wondered then if they could decipher the signals at all, or if the clouds had made it too dark to see. Then, a few minutes later a flag went up.

"She's acknowledging, sir," the yeoman said.

"Very good," I replied, then walked back down to the quarterdeck. The *Forêt Argonne* approached from the shadows of the clouds about a mile back, and I waited as she grew larger and larger, until her monstrous bows gently touched the *Cassandra's* flank.

I found Lieutenant Wilson standing by the hammock netting on the *Forêt-Argonne's* quarterdeck. He looked exhausted, with red eyes and his hair all in a tangled mess. "Sir," he said, raising his knuckles.

"Captain," I said, acknowledging that as the commander of a vessel he had earned that title, despite the fact that he still had to obey my orders and technically held the rank of lieutenant. "Your vessel appeared to be heavily-laden. I wanted to lighten the load by transferring some of the French prisoners to *H.M.S. Cassandra*." As an experienced seaman, I knew that being heavy-laden in this weather would actually be beneficial, as weight below would stabilise the ship and minimise the action of the waves. The real reason I wanted the prisoners is because it would mean that fewer lives would be lost if the *Forêt Argonne* sunk and we couldn't rescue her crew. "Now, Captain Wilson," I said. Brooks looked on over my shoulder in jealousy, though Wilson's expression only hardened in response. I could tell he was under tremendous stress, and that his true love Angeline's injuries only caused him more worry. "We're about to be struck by the storm. I understand that the *Forêt Argonne* took heavy damage to her hull during the battle," I said. "I'm not willing to give her up without a fight. I want you to stay within a half mile to leeward of me at all times. If at any point you feel as though she is in imminent danger of sinking, have your men fire your bow chasers repeatedly and keep sailing straight, I will come downwind and get you."

"Aye, sir," he replied. "Thank you, sir," he added, turning back to his ship.

I watched as the French captain hesitated at the hammock netting. He was on crutches, having lost his leg. The boy stood at his side, a worried expression on his face. Five marines were escorting them, and suddenly one struck the captain with the butt of his musket. I hobbled over then drew my sword. "Leave the captain alone!" I ordered fiercely. "We are not savages! He's lost his leg, he can't get over the netting." I took Captain Valeurais' hand and helped

271

him as he struggled to climb the netting, and the boy followed right beside him. "If any of you even so much as touch him again I'll have you flogged," I added, hissing to the marines.

"Tell your father that I most humbly apologise for the poor conduct of my men."

The boy translated. "He says he understands," he said after a long pause. I knew that my men had lost friends and comrades to the French, but I in no way condoned them behaving as barbarians.

"Ask him if they hurt him," I told the boy.

He translated for me, then after a long conversation with his father he finally spoke.

"Captain Valeurais told me to say no," he said. Then, after a pause. "They refused to feed us. Three of the men came into our cabin. Father was helpless. They started beating him. Then the lieutenant came in, the one with blond hair and brown eyes, and a small nose. I asked him to help, but he just stood there. One of the men hit his leg. He begged them to stop. They still beat him." I had seen that the Frenchman had been badly bruised about his face, in particular around his eye.

Wilson, I thought when he described the lieutenant, *because of Angeline*. "Tell your father that we have a nice cabin for him, just down two flights of stairs and across the deck. Tell him that he should expect no further ill treatment now that he is aboard *H.M.S. Cassandra*. I shall lock your door for your own protection."

"Thank you, sir," the lad said, then translated for his father.

"Follow me," I said, climbing down the steps. I hurried into my cabin and found a pair of manacles and their key, then rejoined the Frenchmen outside. I escorted Captain Valeurais to the gunroom, then to Lieutenant Wilson's cabin. *See how he likes that,* I thought with chagrin. His hammock was gone, along with his sea-chest, but his vanity and a desk with a chair still remained.

"I will talk to the purser, get you a hammock and some clean clothes, then I'll have the cook fix you some dinner," I told them. The boy nodded, helping his father lower himself into the chair. I shut the door, then fixed one end of the manacles to the door handle and the other to the base of one of the lanterns that hung on the wall. I climbed down another ladder to the aftermost hold platform, finding Mr. Gailden in the slop room. "I need two hammocks with bedding, a large clean nightshirt and a small one, along with soap, a brush, and a razor, if you please."

"That's a big order," he said, finding them from his stash. "Did another one of the men lose a sea-chest?" He asked. I knew that a few had been jettisoned before the battle and their owners had needed to be compensated.

"'Tis for the French captain and his son. I'm quartering them in Lieutenant Wilson's cabin."

"Wilson…" he chuckled. "You have a subtle way of revenge, don't you Captain?" He said.

"If you please, could you carry the purchases for me?" I asked, finding a bag of shillings in my coat pocket and setting them on his desk.

"Of course, sir," he said.

I hobbled back up the ladder then finally reached Wilson's cabin where the prisoners were quartered. The French crew and the other officers were at the far end of the upper deck. Lieutenant Reid was supervising the pumping of the bilge. I knew he was trustworthy, and not too cocky. He would not allow anyone to hurt the prisoners. I doubted that any of the men would dare to when they knew that I was wandering about the ship watching their every move. They knew that I would unhesitatingly flog the lot of them if I so chose, and that my heart had no place for wrathfulness at the expense of civility. I passed the officers' cook on the way up to find he was making a stew.

"Hello, sir," he said, raising his knuckles.

"Could I have two bowls of that, along with a couple of pieces of bread?" I asked.

"Oh, yes sir, there's plenty enough to share," he replied, ladling the stew into two bowls. He handed me two spoons, then followed me with the bowls.

I found the key and slid the spoons into my pocket, then unlocked the manacles and opened the door.

"I'm back," I said to the boy who was sitting on the deck. "I brought dinner," I added, setting down the spoons. The cook set the bowls on the table with the biscuits already dissolving inside. "Thank you," I told him. "If you please, sling the hammocks for them," I said to the purser. "Don't worry," I added to the Frenchmen. "You can trust him." I walked back up to my cabin. I had no brandy, and I thought that champagne would be inappropriate, but I did find a bottle of apple cider. I slid my last two unbroken glasses into my pockets and walked back down. Gailden had finished slinging the hammocks and was now making the beds. I set the glasses on the table, then poured the cider and left them the bottle. The Valeurais' were eating hungrily. Gailden left the room with the beds now ready and a bowl of clean water to shave resting on the vanity. "We're about to enter a storm," I told the Frenchmen. "Pour the water out your window when you're done shaving and washing yourselves, then secure all the glass objects in the drawer under the vanity. Make sure the window is closed. You'll be most comfortable lying in the hammocks."

"Thank you, sir," the boy said. "For everything."

"That's quite alright," I replied.

I found the purser just outside. "Mr. Gailden, if you please, could you keep the key and allow them out if they'd like to leave their cabin?" I asked him.

"Aye, sir," he replied, taking the key from me.

I turned to go walk outside to the quarterdeck. Brooks met me on the ladder halfway. "I was looking for you, sir," he said. "We're about to enter the worst of the storm."

"Just what I was coming on deck to see," I said, climbing the rest of the way up the ladder. Brooks followed me up the ladder.

"Mr. O'Hare," I said, "how far are we from Portsmouth?"

"Twenty-five miles sir," he replied. We had travelled quickly throughout the day. "That's by dead reckoning," he added. "I've not been able to get good celestial readings since three nights ago."

A sudden fear gripped my chest, that we might be turned around and headed straight towards France, or out onto the open Atlantic Ocean, but I ruled that out by glancing at the compass, which pointed north towards England.

I felt the rain intensify as it beat against my hat and coat, then watched as the top-men climbed down the masts back to the relative safety of the deck. A wave splashed over the bow, spraying droplets of white water on the deck. I watched as two of the men tied down the hatch over the

ladder leading from the forecastle to the upper deck. Now
the only way in or out was through the hatch back aft just
in front of the quarterdeck. The men clung to the hammock
netting, working their way aft where the motion of the ship
would be the least. Haynes remained with me, but Larson
was below with Reid at the pump, along with most of the
men. The ones not at the pump at any one time would be
huddled about on the upper deck, frightened and helpless.
By this point the two cooks would have doused the galley
fires, so there would be no hot victuals until we reached the
safety of Portsmouth harbour. "The map, if you please," I
ordered Mr. O'Hare.

      I unfolded it and studied the many twists and turns
we had taken during the battle, then the beeline course
we'd turned on to head for Portsmouth. I questioned the
accuracy of our position. Dead-reckoning during a battle
was always flawed, and O'Hare would not have been able
to take the hourly speed reading for the time we'd been in
combat. How long had it lasted? Thirty minutes? An hour?
Five hours? With the break in our navigation and the poor
weather, we really didn't know where we were. I folded the
map. I saw that the ink lines were beginning to get wet and
smudged in the rain. I handed the map back to O'Hare, who
stowed it away in a drawer fixed to the binnacle. To make
matters worse, only one of our trained helmsmen remained.
The other on Brooks' watch had been wounded during the

battle, and the two on Wilson's watch had gone with him to the *Forêt Argonne*. Brooks had found one of the men to take the place of the cockney fellow, but with little experience he would not be as effective.

  The rain pounded on my head and now the wind was driving it from the larboard side. To my shock an horror, the sky around us turned suddenly dark and the waves grew fiercer. The bow jerked sharply up then crashed back down again, almost knocking me off my feet. Water splashed over the bow, and for a moment the bowsprit was entirely submerged, then the seawater rolled across the deck. It splashed at my shoes, soaking my stockings up to the knee, then fell around the aft hammock netting. The waves must have been a good ten feet high, as they were now three feet higher than the deck. I clutched the mizzenmast for dear life, then stumbled back down to the upper deck and into my cabin, throwing the cane in my sea-chest so I could have my good hand free. I went back outside into the torrential rain, scanning the horizon for the *Forêt Argonne*. Seeing nothing I stepped up to the quarterdeck for a better view, only to find more rain and waves, and no ship. I held my glass to my eye but the deck was moving too much for it to be of any use at all. The motion of a wave buckled my knees and I fell backwards, having no free hand to hold onto anything. The deck rose up sharply to meet me, and I landed on the back of my left shoulder, momentarily stunned. My wrist hit the deck and I dropped the telescope, then scrambled to pick it up again, only to see it roll off the deck on the starboard side inches from my grasp.

I stood on shaking legs, clutching the hammock netting, then finally caught sight of the *Forêt Argonne*. It was at least two miles back, and grey rain and clouds shrouded it again. A roll of thunder boomed in the distance, and I watched as a streak of lightning touched the sea to larboard. It was too far away to do us any harm. I then saw orange flashes spurt from the *Forêt Argonne's* guns; a distress signal. Mr. Larson approached me then. "Sir!" He shouted over the cry of the wind.

"What is it, Mr. Larson?" I asked.

"The pump can't keep up, sir!" He cried. "We're in danger of sinking!"

"Keep bailing her with all we've got. Have the men use buckets if they have to!"

"Aye, sir," he replied.

"There's no way out of this. If she sinks we'll all die!"

"Aye, sir!"

Another wave shook the deck and I clutched the hammock netting until my knuckles were white and I felt the rope burn my hand. The water again surged over the bow and ran across the deck, soaking my legs up to my knees. The splinter wound on my left leg stung as saltwater soaked through the bandages. I felt weak and lightheaded, having not yet recovered from the blood-loss of yesterday and still with a raging fever. My breaths formed white clouds it was so cold, and my fingers and toes were numb.

"A hundred and eighty degrees to larboard!" I ordered the helmsmen. "The *Forêt Argonne* is in distress!"

"Begging your pardon sir," Brooks said with an air of humour, "but *we're* in distress!"

I chuckled at that. Here we were on the verge of death and he found it funny. Brooks' attitude would have disgusted me if I didn't find it so comforting. The ship turned, and for a precarious moment we were running parallel with the waves. A large swell knocked into our starboard side, and we heeled over so sharply that the leeward hammock netting brushed the water. I clung to the windward hammock netting, my throat tightening. I clamped my eyes shut as my feet slid off the deck and I hung in midair, anticipating that we would capsize and sink. I waited for the rush of water around me then the waves to suck me under to my death. Only moments later, however, the ship stabilised and went back to face the waves head-on. I collapsed to the deck, gasping for breath.

We charged up and down through the waves, now heading in the direction of the *Forêt Argonne*, further into the danger of the storm, further away from the safety of home.

The guns still fired and on the crests of the waves I still saw the flashes. They were getting larger. *That's good*, I thought. If she could still fire her guns then her powder was still dry, so presumably the orlop deck had not yet been inundated.

The wind blew into my face with such ferocity that it seemed to drive needles into my cheeks, and I could not keep my eye open facing the bow. I stepped forward, and it felt as though the wind was an invisible wall pushing me backward, ready to throw me to the ground. The waves had grown higher now, up to fifteen feet in places, and now I could not see over them in their troughs. There was darkness all around, and clicking open my watch I squinted to read that it was only 3:45 in the afternoon.

The ship suddenly smashed down into a wave, and seawater surged in a giant wall over the bow. I clutched the hammock netting for dear life, then clamped my eyes shut as an icy coldness vigorously washed over me. Suddenly the water receded and I found myself lying on the quarter-deck, gasping for breath. Brooks helped me up. I counted the men whom I had stationed on deck, to find that all were safe. "Helmsmen, stay at your posts. All other hands, go below. I don't believe we'll need to adjust the sails any time soon, and 'tis not safe out here."

"Aye, sir."

"Aye, sir," they replied.

"Mr. O'Hare, that includes you. "Lieutenant, I'd also like you to go below."

"With your permission, sir," Brooks said, "I'd like to remain on deck with you."

"Very well then," I replied. "You may."

The others climbed down the ladder, then the hatch closed with a thud. The helmsmen remained diligently doing their duty, and though there were at least 150 souls aboard, including the prisoners, I felt entirely alone. Thunder rumbled once again in the distance, and though I saw no lightning bolt the sky lit up suddenly. Another wave crashed over the bow, and the deck was momentarily submerged. The water rolled across, and once again I was buffeted by a wall of icy froth, almost losing my footing until it receded and I could catch my breath.

"Tie yourselves to the helm," I ordered the helmsmen. There were lines aboard for such purposes, and they quickly found two on the binnacle. I could see the white ensign hanging drearily from the mizzenmast, now soaked through and plastered to itself, and the three stern lanterns on the aft-most part of the quarterdeck, put out by the water.

The *Forêt Argonne* fired off another shot, though it was still a mile distant. She heeled over sharply, and her lower gun deck was so close to the water that waves now submerged the gun-ports. Luckily, they had been closed and secured. Or at least they were supposed to be.

I found a line hitched to the aft hammock netting and with one hand and my teeth I managed to tie myself to the mizzenmast. I realised then that I had lost my wig and hat somewhere in the fray, along with my eyepatch. The scars were now revealed clearly and openly, though the only one to see them now was God. Still, I felt self-conscious of the old wounds. My hair was plastered to the sides of my head, and I felt shivers run up my arms as chills racked my body. My teeth began to chatter, and the cold seemed to reach through me, extinguishing any warmth that I had left within me. I leaned against the mast, taking weight off my bad leg, and shut my eye. There was nothing more I could do. The thunder rolled menacingly all around me and the ocean roared in violent fury.

I opened my eye again, then shifted around to the front of the mast, searching for the *Forêt Argonne*. In some desperate attempt at a signal, all the forecastle, main deck, and quarterdeck guns fired, then, after a few minutes of waiting, they remained silent. The *Forêt Argonne* was finished.

Finally, we reached her, and the seventy men waiting on her deck. "Come aboard! We're here to rescue you!" I called from the *Cassandra*. The sailors climbed gratefully

surface and the water washed over the le
ship pitched violently to larboard then b
gasped for breath, my lungs burning. I w
skin and shivering. I tried to speak, but a
interrupted me, then a flash of lightning
deadly bolt and ignited the sky. The wav
me, and I wiped the rain from my eye. 2
to myself.

"Lieutenant Brooks," I began, cl
My voice came out raspier than I'd inter

"I'm sorry, I can't hear you!" He
sound of the wind.

"Lieutenant Brooks, I leave you
ship!" I ordered him, then without hesit
ted over the hammock netting, swinging
Argonne.

"Captain!" He cried.

I immediately ran for the helm a
as hard as I could on the righthand side,
to point the ship on a beam reach away,
could sail for home.

A gap emerged then widened be
Portsmouth!" I shouted to my lieutenan
sandra! It has been my honour to serve
one who asks, that I perished in the line

over the railing. "Go straight to the upper deck!" I ordered, my voice hoarse from cold. When the last seaman was aboard, Wilson climbed over the netting.

"The damage to the hull was too great, sir," he admitted. "Two of our patches failed and water started pouring in. There was nothing I could do."

"That's fine, I never expected the *Forêt Argonne* to survive the storm. That's why I moved the prisoners earlier," I explained. "Now, go below and get warm," I ordered him. He, too, was soaking wet, freezing, and miserable.

"Helmsmen, head due north," I ordered them, shouting below. "We're going home now!" It pained my heart to give up the prize, after so many lives had been sacrificed to obtain her, but to try to save her now would be folly, and only cause the deaths of more of my men.

I felt the rudder turn, but we stopped, the *Forêt Argonne* blocking our movement. Wilson followed the rest of the men below. I remembered suddenly that I'd locked his cabin, but none of his things were in there anyhow. I untied myself from the mizzenmast and walked across the quarterdeck. I cringed as we hit a wave, and the *Forêt Argonne* crashed into us, risking immeasurable damage to our hull.

The ship began to turn, though not in the way that the rudder was directing it. We were being pushed by the *Forêt Argonne* to head at a parallel angle to the waves. I ran

down to the helmsmen. "Hard-a-larb
free of her!" I shouted.

"Sir, we've lost all steerage w
helmsmen replied.

The details of the situation fla
my mind. The *Forêt Argonne,* now e
drifting in the direction of the wind, v
pushing us at an odd angle as she trie
downwind approach. As she was muc
than us, and we had stopped moving
had lost momentum and no longer ha
ship. Essentially, she was steering us
ection, that also happened to be paral
we would capsize in only minutes. If
souls would be lost. I knew that there
be done, and that was to send a man a

"Lieutenant Brooks," I ordere
He was my most competent officer ai
ience with seamanship, short of Mr. (
tightened in anxiety.

"Aye, sir?" He asked.

I felt the deck roll under my fe
crashed over the bow at an odd angle.
over the deck and he took my arm as
over my head, holding me so I would
salt and spray pushed me about until

A clap of thunder followed my words, and lightning flashed across the sky. The *Cassandra* sailed on a northward course bound for home. My heart filled with a mixture of emotions; hope, joy, pride, melancholy, a mounting fear. Was I really certain what would happen when I died? Part of me wanted to take my cutlass and drive it into my own chest, as I would be dead in seconds as opposed to the agonising minutes it would take for me to drown. Survival instinct held me back. I did not want to die. When the *Cassandra* had disappeared in the distance, I turned the helm to bring the *Forêt Argonne* back onto a broad reach into the waves. I was not done fighting for my life yet. I didn't know how fast water was leaking into the hull, or precisely how far from shore I was. Perhaps I was only a few miles away, and the *Forêt Argonne* still had the stamina to take me within swimming distance. I tried to remember the charts from my cabin, the details of the English coastline. France was more prone to rocks and dangerous shoals than England, but if I managed to beach the *Forêt Argonne*, perhaps I could buy myself some time. When I scanned the horizon, however, all I saw was the wind and the rain, and the monstrous swells growing higher by the minute.

I held out hope, fear gripping my chest that something might have happened to the *Cassandra*, and I had strung my own noose by jumping onto a sinking ship for no reason. The French had jettisoned all of their small boats before the battle just as we had, so there were no such vessels that I use for a lifeboat. I could not take my eyes off the horizon for a moment, else risk capsizing the *Forêt Argonne* by turning her in the wrong direction, so could therefore not check my pocket watch, but I did check the binnacle every now and then. The minutes ticked by quickly, five, ten, now twenty. As I felt the *Forêt Argonne* drop lower and lower into the swells I wondered how many I had left. My heart beat desperately. Waves now splashed regularly over the bow, only driving the ship down further. Each time it soaked me to the skin, and I tied a line around my waist and the helm so I would not be washed overboard. The rain and clouds were so thick that I could hardly see a hundred feet in front of me, but each time I looked up hopelessness crowded in closer and closer. Some last instinct kept me searching for strange patterns in the waves, for the dark shapes of rocks, the lights from a ship, a static grey edge that would indicate land. I saw nothing.

I was going to die. The rate of sinking had increased so that the bow of the *Forêt Argonne* did not resurface when it came out from under the waves. The water was up to my knees. I was so cold that my body felt as though it were badly burned, and I could no longer feel my limbs. I struggled to move the helm, and my teeth chattered endlessly. A tear slipped down my cheek. I knew I had only minutes to evacuate the ship, else sink with her, but there

was nowhere to go but the twenty-foot swells. I thought of
the church my family went to when I was younger, the sunlight in the windows that warmed the back of my neck, my
father's big bear-claw hand holding mine, my mother next
to him and my brother Oswald beside her. The Bible had
said bits and pieces about death; that God would protect
me, that I would return to dust just as I had come, that I
would go to a land of eternal happiness. My mother had
told me after I was wounded the first time that Father was
watching over me, and that he would be there for me when
I was ready to join him. I tried to think of my parents and
my brother, tried to find peace thinking that I would soon
join them. Perhaps when I became an angel they would
give me my arm back, or even my eye, and erase the scars.
Yet I felt no comfort from these final thoughts of spiritual-
ity.

I did not deserve heaven, I had ordered twenty-three
of my own men to their deaths, perhaps more who would
not survive their injuries, and that was not counting the
Frenchmen who had also perished as a result of my command. Many of them were likely innocent, as young and as
oblivious as my lads. They were fighting for their country,
that was all they knew, and some of them were also con-
scripts and had had no choice. I had pressed men away
from their professions in the merchant service, their homes
and their families. I had flogged men until they lay bloody,

unconscious heaps. I had killed and mutilated countless Frenchmen. But my worst decision had been to attack a ship a hundred men and eight guns larger than the *Cassandra*, starting a battle in which a third of my dearly beloved crew had been killed or wounded, officers and their families, young lads who loved me and trusted me. For God's sake, my orders had even resulted in the mutilation of a *thirteen year old*, on a ship that fought for a country that wasn't even his own.

It was then that I remembered that Matrose and the eleven other Austrians aboard would be dead if I'd not liberated them. I had failed to save three of them, it was true, but twelve lives had been preserved by my taking the ship that held them prisoners. I had united lovers and families, like Rosie and Morgan, and the Brooks'. I had given second chances to men who did not deserve them, like Jameson. I had given a future to a lad who should have died two years ago, little Matrose, who would now live in comfort for the rest of his days from the fortune I'd left him and would have the status of the well-to-do off of my name. I'd saved a convoy of our merchant vessels, filled with innocent people, and had prevented more wealth from flowing into Napoleon's empire and fuelling his ambitions of domination. I'd shown mercy to my enemies, loving them as I loved my own officers and crew, despite the fact that they had wounded me and I them. I'd given everything I had to my command, and I'd lived my life selflessly, with only my duty in mind. Now it was only fitting that my last gift should be my life.

Fearing God and nothing else, I untied the knot around my waist, knowing that on the next wave the *Forêt Argonne* would sink down to her icy grave, and I would be sucked in with her. I knew that drowning would be excruciating, and my blood ran cold at the thought, but though sheer terror coursed through my veins as I watched the foaming, merciless mountain of water descend, I accepted my fate.

The water closed in around me and I was immediately sucked under. The force of the wave was so strong that I felt it would rip me to pieces. My lungs burned, and I struggled to swim upward, then finally my survival instinct forced me to open my eye. I was forty feet below the surface, the foaming water still all around me, and I felt my strength began to give. The last of the *Forêt Argonne's* masts fell to the side as she sank into darkness below. Black murky water closed in around me. My chest throbbed for air and sheer panic filled my body, though I knew that despite my desperate attempts to swim, I was too far down; it was over, and there was nothing I could do. My life flashed before my eyes— my mother's fingers on mine teaching me to play the harpsichord, walking along the beach with my father holding my hand, my brother and I racing each

other swimming. He would always win, despite the fact
that I was the one destined for the navy. The first time I
tried on my midshipman's uniform, the day I'd received my
Nile medal, the time I'd seen Haydn in concert and the
Austrian girl who had given me flowers. The thrill of my
first command, the time I'd bought a house of my own to
live in in Portsmouth, my dreams of raising a family in that
house, perhaps with the Austrian girl and Matrose. The letter I'd received assigning me to the *Cassandra*, the parties
I'd had with my officers along with Dr. Burke, the day
Matrose had told me he'd wanted to stay with me, and that
I was like a father to him.

  I saw a bright light in front of me, and knew the end
must be near. My body had gone limp and I had stopped
struggling, for all it was worth. At the end I felt a sense of
pride, and of peace. I'd sacrificed my life so that my men
might live. The light grew brighter, and suddenly I felt
warm and comfortable all over my body. The light engulfed
me, then my life was extinguished, my hopes, my dreams,
my future, all put out by the sea like the delicate flame of a
candle set adrift on the waves.

Epilogue

"Cough, darling," a gentle voice said, that of an Englishwoman. "You need to cough now, dear." She held me propped up on my side, rubbing my back with her hand.

I coughed, saltwater gushing from my mouth. I fell into the wet sand, gasping for breath, my lungs still filled with water. I saw I was on a beach, the sand was grey. A wooden cage and bits of wreckage rested near me, and I recognised my chicken and her three chicks running about willy-nilly amongst broken pieces of oak planks and bits of furniture that had washed up on the beach.

"Good, that's very good, darling," she said. "I'm going to take you to hospital now..." her voice trailed, and I again lost consciousness.

I woke to the sound of rain on the roof of a building, disoriented and confused. Someone had tucked me into bed and covered me in blankets, and I heard a furnace crackling peacefully in the centre of the room, though curtains surrounded me on three sides to give me privacy. On my right was a window that faced out to sea. I recognised the long peninsula with water on all sides, but for a thin strip of land with a road leading back to Portsmouth, and decided that I must be in Haslar Hospital. The view was similar to my last stay twenty-four years ago. It took all my effort to turn my head, and I found that my muscles were stiff and sore. Every movement seemed painful. I saw on my right that I had a bedside table. To my surprise, in addition to the standard pitcher of water and cup that rested on the table, wrapped bundles of gifts and bouquets of flowers covered both the tabletop and the floor. A stack of letters a full six-inches high rested next to a vase of white and yellow roses, and I could smell the flowers from here. I felt silk touch my body, and a comfortable silk eyepatch with padding under the strap covered my left eye.

The curtains shifted and I jumped, startled, only to see a nurse walk in carrying a tray of food. "Good morning, Captain Herrick," she said. "How are you feeling?"

"Wh-where am I?" I asked, confusion taking over. I was supposed to be dead. I'd been forty feet under water, I had died. I *remembered* dying.

"You're in Haslar Hospital hospital in Portsmouth, dear." She took my hand. "A nice lady found you on the beach and took you here because of your uniform. Then a man said he recognised you, someone named Dr. Burke. Do you know him?" She asked.

"Aye," I replied hopefully. "Morgan— the doctor, is my best friend. He was my ship's surgeon. Have you had any men from the *H.M.S. Cassandra* sent here? A frigate, 36 guns?"

"Yes, it arrived three nights ago, along with some of the men. When word got around that we had a patient named Captain Herrick who had washed up on the beach, they all wanted to see you. The story's been all over the papers about how you took a French man-o'-war when it was going after an East India convoy whose cargo was worth over 200,000 pounds. You're famous now. Rumour has it that you're to be presented with a sword from Lloyds of London. There were loads of people who wanted to visit you, but Dr. Burke sent them away so you could get your rest. We allowed people to send gifts in the meantime."

"Are the flowers… are they for me?" I asked, still shocked.

"Yes, sweetheart. They're all for you. The large bouquet of roses came with a note," she added, handing it to me. "I'm going to leave your breakfast here, alright dear? You seem like you need some time to yourself."

She left me then, and I saw that on the plate were two delicious blueberry scones. I ate half of one of the scones, the delicious fresh flavour filling my mouth and warming my chest, then sipped the cup of tea that had come with them.

I read the note, and my heart swelled with affection. *Captain Herrick,*

We will never be able to repay you for risking your life to save ours. You are an excellent captain and we are proud to have served under you. We were overjoyed when we heard that you were alive. We hope you recover quickly from your wounds and you soon return to good health. We

295

pooled our funds to buy you the flowers. We hope you re-
ceive your next command as soon as you have recovered,
and we will gladly serve under you again.
    Signed, Ship's Company, H.M.S. Cassandra

Made in the USA
San Bernardino, CA
14 August 2018